To Anne
Thank you for your
encouragement and support
Dermot
June 2012

DredgeMarsh

The Reluctant King

D0814470

i

Dredgemarsh

The Reluctant King

by Dermot McCabe

Axletree
Press

Ebook version at
http://xrl.us/bmwx67

Copyright © 2012 Dermot McCabe
All rights reserved

Typeset: 16/12/10pt Garamond
Cover: based on Warrior with his Equerry
by Giorgione da Castelfranco c. 1509
Original at Galleria degli Uffizi, Florence

Chapter 1

Half opening his eyes to the glimmer of light seeping through the ivy covered windows of his bedchamber, Cesare Greyfell tried to remember what it was that weighed so heavily on his mind. He turned over and gathered his knees up to his chest, attempting to create a cocoon of warmth around himself. But his body remained cold and his mind, swimming from the depths of sleep, flitted around the duties of office that awaited him until finally, the real cause of the sadness in his heart flared painfully into consciousness. He could picture her now with startling clarity: Lucretia Beaufort, strolling along the bank of the Yayla river with her companion Celeste, while he, hidden, feeling guilty, but unable to take his eyes off her, watched from Hazel Wood where he rambled each evening with old Thunder. Her laughter, her sweet rippling laughter, tormented him. He pictured again the exquisite curve of her breasts and hips under the clinging samite caftan that she wore with such casual grace. A hot flush suffused his whole body. He felt dizzy and angry; angry that she could make him feel like that, and angry at her apparent happiness that had nothing to do with him. He despised himself for that selfish impulse.

Delighted! That's what Chancellor Tancredi said. Lucretia was delighted with her father's proposal that she should marry Albrecht Pentrojan of Brooderlund. Shortly she and her father would be seeking royal permission, Cesare's royal permission, to proceed with this alliance. That's what Tancredi said. Cesare could not bear to think of her with any other man. He rolled onto his back and flung the heavy musk ox blankets from him.

'Father, this is not what I wanted,' he spoke to the empty room.

It was five years since his beloved father, Philip the Wise, died of a wasting disease contracted in that accursed Manchian campaign that sowed the seeds of death in his lungs. It was five years since Cesare's life as a student in Anselem had so abruptly ended. Five long years since he was compelled to take his father's place. He thought of the solemn promises he had made when Tancredi –it was always Tancredi– told him that his father's dying wish was to see him form a marriage alliance with Manchia. It made sense. But now … since Lucretia's return … seeing her again, even after all these years …'Oh father, if only you were here. But what does it matter? She is happy to marry the Brooderstalt.'

No, Cesare did not want any of this. Even now he still felt the bitter loss of his father, as did every other soul in Dredgemarsh. They were so secure under Philip's benevolent rule. How could he possibly measure up? How could he even try, when he had bound himself to his beloved father's request that he would be guided, in all state matters, by Chancellor Tancredi until he reached his twenty first year? His hands were tied. He should have been allowed to continue his studies at Anselem; there would be none of this torture. Besides, the Chancellor, Demetrius Tancredi, revelled in the minutiae of State business; that's why he was Chancellor. Leave it to him.

'Up, up,' Cesare chastised himself and rolled into a sitting position on the side of the bed. He could hear the rooks clamouring on the spires and turrets of Dredgemarsh, waiting for spillage from the offal pumps that filled the swine vats from the kitchens. The raucous squabbling lifted his spirits slightly. It signalled life and activity, even if it was in the bowels of Dredgemarsh where the kitchen serfs would already be preparing breakfast for the soldiers coming off night watch. He could just imagine the irascible Cook Meister Clutchbolt bawling out the morning orders to his sleepy menials.

He dressed quickly in black hose, long black jacket, silver girdle belt and soft leather boots, all laid out for him on the previous evening by his squire. His bedroom opened onto his solar where Thunder, his father's favorite alaunt, dozed away his declining years amongst the clutter of books, manuscripts and scientific instruments. Thunder wagged his ragged tail and, moving only his eyes, followed his young master's progress as he entered the solar.

'Stay, old warrior.' Cesare reached down and stroked the grizzled head. 'Stay.' He sat into the carrel where he spent hours every day studying the complexities of the science of Optiks, an obsession inherited from those happy days with the learned monks of Anselem, especially the renowned Peregrinus. He picked up a scroll, then dropped it with a sigh and reached for the oil lamp and tinder box. After a few half hearted attempts to light the lamp, he put it and the tinder box aside. He sat there, motionless, staring into the grey penumbra. Thunder whined as if he sensed some unseen threat. In the distance, the grinding of iron-rimmed wheels across cobbles heralded the arrival of the first mercer bound for the market square. Or perhaps it was the fishmonger with the night catch of mullet from the Yayla river. Gradually, the sounds of early morning activity began to multiply. The impenetrable shadows slowly dissipated and still Cesare sat unmoving, silent, eyes open but not seeing anything.

Thunder lifted his head and looked towards the main door of the solar. Moments later it opened and Jakob, Cesare's squire, entered quietly and made his way past the carrel where Cesare sat. Jakob stopped at the open door of the bedchamber.

'Sire,' he called quietly and tapped gently on the door frame. No answer. 'Sire,' he called again, and knocked louder. Cesare, invisible where he sat in the shadowed recess of the carrel, watched his squire as if what was happening was not real but a dream where he, Cesare, was simply a remote and uninvolved observer.

'Sire?' Jakob called out more urgently and entered the bedchamber. Seconds later, he rushed back into the solar.

'Jakob!' Cesare said at last and his startled squire turned to peer into the carrel.

'Sire, what ...' Jakob moved closer. 'Are you unwell, Sire? You look ... pale.'

'What?'

'You look pale, Sire. I wondered if you were feeling unwell.' Cesare gestured to the carrel seat opposite him. Jakob slid onto the seat and faced across the worktop where the discarded scroll and flint box lay amongst the confusion of books and manuscripts.

'Tell me, Jakob, who rules Dredgemarsh?'

'What do you mean, Sire, I'm not sure ...?'

'It's a simple question, Jakob. Who rules Dredgemarsh?'

'Well, you do, of course.' Jakob looked at his young master with raised eyebrows. Cesare leaned forward, elbows on the table, hands, fingertip to fingertip, forming a steeple, the pinnacle of which he pressed against his pursed lips. He stared hard at Jakob, whose expression began to change from quizzical to a frown of uncertainty.

'Of course, with the help of others ... ' Jakob began. 'I mean ... there's the Chancellor, Demetrius Tancredi and ... and the council and ...' Jakob stared intently at Cesare, looking for some affirmation that he was saying the right thing, but it was not forthcoming. He shrugged his shoulders. 'Sire, these matters are beyond me ... shall I arrange breakfast, Sire?' With a slight nod and perfunctory wave of the hand Cesare gave his permission. Jakob sighed and left his despondent young master without further discussion. Thunder rose stiffly, came to Cesare, stared up at him with his one good eye and whined softly.

'Poor Thunder,' Cesare said, stroking the hound's head tenderly, 'it will not be long 'til you join father in the Elysian Fields where you can run and hunt once more to your heart's content.'

****

'She may not like it, uncle, but you must convince her.

Young ladies of her age hardly know their own minds,' Demetrius Tancredi, Chancellor of Dredgemarsh, said to Arnulf Beaufort as the pair took a dawn stroll through the walled orchard garden attached to the Chancellor's residence.

'If only her mother were alive.' Beaufort sighed.

'Uncle, you will be one of the most influential men in the region when this union takes place. A young girl's fantasies cannot be allowed to jeopardise the peace of great nations. I have already told his highness that the matter is settled.'

Beaufort stopped and turned to Tancredi with anxious eyes.

'Is his highness happy with this marriage?'

'Of course, why should he not be?'

'No reason, no reason at all. But I can't seem to get through to Lucretia. Maybe, Lord Chancellor, Lucretia would listen to you. After all, you are her cousin. I hardly recognise her now after her four years in Nuvarro. She is no longer a child, but she is just as headstrong as she always was, more so and –'

'Uncle, you are the head of the family; you must insist that she ceases her malingering.'

'Yes, you are right of course; I must do it ... and I will.'

Tancredi took Beaufort firmly by the arm and walked him towards an iron gate set in the twenty foot high wall surrounding the garden. The gate was almost hidden by a luxurious canopy of the late flowering clematis vitalba, still heavy with morning dew. He partially opened it and checked outside; then stood aside to allow Beaufort to exit onto a cobbled square set in the centre of the courts and chancery buildings.

'Uncle,' Tancredi called after Beaufort, 'have the details of the union drawn up and be at the Court of Petitions before the tierce bell ... with Lucretia. I have listed your petition for hearing this morning.'

'And you are sure that his majesty approves of this union?' Beaufort looked back anxiously at Tancredi.

'I told you, there is no problem; his majesty understands the necessity of this marriage. He will probably not attend the court this morning; I will approve the marriage on his behalf.'

****

When Jakob returned with Cesare's breakfast of hot frumenty and a jug of posset, he also brought a list of the cases to be heard before the court of petitions later that morning and several documents requiring the royal seal.

'What have we here?' Cesare said. 'More dismissals from the royal household? I hope Tancredi knows what he is doing. Efficiency, he calls it. I sometimes think the man is a fanatic.' Cesare barely scanned through the documents requiring his seal and handed them back to Jakob. 'Wax,' he said. Jakob, anticipating his master, was already heating a stick of wax in a candle flame. He dropped a hot blob of wax on each document and placed them, in turn, before Cesare, who was now reading through the list of cases for the Court of Petitions that morning while, at the same time, casually impressing the hot wax with the royal seal. Without warning, Cesare's face reddened and he crumpled the list in his fist.

'Court of Petitions! Ye Gods, must I endure this?' He flung the list to the floor. 'I'll not go. Inform the Chancellor.' Jakob said nothing. '...endless petty complaints between feuding neighbours: whose dog did what, which merchant watered his wine, which fish monger diguised stale fish with pig's blood ... and who wants to marry whom. No, I will not waste my time on such nonsense.' Jakob was still silent. Cesare glared at him. 'What is it? You're usually quick enough with your opinions.'

'Nothing, Sire. It is your decision.'

'Yes, it is my decision.' Cesare rose abruptly, his breakfast barely touched. 'Have Gargantu saddled immediately. Come, Thunder.' He made towards the main door, with the old alaunt trotting stiffly behind him. As he was about to exit, he said, 'I will ride alone. You will go to the court and inform the Chancellor that the matters before it are too trivial to warrant my attendance.' Jakob shook his head slowly from side to side and picked the crumpled list of petitions from the floor.

Chapter 2

Lucretia barely glanced at her father, Arnulf Beaufort, and said, 'Father, it is much, too soon to discuss such matters. I am but a few weeks back and barely settled.' She turned in her seat in the oriel window of the belvedere and resumed reading.

'Is this what they taught you in Nuvarro; to ignore your father?' Arnulf Beaufort's jowls reddened. He grabbed the book from Lucretia's hand. 'How dare you turn away from me when I am talking. What is this nonsense they have you reading? Ars Amatoria.' He scanned the title, spitting out the words, and flung the book to the floor. Lucretia stood and faced her father. Her eyes were on a level with his. She glared at him, a delicate tinge of red blossoming on her cheeks. Celeste, Lucretia's companion and lady in waiting, instantly laid aside her embroidery tambour and stooped to pick up the discarded book which had landed by her foot. 'Leave it, and leave us,' Beaufort, without looking in her direction, enunciated each word as if his teeth hurt. Celeste looked anxiously at Lucretia, who, still glaring at her father, nodded and said.

'You may go Lettie.' Celeste tiptoed from the room and closed the door quietly.

'Father,' Lucretia said, 'I have been away a long time, but I do not remember you like this.' She continued to stare at him but the initial anger in her eyes had turned to one of hurt.

'Girl,' he turned away from her unrelenting gaze, 'you will not sway me with that innocent look of yours. You are well versed in your duty. It is time, and you know it. Captain Pentrojan is a fine man, a worthy match.'

'He is a Brooderstalt, father. Have you forgotten your history?'

'No, by God I have not. And that is the very point, young lady. Pentrojan is one of the most powerful men in Brooderlund; next only to Cawdrult himself. You will be the most powerful woman in the region. Think of it, daughter.'

Lucretia moved over to the vaulted window that overlooked the western battlements of Dredgemarsh. She gazed at the sparkling Yayla River that zigzagged gently from the multicoloured autumn finery of Rim Wood. It flowed down directly onto the western battlements, then south along the castle wall to feed the Meregloom marshlands. She could see a thin column of white smoke curling up into the translucent air from somewhere deep within the woods: a charcoal collier tending a forest kiln, she surmised. Her father was still speaking, but the words meant nothing. Her heart filled with longing for the carefree days when she raced through those bright woods and swam in the Yayla's clear water with her boisterous companions. She imagined Lake Tranquil beyond Rim Wood, the surging Maulin Weir that frightened and fascinated her as a child, and the outings she had there with her dear departed mother. Beyond these, she could see a purple haze on the slopes of Anselem Mountains with its majestic pinnacles piercing a low cloud that encircled them like a collar of ermine. For an instant she was back listening to her mother telling her tales of the mysterious Knights of Anselem in their mountaintop monastery. But gradually her father's prattle intruded on the pleasant daydream.

'Father, do you miss mother?' She interrupted him.

'What are you talking about, girl?'

'You know.'

'No, I do not,' Beaufort raised his voice, 'I will not be diverted. We must settle this. If not to me, you, at least, have a duty to your king and country.' Lucretia flinched visibly at the indirect mention of Cesare.

'Does he know?' She asked tentatively, almost as if she dreaded the answer.

'Does who ... oh, you mean the King. Well yes, the Chancellor keeps him fully informed of everything.'

'And he approves?' She barely whispered the words.

'Approves ...? Of course, of course. Why would he not approve? He knows the power of Brooderlund, knows they can crush us at will. He may even be present at the court of petition this morning when the matter is put formally.' Beaufort did not see how her body wilted or the tears welled up in her eyes. With a look of mingled triumph and guilt, he turned to leave. 'So be it. Be ready, daughter. You must attend the court with me at the tierce bell.'

'Make your petition father, but I will not attend.'

'Curse of Grak, girl, just be ready. I'll have no more of this; you are not being cosseted in Nuvarro now.' He slammed the door on leaving.

Celeste re-entered as silently as she had left. She picked the book of poetry off the floor.

'My lady, what troubles you so?' She crossed the room and sat beside Lucretia at the window. The weak autumnal sunlight flooding through the rippled glass glistened on Lucretia's dark tresses and Celeste reached out to gently push back a wayward strand. Lucretia turned her face towards Celeste, as if she had only become aware of her presence, and her eyes, though tearful, were defiant. But the defiance melted instantly when Celeste put her arm around Lucretia's shoulder.

'It is so unfair, Lettie. My own father and my cousin Tancredi ... I don't trust him ... I never did ... he acts like he was king. What right has he got to interfere in my life? It's my life, mine, that these men are bartering with as if I were a mere slave. I won't allow it. I will run away.'

'Calm my lady, calm.' Celeste reached out with her free hand and patted the clenched fist of her mistress. 'It is the way of things. We cannot change it, and perhaps you ...'

'No Lettie, I will not accept that. Even he knows ... I thought ... I thought he ...' Lucretia's voice spiralled into a forlorn sob. She slumped forward and covered her face with trembling hands. Celeste put her arms around her weeping mistress and drew her closer.

'You mean his majesty, the King?' she whispered. Lucretia nodded her head without removing her hands from her face.

'Perhaps he doesn't know how you feel?'

'It makes no difference how I feel,' Lucretia straightened up and wiped the tears from her cheeks. 'It's how he feels that matters. I thought, I always thought that no matter how far apart or how long we were apart, there was something special between us. I don't even know why I should be so foolish as to think that.' Lucretia rose from her seat and stood staring out towards the Anselem mountains as if trying to recall something.

'The first time I really met him, I was with my father. We saw him racing across the Vildpline?'

'The King?'

'Yes and he caused my pony to throw me, and father was so angry and Cesare ...' Lucretia winced as if she experienced a sudden sharp pain and for a moment she was silent. Then taking a deep breath she continued. 'Cesare took my hand and helped me to my feet. He apologised, said he could not forgive himself if I was hurt. And the look in his eyes, Lettie. There was no mistaking that look. He knew and I knew: something passed between us.' Lucretia turned from the window. She looked animated, joyful, as if she was reliving that day. 'A pledge, Celeste, a pledge was made, though no words were spoken. And then this brooch, you remember this.' She touched a beautiful rose-shaped brooch that she wore over her heart. 'There has not been one day in the whole four years we were in Nuvarro, that I did not think of that day. And I thought,' her voice was quiet once more, 'I thought he would not have forgotten.' The tears began to fill her eyes once more and she stood with her arms dangling loosely by her side, not caring any more to hide her anguish.

Celeste, still seated, reached out and took her hand.

'You were both so young, my lady. And people change. Maybe he does not remember things as you do.' For an instant, Lucretia's eyes flashed with anger. 'Or maybe,' Celeste quickly continued, 'maybe he has not the luxury of following his heart. A king can also be a slave, my father always said.' Neither spoke for several moments. Lucretia wiped away the remaining tears from her flushed cheeks with the heels of both hands. She sat once more and looked directly at Celeste.

'A king may be a slave, Lettie, but I will not be one, not to anyone, not to my father, Chancellor Tancredi ... or the King.' Her voice trembled. 'And certainly not to a Brooderstalt.'

'But my lady, what can you do? These matters are beyond your control.' Lucretia turned her gaze towards the window once more, as if there was some inspiration to be found on the faraway mountains of Anselem. After a short while she spoke.

'Pretend, Lettie,' she said. 'We will pretend that we are delighted with the prospect of marriage. Dissemble and delay as much as possible, and when the opportunity presents itself we will go away.'

'Go away?' Celeste's eyes widened. 'Where would we go? Where could we go?'

Lucretia threw her hands up. 'I don't know. Back to Nuvarro maybe. I don't know. But for now, I must be a dutiful daughter and attend the Court of Petitions.' Lucretia stood once more. 'Come, Lettie. No tears or frowns. Let the game begin.' She smiled a bitter smile.

Chapter 3

The old groom said, 'He will kill himself on that brute,' as he squinted, with semi-opaque eyes, at the departing Cesare, who was struggling to control a mud coloured cob with a large club head, tiny ears and pale wild eyes. 'I told him, begged him not to. You heard me, but he insisted on Gargantu.' The groom poked a tiny freckled stable lad with a stick.

'You told him. Yes, you told him.' The lad squirmed and moved away from the groom.

'Can't listen, won't listen. But I'm just a half blind old fool. What would I know?' The groom prodded his stick once again in the direction of the stable lad but made no contact.

'Bah,' he said, then turned and began to fumble his way back through the stables, lashing his stick from side to side.

Cesare hauled viciously on the reins as Gargantu plunged and jinked across the cobbled stable yard. Behind him, old Thunder trotted stiffly, unperturbed by the noisy and boisterous tussle between man and horse. Another alaunt, almost a replica of Thunder, but young and supple, ran wildly around, tongue lolling as if in laughter and eyes glistening with excitement.

'Heel, heel, Lightning,' Cesare shouted. At the same time, he stood up in the stirrups and hauled the bit back in the foaming mouth of the cob. The young alaunt dropped back momentarily beside Thunder but it was clear that his master's rebuke would not restrain him for long. By the time Cesare had emerged into the grand plaza, Lightning was dashing around in all directions again, scattering the scavenging mongrel dogs that slunk behind the carts of the traders making their way to the market. Gargantu swerved and dodged through the morning throng at a dangerous canter.

'Damn that idiot,' a carter shouted out as his mule shied sideways in fright. But he instantly went quiet when he recognised Cesare.

It seemed as if the young King was unaware, or simply unheeding of the panic he was causing. When he reached the postern gate, some foresters with their women and children were streaming through, carrying pelts, herbs, fruit and fresh meat. They scattered, children and women shrieking in fright, as the foaming cob thundered through the short tunnel of the gateway and burst forth onto the promenade, raced down the glacis and onto the great grassy expanse of the Vildpline. Cesare gave the cob his head and they galloped away from the castle, as if they were being pursued by demons. Thunder was gradually left behind but limped on regardless, while Lightning doubled back and forth, in front of the charging cob, in wild excitement.

Had the tower guards or those doing duty along the northern allure of Dredgemarsh Castle been watching, they might have seen the distant figure of their King rein in his mount to a slithering halt, moments after the bells of the cathedral pealed out across the Vildpline, announcing tierce.

At that very moment, Chancellor Tancredi had just seated himself on the court dais, and was arranging the various petitions on the bench before him with the help of the two Dredgemarsh legal scribes, Henri Dipslick and Marten Havelock. Arnulf Beaufort, his daughter Lucretia and her companion Celeste were making their way through the noisy gathering of petitioners. They sat in the very first row of seats facing the dais. Beaufort looked happy. He smiled and nodded to the Chancellor, who nodded back and then glanced at Lucretia, who appeared to be as happy as her father. The Chancellor looked surprised. After a few minutes the scribes moved to a lower bench and prepared themselves for recording the transactions of the court. Tancredi nodded to the court distaff, who pounded the floor with a great decorative mace until the room subsided into silence. As the Chancellor was about to speak, the door to the vestibule of the court was flung open and the King's squire, Jakob, entered, breathless and flushed.

'What is the meaning of this?' Tancredi glared at the intruder.

'Sorry, Chancellor, but my master bid me tell you that he will not attend this morning. He says the matters before the court are of minor concern and his presence is unwarranted. He begs you to proceed in his absence.'

'My lady, I'm sure he did not mean...' Celeste reached out discreetly to take her mistress's hand. Lucretia pulled away abruptly. Tancredi glanced in their direction. Lucretia smiled icily at him. She turned and, still smiling, addressed her companion through clenched teeth.

'Lettie, hold your tongue and smile.'

Tancredi raised his hand to quell the rising murmur of voices in the court.

'Thank you Squire Jakob, you may leave,' he said. 'The court of petitions is now in session. Call the first petitioner.' He nodded to the court bailiff.

****

Cesare Greyfell's wild and reckless charge across the Vildpline unravelled something in him. The years of study and disciplined physical training in Anselem had not prepared him for the fire that coursed through his veins when he thought of Lucretia. Now there was hardly a moment when he was not thinking of her. It was the clear plaintive tolling of the Cathedral bells, announcing tierce, that brought him to a shuddering halt. In that moment all the anxieties and tangled thoughts of duty, decorum and responsibilities fell away, leaving one startlingly clear thought; I love her. Nothing else matters.

'I love Lucretia Beaufort.' He shouted it to the empty sky. 'I love her,' he repeated quietly and turned the frothing cob back towards Dredgemarsh. At first he set out at a slow canter. He was smiling and shaking his head. What a fool I have been, he thought. Suddenly, he remembered the significance of the bells that had triggered this transformation within him.

'The Court of Petitions!' he thumped his forehead with the heel of his hand and instantly set the cob to a furious gallop.

****

'Arnulf Beaufort,' the court bailiff called out, and Marten Havelock, the larger of the two court scribes, noisily turned over a new leaf in the court journal, while his companion Henri Dipslick finished off a certificate and handed it to the previous petitioner. Beaufort rose and approached the dais.

'Lord Chancellor, I have here a petition, requesting that my daughter Lucretia Beaufort marry Albrecht Pentrojan of Brooderlund.' He spoke loudly and confidently. There were some 'oohs' and 'aahs' from women in the body of the court, followed by a noticeable rise in volume from the half-whispered conversations that ensued.

'Silence,' the court bailiff banged his mace on the floor again. He then took the petition from Beaufort and handed it to Chancellor Tancredi. Tancredi read carefully through the document.

'Is the bespoken bride present?' he asked without lifting his head.

'Why yes, of course Lord Chancellor, have you not—' Beaufort began.

'Is she aware that any commitment given before this court is a binding commitment and will she confirm, here and now, that she understands and agrees to be bound by such a commitment?'

'She does, Lord Chancellor, she is only too happy—' Beaufort began but Tancredi silenced him with a wave of his hand and stared down at Lucretia.

'Does she understand?' Tancredi began again.

'I understand only too well what has been decided for me,

19

Chancellor.' Lucretia rose from her seat. Tancredi glared at Beaufort, who shrugged his shoulders and looked anxiously at his daughter.

'Is the young lady, Lucretia Beaufort, agreeable to the proposed marriage to Albrecht Pentrojan of Brooderlund?'

****

Cesare cursed himself for choosing to ride the cob that day. The great beast was slowing and gasping for air as he ascended the castle glacis and pounded across the promenade to the postern gate. Long before they got sight of the cob, those in his path felt the ground tremble, heard the thunderous hooves and the frightening bellows of his lungs. Once more, the young King scattered all before him until he finally reached the steps of the courts, where he leapt from the saddle, as the exhausted cob, in a blaze of sparks and stone chippings, clattered to a halt. Cesare stumbled forward on dismounting, and was saved from falling by a strong arm that reached out and held him upright in a powerful grip. Cesare recognised the owner of that arm immediately.

'Jerome,' he said to a tall gaunt monk of Anselem 'I thank you. Forgive my haste. I will explain later.' The monk released his hold and Cesare, taking the court steps three at a time, entered the vestibule of the court of petitions. A young sergeant of the court, not recognising Cesare, admitted him into the back of the court and held his forefinger to his lips, requesting quiet.

'I declare before this court that I commit myself to marry Albrecht Pentrojan of Brooderlund, and request that I am granted leave to so do.' Lucretia's voice carried to every

corner of the hushed court. The words were like a sledgehammer blow to Cesare. So Tancredi was right after all, he
thought. Lucretia really does want to marry Albrecht Pentrojan. What a fool I am.

'In the name of, and on behalf of King Cesare Greyfell,
the petition is granted,' Chancellor Tancredi said, closing the
book of petitions before him. Beaufort rubbed his hands
together, smiled and turned to look at the body of the court,
as if expecting the approbation of those present, but a mild
look of disappointment crossed his face when he discovered
that the majority of people had either already left, or were
leaving at that moment. He spotted Cesare. The disappoin-
ted look vanished instantly.

'My dear! Lucretia! Look! Look! The King has graced
us with his presence. Come, come! We must pay our respects.' He grabbed Lucretia's hand. She glanced over her
shoulder. The tall commanding figure of the young King,
his black clothes spattered with mud, stood motionless as
the people made their way past him, some with heads down,
absorbed in their own thoughts and schemes, others elbow-
ing their companions or spouses to take notice of him. He
was oblivious to them all. He was staring directly at Lucretia.
Their eyes locked, and for an instant they made that inex-
plicable connection that affirmed once more the unspoken
bond between them. But almost immediately, the turmoil of
youthful confusion, pride and uncertainty broke the spell.

'Father, I want to go home now, this instant ... now ...
please.' She dropped her head, and turned to walk towards
the exit furthest away from where Cesare stood.

'But, the King! We must pay our respects, daughter,'
Beaufort said.

'You do so if you must, father.' Lucretia walked away,

grasping Celeste's hand so tightly that her companion winced. The startled Beaufort turned and walked towards Cesare. Chancellor Tancredi was already ahead of him, also approaching the King.

'Greetings, your highness. I am glad you were here to witness that. Such an important event for Dredgemarsh,' said Tancredi, smiling. Just then, he noticed Beaufort and continued, 'And of course, for the young lady Lucretia and her family.' As Beaufort approached he began to babble something about his daughter not feeling well and how she would have been delighted on this happy occasion to pay her respects and so on and so on. Cesare paid no attention to either him or the Chancellor but followed Lucretia's progress as she rushed from the court.

'I am sure the young lady Lucretia is simply overwhelmed with the prospect of marriage and no doubt wants to start planning immediately. You know what these young ladies are like.' Tancredi laughed heartily and clapped Beaufort on the shoulder. But Cesare was still not paying attention to either him or Beaufort. Tancredi could see the object of Cesare's attention. His laughter died, and the tightening muscles at the corner of his mouth and the narrowed eyes belied the smile on his lips.

'Your daughter,' Tancredi addressed Beaufort in a loud voice, while still looking at the distracted Cesare, 'your daughter seems overjoyed at the prospect of her marriage.'

'Overjoyed? Yes, of course, she is overjoyed. She cannot wait for the happy day.' Beaufort looked uneasily from Tancredi to the still inattentive Cesare who, as if only then becoming aware of him, turned and stared uncomprehendingly at Beaufort. Beaufort lowered his eyes immediately. 'Thank you, your majesty, for granting this petition. That is, allowing it to be ... I mean the Chancellor on your behalf allow-ing–'

'His majesty understands.' Tancredi interjected. 'Now I suggest you go to your daughter and help her prepare for her happy day. In the meantime I will send a missive to Brooderlund and Albrecht Pentrojan. Your majesty,' the Chancellor turned to address Cesare, but the young King was already departing without a word.

Dredgemarsh

Chapter 4

Deep in the bowels of Dredgemarsh, Verm Bludvile could walk blindfolded through the endless maze of underground corridors and tunnels. The Great Hall of Echoes was the centre of this bleak underworld. Every utterance, every closing and opening of distant doors, every crack and creak of disintegrating stone in this dark labyrinth splintered into shards of noise, that endlessly flowed into that ocean of whispering sounds.

It was rare for anyone to descend to Verm's dark sea of echoes, except on those odd occasions when an ancient ritual or ceremony entailed a visit of dignitaries or members of the royal household. These events had become even more infrequent over the past five years, since Cesare Greyfell had returned from Anselem to ascend to the throne of his dead father. This neglect of the old rituals did not worry Verm in the slightest. All he cared about was lighting the candles, his one function in life. That's what he was: the candle lighter.

Verm could not remember why, but he hated "them above". It was in his blood, some old long-forgotten grievance or dreadful wrong done to him. 'Degenerates and fornicators,' his father, old Wat Bludvile, used to fulminate at the mention of the royal household and its staff, never explaining, even on his deathbed, the reason for his obsessive hatred. He had also been the candle lighter. Verm knew nothing of his mother, but in his grim world of flickering candlelight, the only kindness he had ever experienced was from old Wat. Now, the passing years had almost extinguished that trembling flame of affection and left in its place an emptiness that, on occasions, even the hard armour of bitterness could not repel. But as long as he had his candles to light, the squalor of Verm Bludvile's existence could be endured.

Every second day, he set out with a supply of candles from the storeroom below the Great Hall, hauling them in a tall shambling contraption that bore a vague resemblance to a barrow. Its small iron wheels that continually stuck in the ruts and cracks of the cobbled floors, and the noise it made as he hauled it through the flickering shadows, was excruciating. Verm seemed not to be affected by it. He was not deaf. In fact, his sense of hearing was acute as was his sense of smell. He could differentiate between all the rank and poisonous odours that percolated into the tunnels from the canals and settling tanks of lower Dredgemarsh.

It took him two days to check and replace the candles. On the morning of the third day, he would arrive back at the storeroom below the Great Hall of Echoes and commence the process once again. Every minute of his life was accounted for in this endless ritual of replenishing the candles.

Now in the autumn of the fifth year of Cesare's reign, something startling and strange began to happen to Verm. He was beginning to feel some vaguely unsettling emotions. Ideas, totally alien to him, began to hover and flash indiscriminately across his mind. It took him some time to realise that his unease was growing as the stock of candles, in the storeroom below the Great Hall of Echoes, was diminishing. It was unprecedented. The supply of new candles to the storeroom had ceased. These emerging feelings grew, and changed to fear, and finally terror. It was as if the candles were burning away the hours and minutes of his life. And yet, with the terror, came a gradual awakening of a mind long sunk in a state of unconsciousness, punctuated by the odd frenzied outburst of invective against 'them' – the degenerates and fornicators.

Verm began to think. He started replacing only every second candle; later on every third and then fourth. As the gloom and darkness began to close in about him, his mind became more illuminated. His initial terror was being displaced by his growing fascination with these new and strange emotions. If there were no more candles, he could no longer be the Candle Lighter. Verm was compelled towards self-awareness for the first time, since his barely remembered childhood. Images of that far off time, glimpsed, as if through a turbulent mist, disturbed his awakening self; images of dusty schoolrooms, books, reading, learning, unfamiliar excitement, and maybe even happiness. Words and phrases bubbled up from the deep sludge of memory; 'He'll do well. ' Who had said that? His father? No. 'We'll prepare him for the scriptorium. He's clever.' Was that said about him? Then nothing. Nothing but a life of endless drudgery, as assistant to his increasingly embittered father. When he, old Wat Bludvile, lay dying, he cursed "them above" in his final agony. Verm continued as candle lighter. It was all he knew; all he was, all he wanted.

The hope in his awakening mind that these events were merely a temporary disruption; that he could slide back into the comfort of mindless routine, was sundered for once and all, with the shattering discovery that his food supply – slops lowered in pails from the kitchens through a crude shaft – had been, without warning, stopped. It took him two days to decide what to do next; he would visit the provisioner Sledgedrain.

With this one idea, he became animated and started mumbling and whispering to himself, as if to practice talking again before confronting the provisioner. With several lengths of dirty twine, he strapped an enormous ledger to his back. This ledger had a record of every single candle supplied to and subsequently used by Verm. Sledgedrain filled out the supply side of the ledger every month, when he restocked the candle storeroom, and Verm filled out the candle withdrawal side.

Unencumbered with his antique barrow, it took Verm only three hours to reach his destination. There were the unfamiliar feelings of apprehension and excitement, as he climbed the rickety staircase to the office of Sledgedrain. He had to tear aside fistfuls of cobwebs before lifting the creaking latch on a tiny woodworm-infested door. He pushed. It shivered, groaned and opened to what appeared to him to be a dazzling light. In fact it was a rather grim, dreary light, but all things being relative, Verm's transition from the murky arteries of Dredgemarsh to this dismal room blinded him for several moments. He stood in the doorway, darting his head this way and that, blinking and sniffing the air with quivering nostrils.

'Knew you'd come, had to,' a thin whining voice seeped out from behind a cabinet brimming over with ledgers. Verm tried to focus his small pink eyes on the source of the whine. There was complete silence for several moments. A long head looked out from behind the cabinet. Two small moist eyes were magnified in a pair of round metal-rimmed spectacles, broken at the bridge and tied together with a piece of frayed string. The only colour in the off-white face was the thin purple line of a drooping mouth.

'Sledgedrain,' said Verm.

'Here, read that.' The apparition snapped his long bony arm towards Verm, with a fine parchment dangling from his thumb and forefinger. Verm snatched it and began to slowly read the lines of delicate calligraphy. He was confused by the officious jargon until he read the last few lines with a shock:

... and forthwith the practice of maintaining the constant illumination of all sub-terra regions, used heretofore for ceremonial occasions, will cease. The supply of candles will cease immediately and the functionary called Verm Bludvile, being no longer required, is to be dismissed from his duties forthwith.

By order of his Majesty King Cesare Greyfell

Pp Demetrius Tancredi

Summa Administrator

The signature, Demetrius Tancredi, was written with a great flourish in blood-red ink. While Verm was reading, Sledgedrain flicked through a dusty yellow tome. Then he stopped, leaned out further from behind the cabinet without moving his feet, and, in this gravity-defying position, stared at Verm.

'Leave the ledger,' he said, and waited for some response.

'Degenerates, fornicators, bugger them all.' Verm crumpled the parchment, stuffed it into his vest and was gone, the discarded ledger still sliding across the floor towards the startled Sledgedrain. The appalling stench of the candle lighter lingered and wafted through the room.

'Ugh ... good riddance to that.' Sledgedrain kicked the ledger under a large cabinet. 'Maybe next week,' he mumbled to himself and disappeared behind the filing cabinets.

That seemingly minor incident, in Sledgedrain's office, unleashed the virulent hatred, that had been incubating in the bones and blood of Verm from childhood. Verm was unshackled, loosed from a lifetime's servitude. He returned immediately to the centre of his subterranean maze where he read and re-read the words 'the functionary called Verm Bludvile, being no longer required, is to be dismissed from his duties forthwith.' He cursed and howled with rage, until, eventually, a deadly calm took hold of him and he began to plan his revenge on Cesare Greyfell, author of his misfortune.

Chapter 5

It was Nellie Lowslegg, the scullery maid, who first noticed the absence of Sling the cat. Lazarus Clutchbolt,
Cook Meister and master of the greasy chaos of sculleries, pantries, larders, pots, pans, fires and fat, completely dismissed her concerns about the missing mouse catcher.

'That flea bag, Lowsleggg, is swyving every she-cat in
Dredgemarsh. He'll return when his pizzle is as limp as this.'
Clutchbolt picked up a sippet of toast soaked in gravy, and,
pursing his lips, sucked it slowly into his upturned mouth.
'You do know what I mean, Lowsleggg,' he laughed.

Slowly, like the revolving figurines on a clock, different
emotions wound themselves on and off Lowsleggg's normally blank face. Comprehension crawled across the pasty
forehead, lifting first the left and then the right eyebrow;
shock began to push and bulge the listless eyeballs; scarlet

embarrassment rose like mercury behind the pale neck and face, and timid anger tightened slack lips until finally, like the clock, the display ended. Clutchbolt winked at his skinny Assistant Cook Meister, Leopold Ratchet, whose lips had curled into a lewd smile as he gazed longingly at Nellie Lowsleggg. Ratchet had long harboured desires for Miss Lowsleggg. He hoped that the bawdy talk of Clutchbolt might arouse this Venus of the sculleries, and that he might somehow benefit. His lurid thoughts, however, were instantly doused when Bella Crumble, the Kitchen Mistress, bawled out from scullery four.

'Lowsleggg, get in here this instant. These skillets are a disgrace, a living disgrace. Oh it is useless talking to you. Have you learnt nothing? I'm wasting my time. Is there no end to it ... no end? Is it any wonder our dear King Cesare is not eating properly?'

'Coming, Mistress Crumble,' Lowslegg said and went to submit to another of the endless tongue-lashings that filled her days.

Ratchet, now subdued by the uneasy feeling that Mistress Bella Crumble had knowledge of his obscene thoughts, tried to concentrate on his job of chopping the carrots, but every now and then when he glanced across at Clutchbolt, a high pitched whinny of laughter burst forth from his tight little mouth.

Clutchbolt, the maestro of Dredgemarshian cuisine, and prima donna of pastry makers, began to sing a scurrilous ballad at the top of his voice. This rotund dictator of the kitchens enjoyed teasing and embarrassing his staff. But, like all dictators, his moods could change instantly. He was basting a couple of swans and singing merrily when a large rat slithered across the far end of the pastry worktop, grabbed one of his delicate creations and headed back from whence it had come.

'Yaauk!' With an ear-piercing shriek, Clutchbolt grabbed a meat cleaver and hurled it after the fleeing rat.

'Where is that bastard cat?' His face began to turn scarlet. 'That useless whore-mongering bastard cat. Where is he? Get him, someone. Get him now, get him, get him, I'll skin him alive.' Clutchbolt began to foam at the mouth.

Leopold Ratchet, Bella Crumble and Nellie Lowslegg stood together in a huddle, watching this transformation. They had seen it before, but it always mesmerised them with its intensity and passion. They knew what would follow, and there was joy in their hearts. Yes, joy. Clutchbolt was on the verge of another collapse, another little turn that would put him out of action for several days, perhaps more.

With a great moan, the Cook Meister sped from the kitchen, and they could hear him making his way down to the cellars. They remained transfixed, waiting, exulting, and listening to the frenzied noises from below.

'Here he comes,' Ratchet said, winking at Lowslegg, behind Bella's back.

'Poor man,' Bella Crumble said, with a look of unctuous satisfaction on her expansive face.

'Did you hear what he called Sling?' said Lowslegg, feeling suddenly brave, but trailing off just as quickly, when Clutchbolt stormed back into the kitchen with two massive flagons of vernage under each oxter.

'Get him, do you hear,' his lips were trembling, 'or you're all in dung, all of you.' He vanished into his own small living quarters off the main kitchen, and his underlings gave a combined sigh of relief when they heard him slam and then bolt his door.

Complete silence reigned. Then, from the furthest corner of the room, they heard a low sniggering. It was Burstboil, the scullery boy, who had been hidden all the while, watching the commotion. Miss Lowslegg began to titter, and soon Mistress Crumble erupted into coarse laughter, while Ratchet grinned and leered like an idiot. The ensemble's mirth grew and grew till they were all howling with laughter.

Finally, as the merriment began to subside, Ratchet, Lowslegg and Burstboil focused their attention on Bella Crumble, who was now clearing her ample throat and wiping her tear-stained jowls with the end of her apron.

'Leopold,' she commenced, and Ratchet snapped to attention.

'We must get that cat back, before his highness emerges.' She nodded significantly in the direction of the closeted Clutchbolt.

'Yes, Mistress Crumble,' Ratchet said, 'you are right, as always.' Then, in as stern a voice as his rather scrawny vocal cords could muster, he rapped out the order. 'Boy, search for that cat. He must be somewhere below in the tunnels.'

'Go yourself,' said Burstboil. 'I'm not going down there after a rotten cat, not me. There's not a glimmer of light down there.'

Ratchet wasn't quite sure what to do next. He was furious that the pimply kitchen boy was defying his authority in front of Nellie Lowslegg. Fortunately, and to his great relief, Bella Crumble dashed across the room, with unnerving speed for a woman of her proportions, and delivered a resounding thump to Burstboil's left ear, which left him squealing in agony.

'You ... you, you snot,' she screeched. 'Do as Leopold ... er ... Mr Ratchet commands. He is in charge now,' at which point she attempted to look demurely at the would-be masterful Ratchet.

Ratchet's discomfort at Burstboil's insubordination was a trifle compared to the utter consternation and terror he felt at the prospect of Bella Crumble blushing and sneaking girlish looks in his direction, but he did like the idea of being in charge. He braced himself, filled his scrawny lungs with the sultry kitchen air and intoned, 'Go now, my good fellow, or I shall have to exercise my authority.' Anxiously he waited for the response, and oh, what relief when Burstboil whined, 'I get all the poxy jobs around here,' and glanced nervously towards Bella Crumble, who looked set to thump his other ear.

'That's better,' Bella Crumble exclaimed in a loud, satisfied voice, and then, turning towards Nellie Lowslegg, whispered, 'Waster of a boy.'

At this stage, Ratchet felt it was safe enough to assert his authority.

'Very well, let's see ... get yourself a lantern and a bag of scraps, young sir. Start searching immediately. And now, ladies, I suggest we carry on with our duties.' Ratchet's voice took on a superior tone. Quickly, lest there be any dissent, he set to at basting a giant tray of swans and hoped that everyone would obey him. A sideways glance confirmed that Burstboil had vacated the kitchen.

'Brat,' Bella said out loud, hoisting several large cauldrons onto the main stove. Just then, the 'brat' reappeared with an oil lantern and a paper bag filled with kitchen scraps. With protruding lower lip and hurt glare at Bella, he sidled towards the rarely opened door to the tunnels and passed through into the dark labyrinth with a curse of defiance.

Dredgemarsh

Chapter 6

Burstboil, normally brash and cheeky, was frightened as he stepped from the steamy hot kitchen into the cold damp air of the tunnels. His fear heightened when the kitchen door was slammed shut by Bella Crumble, leaving him stranded in the small sphere of light cast by his own lantern. Inquisitive as he was, even Burstboil had never ventured into these tunnels further than the light from the open kitchen door would permit.

He could feel the skin prickling along his spine and neck, and was on the verge of rushing back into the kitchen when the thought of Bella and his throbbing ear made him pause. No, he would not give them the satisfaction of taunting and jeering at his cowardice. So he just sat down where he was with his back to the wall. He would spend just enough time in this frightening darkness to convince Bella Crumble and the others that he had made a serious attempt to find Sling.

Gradually his eyes adapted to the darkness. On either side of him the tunnel, with corbelled ceiling, vanished into impenetrable shadows. From the darkness on his left-hand side he became aware, as his panic subsided, of a sustained whispering creeping up along the stony cavern. This sound began to dominate his senses until it swirled around and washed through him in slow hypnotic rhythms. He concentrated, trying to decipher what it was.

'Voices, it's voices, there are people, hundreds of people down here'. Burstboil shouted into the blackness. His astonishment masked the fear, and he decided he would investigate. Why should he remain all alone in that hideous place, when he could be with a crowd? He set forth, at first tentatively, but then with more assurance as the whispering became more pervasive. The more he moved towards the source of those sounds, the more unpalatable was the idea of going back, and the more urgent was his desire to be amongst the throng.

Strangely, the sounds, although appearing to increase in intensity, were still oddly muffled and unintelligible. Burstboil became anxious again. He broke into a trot, and finally a headlong gallop. And as he ran, the slap of his ill-shod feet on the stones, and his pained breathing, mingled with those waves of sound washing up from the Great Hall of Echoes.

It was empty. Burstboil, in panic, ran into that grim arena of sounds, where, even in the murky blackness, he could sense the vastness around him. He had an unnerving sensation that he was drowning in a dark, noisy ocean. He could not fathom the conflict of sensations between eyes and ears. All around, he heard a contagion of whisperings, totally unintelligible, but there nevertheless. Yet he could see nothing, could sense no presence whatsoever. His legs began to tremble uncontrollably, and his small eyes bulged in fright as he probed the shades and contours of the hall. He noticed that there were a few candles that sputtered and flickered in the murky penumbra.

'Where is it, where is it ohhh ohhh ... .' He spun round and round, trying to to find the tunnel from whence he had come. All he could see were innumerable black openings, all similar, around the periphery of the hall. Which one to choose? Then, horror of horrors; from one of those dark orifices, a stooped shadow scurried. It weaved in and out of the shades and semi-shades, all the while moving with uncanny speed towards him. He stood transfixed, unable to move, his mouth open, his lips peeled back from his teeth, frozen in a soundless scream. Before he passed out, Burstboil saw small blazing red eyes and smelt a foul odour engulf him.

It was several minutes before the wretched kitchen boy became conscious once more. When he opened his eyes, he was staring into those same red eyes that had almost quenched the life from his body.

'Mistress Crumble, oh Mistress Crumble, please,' he sobbed, but still the spectre was before him. His poor heart pounded, as if it would beat its way out of his frail chest.

Verm Bludvile had tied him to one of the decaying pillars in the storeroom of the Hall of Echoes. The empty crates that once held an abundance of candles were strewn around the floor. Bludvile sat on one of them, directly in front of Burstboil, observing him with unnerving curiosity. The petrified boy could not meet that terrible gaze, and tried to look elsewhere. His stomach churned. There beside the crate, on which this monster sat, were the grisly remains of Sling, tail and head. The boy spewed. The contents of his bowels turned to liquid and flowed down his trembling shanks.

Chapter 7

I t is impossible to fathom the human spirit, its amazing force, and equally, its amazing weakness and susceptibility. Verm Bludvile epitomised the force, the fanatical focusing of every facet of being on a single purpose, while the bedraggled and terrified scullery boy was, as it were, a blank page, upon which Verm could imprint anything he wished. It was a strange and fortuitous accident for Verm that this pathetic and weak-minded boy should fall into his clutches. It was stranger still that Verm, only recently come to self-awareness himself, could exert so much influence on another human, even of the calibre of Burstboil. Yet, that is what happened. Perhaps it was that the boy never got over the fright of that first terrifying encounter. Suffice it to say Verm had found himself a willing disciple and a slave.

Three days after leaving the Dredgemarsh kitchens,

Burstboil returned. Ratchet, Crumble and Lowslegg could see that he had changed, that something had happened to him which left him withdrawn and sombre.

'Sling's dead.' He held up the tail salvaged from Verm's leftovers. Nellie Lowslegg screamed and ran from the kitchen.

'How?' There was a subdued and apologetic tone in Ratchet's voice. Burstboil just shrugged his shoulders.

'And where have you been all this time?' Bella Crumble asked.

'Lost.'

'Well, sit down, and have some warm braggot.' Bella Crumble, although she detested the boy, had been consumed with guilt over the last couple of days, when he had failed to return.

Burstboil quietly resumed his duties. A new cat was procured, Sling II. A dishevelled Clutchbolt emerged from his retreat, and the kitchen resumed business as before. That is, except for one thing: Burstboil. He was not a perpetual irritant anymore.

Leopold Ratchet, Burstboil's immediate superior, should have noticed the absence of perpetual annoyance, that might have been expected on the return of the kitchen boy. But there were other emotions and personal upheavals that were preoccupying him at that time; Bella had openly declared her undying devotion to him. She had blatantly attempted to embrace him in her fat arms, but he had leapt backwards with a squeal of panic, sat on the hob and burnt a large hole in his trousers. He was ordered to hand over the damaged trousers to the infatuated Bella who, if appearances can be trusted, found the experience of darning Ratchet's trousers an ecstatic one. Ratchet was in deep, deep trouble. He was terrified of Bella. The thought of telling her that he was not interested in her romantic overtures made him tremble in fear. He could only smile weakly in response to her smouldering glances and this, of course, was ample proof, for Bella, that Leopold was tortured with desire for her. Every day she became more frivolous and skittish, and Ratchet faced each morning with a haunted look on his face, dreading her increasingly audacious advances.

'Poor man,' Bella whispered knowingly to Lowslegg, nodding in the direction of, the now desperate, Leopold Ratchet.

'Can't keep his eyes off me, the randy devil. It will be his hands next.' She pursed her lips, which of late she had been painting a bright scarlet, and she threw a hot kiss in the direction of the demented Assistant Cook Meister. Perpetual panic filled those desperate days of Leopold Ratchet. Added to this was his own secret desire for Nellie Lowslegg. Those steamy kitchens virtually swirled with throbbing passions that completely obliterated any curiosity that might have arisen over Burstboil's new personality. He did his chores quickly and thoroughly and disappeared into the tunnels for long periods. He always carried a parcel of food with him on these excursions.

Dredgemarsh

Chapter 8

Grunkite had spent the morning questioning the night guard about missing weapons from the armoury and now here was a varlet of the hounds jabbering on about an attack on the kennels.

'Damnation, what is it, boy?'

'His majesty is there, sir. You're to come immediately,' the panting varlet turned and ran back from whence he had come.

'Wait, wait, what has ... 'struth ... the world has gone mad.' Grunkite set out after the boy, panting and blowing as he went. When he arrived at the garth surrounding the royal kennels, he was dumbfounded by the carnage that greeted him. One corner of the garth looked like an abattoir. There were at least four young alaunts lying like discarded rags in great pools of blood. Their throats were slashed open. A fifth hound, this one a lymer, was still standing with a great gash in his neck and shoulder, his chest and forelegs covered in gore. The King was kneeling in another pool of blood with his back towards Grunkite and for a heart stopping moment, Grunkite thought the King was mortally wounded like the young hounds.

'Sire,' he called and rushed to Cesare's side. Cesare was cradling the old alaunt, Thunder, in his arms. Thunder was alive, despite the gaping wound in his neck. He lay calmly gazing up at his master with his one good eye. Cesare was talking quietly to the hound until it gradually went limp in his arms, the spark of life vanishing from his still-open eye. The King lay Thunder gently onto the ground, rose and turned to Grunkite.

'Tell me, Marshall Grunkite, how long will this go on?' There were tears rolling down Cesare's cheeks.

'To tell you the truth ...' Grunkite was sweating profusely.

'To tell me the truth,' cut in Cesare. 'To tell me the truth. How often have I heard that. It means nothing.' The young alaunt, Lightning, Cesare's own hound, just as Thunder was his father's, whined as if in sympathy with his master. Cesare leaned forward and tenderly stroked the head of the dog. 'Hush Lightening,' he whispered. 'Incompetence, stupidity,' his voice was breaking, 'my best, my finest falcon; strangled ... strangled. Four of our best alaunts, butchered under our very noses. Thunder, old Thunder, the best alaunt we ever had, my father's pride ... this noble creature, butchered ... is this how his life had to end?' More tears welled up in Cesare's eyes. 'He was like a brother to me. Now, swords, arbalests, daggers missing ... and you stand there telling me the truth. What next?' Cesare's face was reddening, and there was spittle at the corner of his mouth. 'Will they walk in and take the halberds and shields from the wall? The truth is, Grunkite, you have failed. Failed miserably. What are you proposing to do; what are you doing? I should not have to deal with these matters. You are the Marshall of the Royal Household.'

'Sire, whoever is doing this, whoever it is, he or they, know this fortress inside out.' Grunkite gasped for breath. The broken tracery of veins and pulpy skin around his nose stood out against the sickly pallor of his face. 'We suspect the culprit or culprits are coming and going from the lower tunnels and canals so we have started ... we have started, Sire ...'

'Started what, Grunkite?'

'A detailed search, Sire, but it may take weeks to ... to ... to cover the whole sub-terra region.'

'Weeks, weeks? We have already endured weeks of this, these assassins, butchers, thieves. No, no, Grunkite, weeks will not do.' Cesare's threw his arms upwards. 'I despair,' he said. 'I'm wasting my breath.' He swept past Grunkite with Lightning slouching behind him. Grunkite stared at the ground like a chastised child. Cesare stopped, exhaled deeply and pressed both hands to his temples, as if to massage the frustration away. He turned and very slowly approached Grunkite from behind. 'Grunkite,' he said, placing his hand on the old man's shoulder. 'Forgive me, I know you are doing your best.' Grunkite's whole frame appeared to wilt under this unexpected show of empathy from Cesare, and it was clear to all present that it was only by grim determination, that the old man did not sink to his knees and weep openly. 'Catch the culprits, Grunkite; catch them,' Cesare said quietly, and left. After a few moments Grunkite shrugged his shoulders and shook his head vigorously from side to side, as if to dispel a fog of confusion from his brain. He was angry now; not angry with his young King, but with himself, with his own officers, his own guards. Every day a new outrage came to light; arms stolen, portraits vandalised, fires breaking out, and each event was a painful and personal blow to Grunkite. He brushed non-existent hairs from his lapel with trembling hands, once-powerful hands that had served Dredgemarsh faithfully for so long.

'I think you could safely go now, Grunkite.' The voice was that of Chancellor Demetrius Tancredi. Grunkite had not noticed his presence up until then. The tone of condescension and subtle malice pierced Grunkite like blade of ice. He glared in hatred at the smiling Tancredi.

'It's not as if you have nothing to do. I think his Highness was quite explicit. We want results now.'

'We! Tancredi, we! Have we suddenly found some royal ancestry? I knew your father, don't forget; a good honest fuller, and your mother. Just as well they are not here now.' At this mention of his parents, Tancredi's cynical smile froze on his smooth face.

'You misconstrue my words; my concern is solely for the safety of this house and our dear King. I trust we both share that concern. If you will excuse me.' Tancredi rushed away.

'Bah!' Grunkite said it loud enough for all to hear, including the departing Tancredi, who, for one instant, looked as if he was about to turn and confront Grunkite, but after a moment's hesitation he moved on.

'Another day, old man, another day,' Tancredi muttered to himself.

Chapter 9

Jakob was anxiously rubbing his palms together. 'But, Sire, really, this is not wise. When all this trouble is cleared up, by all means, but now, with respect, Sire, it is too dangerous.'

'Enough, Jakob. I have had as much as I can endure for one day. I will go hunting, and that is final. I am in no danger. Now get the usual party together; we leave immediately.'

Cesare could not shake off the anger he felt after the obscene killing of old Thunder. It wasn't just anger at the killers; it was the anger of guilt: guilt that Thunder, whom he loved like a brother, should meet such an ignominious end under his care. And when he thought of how he had spoken so harshly to Grunkite, he was ashamed. It was his, Cesare's fault that things had come to such a pass. He had been careless and neglectful of his duties for too long. Not only that, but of late, he had allowed his mind to be consumed by thoughts of Lucretia to the exclusion of everything else. Even now, he could not dismiss her from his mind. It was almost a month since her petition to marry Albrecht Pentrojan, and nothing appeared to be happening.

'What progress on Lucretia Beaufort's betrothal?' he had asked casually of Tancredi, that very morning.

'Like all young ladies, she wants everything to be perfect,' Tancredi said. ' She needs time to plan all the details, will not take any help, wants to do it all herself. But we should be able to set the date shortly.'

Two stable varlets were ready for Cesare when he arrived. They hauled on the reins of a mottled grey stallion, coaxing it towards one of the many mounting blocks in the yard. Every time the sweating boys got the stallion close to a block, it skittered sideways and dragged them into the centre of the circular yard. Cesare looked on impassively, which made the boys more nervous until finally, exhausted, they looked helplessly at their King. Cesare strode out to them and in one graceful movement took the reins and leaped onto the stallion's back. The startled animal reared and clattered sideways. The stable varlets scrambled for cover. Cesare sat easily and confidently astride the beast, holding the reins lightly, his powerful legs locked solidly. Moments later, Tancredi, Jakob, a falconer with a gyrfalcon on his arm, three spearmen, four sleek alaunts and a couple of lymers with two mounted fewterers arrived, ready to follow Cesare.

The small hunting party, with the King at its head, thundered out across the immense cobbled square, enclosed on three sides by stables and barrack rooms that once held a standing regiment of over one thousand cavalry. The square was overlooked by four towers at each corner. Each tower was built from different coloured obsidian, quarried from Grak's Mines. The square was now deserted and unused, apart from a few stables and grooms' accommodation, overlooked by the Blue Tower on the southwest corner. The fourth boundary to this vast square was the north wall and main gate. It was rarely opened now.

The small band of riders veered off to the eastern side of the main square, through an arcade and onto a long narrow road called Sky Road. It was flanked on either side by crenellated granite walls of dizzying height. This man-made canyon swerved and curved with only a narrow strip of heaven visible to the riders below. The thunder of the hooves grew and intensified within that confined space and reached a deafening crescendo as the party dashed through a narrow archway, emerging into a small courtyard surrounded still by immense man-made cliffs of granite.

'Open up!' Cesare called out as he reined in the frothing stallion just yards from a solid iron gate in a corner of the courtyard.

'Hold your horses, hold your horses,' a cantankerous voice called from the grimy window of a tiny guardbox.

'Dungheads,' the owner of the voice did not intend that last comment to be heard, but it was obvious he was drunk, because what started out as a whisper ended in an alcoholic bawl. Cesare was dumbfounded, but at the same time amused. His retinue was aghast. Eventually the owner of the voice staggered sideways from the dark interior of the guardbox, unkempt and bleary-eyed. He steadied himself and, having inspected the 'dungheads' in front of him, he promptly turned a bilious green.

'Scuse, me lor ... shit, horse ... ship, lordshhh ... 'scuse...'

'What's your name, my fine soldier?' Cesare asked.

'Pluck.'

'Pluck, dear, dear, how unfortunate. There was an old soldier called Pluck ... no, no, mm ... There was an old drunkard called Pluck. Ah yes, infinite possibilities. Infinite.' Cesare sat there staring at the unfortunate Pluck, who had now turned a sickly grey.

'Well, my dear Pluck, this is your lucky day; I can't quite think of a suitable ending to my little verse, or to you, so perhaps you might be so kind as to open the gate.'

'Inst ... inst...right away,' and Pluck started to wind the gate winch. The squat iron door of this almost hidden entrance, just east of the great main gate, groaned open to reveal the bright undulating meadows of the Vildpline beyond the sombre walls of Dredgemarsh. Without further delay, or a second glance at the now sweating Pluck, Cesare galloped through.

'You will hear from me soon, you miserable swine,' Demetrius Tancredi pointed and shouted at the gatekeeper as he passed through. The gatekeeper however was, at this stage, pre-occupied with emptying the contents of his stomach all over himself and the gate winch, to which he was clinging like a drowning man.

As soon as Cesare was outside the walls of Dredgemarsh, a calm descended on him. He slowed to a canter and began to recite a Latin verse:

Vivamus, mea Lesbia, atque amemus,
rumoresque senum severiorum
omnes unius aestimemus assis!
soles occidere et redire possunt:

nobis cum semel occidit brevis lux,
nox est perpetua una dormienda ...

(Let us live, my Lesbia, let us love,
and all the talk of the stern old men,
may it be worth a penny!
Suns may set, and suns may rise again:
but when our brief light has set,
night is one long everlasting sleep.)

His retinue followed behind respectfully, casting odd uneasy glances at one another. They feared what they considered strange behaviour. Cesare had this effect on people. These spontaneous outbursts were directed at no one, as if those in his company did not exist. Even Tancredi, who prided himself on his self-control, was unsettled at such moments and he hated himself for it. He preferred to deal with the frustrated young King, when cunning and diplomacy were required. This otherness disturbed him because it made him realise that, ultimately, Cesare would always retain that element of unpredictability that defied manipulation.

Eventually, however, the spell was broken, and Cesare galloped off down the sloping glacis, onto the Vildpline and headed towards Grak's Forest, an ancient forest of gnarled oaks and glistening beech trees that stretched in an unending vista across the skyline to the North of Dredgemarsh. He loved this forest, named after the tyrant Grak, his great-great-grandfather. In contrast to this surprisingly pleasant northern aspect of Dredgemarsh, the east and south was mainly bogland and almost permanently shrouded in an unwholesome fog. Only the peasants ventured to its perimeter to cut and draw turf.

On this late autumn day, swine herds taking their pigs to the forest for pannage watched, with sullen interest, the small band sweeping across the Vildpline. But these were not the only eyes observing that little group and in particular, their leader, Cesare.

From Dredgemarsh, two people, each unaware of the other, watched, from different vantage points, the riders' progress, and there was hunger in each pair of eyes. Those belonging to Verm Bludvile burned with hatred, while the other eyes belonged to Lucretia Beaufort.

Despite all her father's exhortations, Lucretia had found excuse after excuse to delay her marriage to Albrecht Pentrojan. On this fateful day, like most of her days, she was sequestered in a small private room at the top of a belvedere set high above her father's residence, with its lancet window looking northwards over the Vildpline.

When she realised it was Cesare who was riding out with the hunting party, her whole body ached with longing. She recalled when she was first introduced to the young Cesare by her father Arnulf. That was almost five years ago when she was twelve and Cesare fifteen. Her father had taken her riding across the Vildpline on her new palfrey named Blossom. Even now, she could recall vividly the sweet scent of summer grass; could feel again the pleasure of wind blowing wildly through her hair as she galloped ahead of her father.

'Lucretia, look, look,' her father shouted to her. She reined in Blossom and looked to where her father was pointing. A lone rider was racing at a diagonal to them across the Vildpline on a black stallion, flanked by two brindled alaunts. Even from a distance Lucretia could see how at ease the rider sat. She could hear him calling out to the graceful hounds.

'On, on, Thunder, Lightning,' challenging them to run faster and faster.

'By heavens, what a horseman,' her father exclaimed, as they watched in admiration.

'Why it's Prince Cesare,' he said as the rider got closer. The young prince raced at speed in their direction, and did not notice Lucretia or her father, who were partially hidden by a tiny stand of hazel trees, that grew in clusters across the Vildpline.

'Lucretia, watch out!' her father shouted in consternation as Cesare, spotting them at the last moment, hauled his mount to a shuddering stop in a swirl of flying clay and grass. Lucretia's palfrey shied sideways in panic, throwing her to the ground. The next thing she remembered was being lifted to her feet. Cesare was standing directly in front of her, supporting her by both arms.

'Are you hurt? I'm sorry. I did not see you. Can you stand? Please tell me, are you hurt?' There was panic in the young prince's voice.

'Stand back, I think you have done enough harm, stand back.' Lucretia's father pushed Cesare aside. 'Lucretia, my child, let me look at you. Can you walk? Come, walk forward.' He placed an arm around her shoulder and encouraged her to walk a few steps.

'Good, no broken legs at least.' He glared at Cesare.

'I'm sorry, sir,' was all the young prince could say. Beaufort turned away from him and began to examine his daughter's hands and arms.

'Father, I am perfectly all right. Please don't fuss.' She looked at Cesare. He was standing staring at her, arms dangling helplessly, a look of consternation on his face. It was that awkward, boyish vulnerability that filled her instantly with tenderness for him. It was an image that would never be far from her mind. She smiled as she remembered it now, watching once again Cesare's flight across the Vild-pline.

Days after that first brief encounter, the young prince, being of age, was sent to commence his Quadrivium studies in the monastery of Anselem. But before he left, on one of those rare occasions when she was unaccompanied, he appeared as if from nowhere.

'My Lady Lucretia I am sorry if I startled you again. I ... I hope you have recovered from your fall.'

'Yes,' was all she could say.

'Please accept this and my apologies.' He extended his right hand. In his palm was an exquisite rose-shaped brooch.

'Oh, it is so beautiful,' she exclaimed, 'but I could not take it. It's too good ... my father –'

'Please, take it.' He took her hand and placed the brooch in her palm. She did not resist. The memory made her body tremble with pleasure, as it did then when their fingers touched and lingered. Her companion Celeste had arrived at that moment and Cesare, his face flushed, bowed awkwardly and left without speaking another word.

There was not a day that passed during Cesare's five-year absence and her schooling in Nuvarro that she did not think of him. She experienced again the excitement she felt when Cesare was forced to return to Dredgemarsh on the death of his father, and she was recalled briefly from Nuvarro to attend the funeral ceremony. She remembered every detail of meeting him then.

'I hope you have not fallen off any ponies of late,' he said, in an awkward attempt to be amusing.

'No indeed, Sire,' was all she said. A strained silence fell between them. Professor Quickstrain hove into view. She could see the relief on Cesare's face as he excused himself and turned to talk to the Professor. She chastised herself for being so tongue-tied in his presence. Yet she sensed that Cesare, despite all his learning, was equally inept at talking in her presence.

Lucretia was also certain that the overpowering attraction she felt for him then was not one-sided. On more than one occasion she caught him staring intently in her direction. She was well aware, even then, that Cesare, once he became king, would be expected to consider political alliances with powerful neighbouring countries when choosing a bride. But these were not insurmountable barriers in the eyes of Lucretia; love would find a way. On her return to Nuvarro to complete her schooling, she never abandoned the dream that she and Cesare would be together. Her lady-in-waiting, and close companion, Celeste, exhorted her daily to forget about him, indeed, to never put her trust in any man.

'They are all the same. They'll break your heart and not think twice about it.'

If she knew, as she watched Cesare now, that another pair of eyes also watched, but with the most evil intent, she would have been sick with fear.

'Gotcha ... bastard,' Verm crooned to himself, as he made his final calculations on exactly where Cesare would enter and exit Grak's Forest. He then hastily abandoned a seldom-used bartizan on the north wall of Dredgemarsh where he had set up his observation post for the last two weeks.

Lucretia, still seated by her window, was reading her favourite book of poetry: Ars Amatoria. It would be some time before Cesare would return, but she would be there waiting. Had she looked up from her book, she might have

spotted the shadow of Verm Bludvile astride a jennet slipping northwards to Grak's Forest along the eastern edge of
the Vildpline, where stunted trees and hedges separated that
glorious grassy plain from the rim of Meregloom Gorge.

When the afternoon cooled and the sun descended behind the Anselem mountains, the hunters turned for home.
The pounding of the horses' hooves drove through the great
forest like war cannon, booming through the maze of leafy
corridors. Cesare dodged through the trees at reckless speed.
The party with him were content to follow at a more sedate
pace.

'Halt! Listen!' Tancredi held up his hand. They drew rein.
The noise of their lord's boisterous progress had ceased.
There was utter silence.

'Call out,' Tancredi commanded and Jakob shouted.

'Sire, where are you?' There was no answer. 'Sire,' he
called again and still there was no answer.

'Spread out,' Tancredi said, 'and move forward slowly. Be
careful.' Within minutes, they found him. He was lying face
down, with the head of a bolt from a crossbow protruding
from his back.

'He has been killed. The King has been killed,' one of the
party shouted hysterically.

'No! no!' another shouted. 'He's alive!' The party gathered
around the fallen King.

'You two, quick, back to Dredgemarsh, bring the hospital
coach and Keenslide. Bring Keenslide. Tell him exactly
what's happened. Go! Now!' Tancredi snapped out the commands while at the same time attempting to raise Cesare
into a more comfortable position. Cesare's back was bathed
in blood and his face contorted in pain. He tried to speak,
but could not. His eyes rolled. He slouched forward. Tan-

credi and Jakob sat on either side holding him in a half-sitting position: three men melded together in a bloody tableaux, illuminated by the slanting spears of light shimmering through the green canopy above them.

Dredgemarsh

Chapter 10

She knew, felt it in the deepest recesses of her heart that Cesare was hurt. She saw frantic members of the royal party racing across the Vildpline from Grak's forest. He was not with them. They were waving their arms and calling out long before they reached the castle or could be understood by anyone. Her heart began to beat so fast she thought it might burst.

'No! This cannot happen.' She was talking out loud without knowing it. Her eyes glistened with the onset of tears and she wished time would stand still, wished that those frantic men would never reach the castle, her mind filling with an unreasonable hate for them because they were returning and he was not.

'Wait. Wait. This is foolish. It's something else. They have discovered something. Yes, it's something else.' She knew she was deceiving herself, but, just then, it was enough to ward off, for a few precious moments, the awful truth that was insisting to be heard. In those few critical moments, she chose action over despair. Almost in a trance, she made her way to the courtyard from whence Cesare had so recently departed. She was totally unaware of how long it took her to get there but when she arrived, a chaotic scene intensified the dread in her mind. As if in confirmation of her worst fears, the long, delicately sprung Infirmary coach was harnessed and preparing for departure. Surgeon Keenslide and Ned Clinker, his assistant, were piling blankets, bandages and an assortment of medical equipment onto the coach.

'What's happened?' She held her breath, waiting for the response. The man she had asked was in the middle of a garbled conversation with some others.

'King's dead ... or almost dead. We think. Assassination.' The man, in the thick of conversation with his companions, casually cast these few words over his shoulder to Lucretia, whom he did not recognise in the turmoil. Lucretia gasped. The despair she felt was as real and tangible as any pain she had ever felt, but infinitely more dreadful. She could feel it creeping through her bones and flesh like death itself.

Ned Clinker was assisting Surgeon Keenslide into the coach, which was now ready to leave. Two Lydian cobs snorted and pranced in the traces as if they knew there was urgent business afoot.

'Wait, wait, I must go with you,' Lucretia cried out and ran to the coach.

'What's this? We cannot delay ...' Keenslide called out in exasperation.

'It's Lady Lucretia, surgeon Keenslide,' Ned responded.
'What?'

'Lady Lucretia. She wants to help.'

'Well come, come, no more delays.'

Lucretia, with Ned's help, climbed quickly into the coach. It lurched forward at the crack of the coachman's whip. They raced across the cobbled Plaza. Sparks flew from the feet of the great cobs. Lucretia heard the coachman yelling as they approached the main gate, which opened wide enough for the coach to drive through without slowing. The loud clatter of hooves changed to a muffled thunder as they passed from the cobbles onto the outer promenade of the castle. They sped onwards across the wide meadowlands of the Vildpline, towards Grak's forest, and Lucretia repeated over and over,

'Not yet, not yet.'

When they finally came to where he lay on the blood-soaked ground, Lucretia, oblivious to everyone, ran to him and took his hand in hers. Tancredi and Jakob, who had remained with Cesare, moved back to allow Keenslide access to the King.

'It is not your time,' Lucretia cried with such fierce intensity, as if she would will life into Cesare. For a few moments, Keenslide, though anxious to examine the fallen King, held back. Very slowly, the eyelids on the deathly white face of the stricken King, opened and for an instant those burning black eyes focused on Lucretia, rolled skywards and closed once more.

'Stay with us sire, stay with us.' Her tone changed to that of a distraught child.

'You cannot leave us ... leave me like this, not like this.' She stroked, ever so gently, the hair back from his forehead. Almost imperceptibly, she felt the Lord of Dredgemarsh tighten his grip on her trembling hand. Even in that moment of agony, her heart swooned with a strange despairing happiness.

'Young lady, we must attend to him at once.' Keenslide directed his assistant Ned Clinker and the coach driver to gently manoeuvre Cesare onto a hide stretcher. They laid him on his side in the long coach, on a thick layer of blankets, wedging more blankets around him so that he could not move and damage himself further.

'Keep him warm, Ned, and don't let him move an inch.' Keenslide said. Ned covered his patient with more blankets, sat on the floor of the coach behind Cesare and, very gently but firmly, grasped the prostrate patient by the shoulder and hip. Lucretia sat on the other side holding Cesare's hand.

'I'm ready, surgeon Keenslide, he'll not budge.' They commenced the long slow journey back to Dredgemarsh with Tancredi and Jakob following in the coach's wake, with Cesare's stallion in tow.

All the while, Lucretia talked to Cesare, talked about their first meeting, about how she thought of him every day and a million other trivial things. When she ran out of talk she crooned nursery rhymes and recited favourite poems. Instinctively this young, inexperienced girl knew that the delicate thread of Cesare's life would break, and he would quietly drift from them, from her, without the anchor of her voice. And all of those present were strangely consoled by her soft melodious speech.

But the spell was broken every now and then, when the normally courteous, Keenslide shouted at the perspiring coach driver.

'Careful. Careful, you oaf!'

With every revolution of the coach wheels, every jolt and shake, their anxiety increased. They were no more than halfway across the Vildpline when Keenslide ordered the coach to stop.

'What is wrong? Lucretia asked.

'The Infirmary is too far, lady. Ned,' he called out, 'Ned, take his majesty's horse and ride ahead as fast as possible. Prepare one of the groom's quarters just off the stables. Fire, water, trestle, cauteries and my surgical instruments. Go now, as fast as the wind, Ned. I'll take over here.' Keenslide lowered himself into Ned's position and took over the duty of holding the patient as still as possible.

'Are you sure you'll be ...' Ned was looking anxiously at his master.

'Go, Ned, there's not a moment to spare.'

The coach moved off once again, but this time the coach driver led the pair of cobs on foot. Slowly, they crossed the Vildpline till at last they rolled through the main gates of the castle and across the great cobbled square of The Four Towers, with Keenslide wincing at every little jolt of the coach. Then, at last, with the tenderest of care, they carried Cesare to a groom's quarters beside the stables under the shadow of the great Blue Tower. Ned had prepared everything as Keenslide had ordered.

'We dare not move him any further,' Keenslide explained to Lucretia.

No one was allowed into that room while the surgeon and his assistant were operating. They were skilful men and set about their business in a restrained, professional manner. Working in silence, it was as though they shared each other's thoughts, Ned anticipating every requirement of his master. A great cauldron of boiling water burbled on a crane and hook over a blazing fire. Protruding from the glowing embers themselves were the handles of several cauterising irons. An urgent knock on the door was answered by Ned. He ushered in the armourer Gawan, who carried a leather sack with the tools of his trade.

'We need to extract this bolt as fast as possible and without moving the patient. Give your tools to Ned first,' Keenslide said. Ned took Gawan's tools and plunged them into the boiling water. Gawan could not take his eyes off the iron bolt protruding from Cesare's fair skin. He looked repulsed and sickened at the desecration of the young King.

'Just tell me what to do, surgeon Keenslide,' he said.

'Remove the head of the bolt, with as little movement of the shaft as possible. Ned and I will hold the patient still. When you are finished, grab those cauterising knives from the fire and be ready to hand them to me when I ask. Do you understand?' A perspiring Gawan nodded.

'Now, we must do this swiftly.' Keenslide took hold of Cesare's shoulder and Ned held the torso and hips in his powerful grip. Gawan worked quickly and to the surprise and admiration of Keenslide, the head of the bolt fell to the floor within minutes.

'Bravely done,' Keenslide said, and immediately gripped the back end of the bolt and slid it out of Cesare's body. Great gobbets of blood began to flow from the wound. Keenslide, perspiration pouring down his face, grabbed one of the glowing cauterising irons from Gawan and inserted it directly into the wound. Gawan squeezed his eyes shut and turned his head away.

'Ned, hold it, I'll do the other side,' Ned held the first cauterising iron in place with one hand while still firmly grasping Cesare's shoulder. Keenslide rushed to the other side of the trestle, grabbed the other cautery and inserted it into the exit wound on Cesare's back. Gawan staggered to the corner of the room, gagging at the smell of burning flesh.

'You did well, Gawan,' Ned called out. 'You did well.' When the cauteries were removed, Keenslide poured warm oil into the wounds and then packed them with compresses soaked in wine. Ned took care of the final bandaging with lint and linen strips.

The operation was over, and Cesare Greyfell lay drained and barely breathing on the makeshift operating table. Ned Clinker began the chore of cleaning the surgical instruments and cauteries. There was so much blood it was hard to believe that Cesare could still be alive. Gawan, ever so quietly, slipped out of the room with his tools and a sickly look on his face.

Breathing heavily, the old surgeon, now almost as ashen-faced as his patient, lowered himself slowly onto a small stool next to Cesare.

'Who did this, Ned? Why?' The old surgeon sighed. 'If this young man dies ... it's the end of everything, everything.'

'You have done all that's possible, sir.'

'I fear it will not be enough. If only we had gotten to him sooner.' Keenslide wearily rose from his seat. 'I almost forgot, Ned. The young Lady Lucretia, she is waiting for word. She was devastated. I never realised ... never realised. I will talk to her now.'

Lucretia had remained just outside the door of the temporary sick room during the operation. Her eyes were full of fear and she seemed not to hear the frequent solicitous comments of the guards posted outside, suggesting that she seat herself next to the brazier they had lit to dispel the chill evening air. After Gawan rushed out, his face grey and drawn, the fear etched on Lucretia's face turned to terror.

Then the door opened again. Surgeon Keenslide, his eyes sunken, a look of exhaustion on his face, stared out at her, hesitated, as if not quite sure what to do or say, but finally beckoned her inside.

Chapter 11

Even in the hallowed council chamber of Dredgemarsh, there was an air of overwrought agitation.

'Has he died?' one asked.

'No, couldn't be, we would have heard,' another answered.

'I'm not so sure.'

'There's no heir.'

In the centre of the chamber was a raised dais, carved completely in black porphyry. It was three steps high, with each level supported by intertwining snakes and lizards with eyes and scales of sapphire, alexandrite, amethyst and lapis lazuli. The reflections from the flickering candlelight—there were no windows—gave the impression that the snakes and lizards were sliding and weaving in perpetual movement. On top of this heaving mass was a throne of carved black oak. It took the form of two griffins whose heads and necks formed the armrests, wings formed the seat, and tails, curled up and around, formed the back. This was Grak's Throne, repulsive and malevolent as Grak himself, who died of leprosy, and still, two generations after his death, induced shivers of apprehension, even at the mention of his name. He was the first and last person to ever sit on that throne. Below the dais and Grak's throne were two more modest seats, used by the current King and his Chancellor.

Around the oak panelled walls of the chamber were rows of intricately carved chairs. The room gave the impression of being carved out of one great oak trunk. Above every chair hung a bronze scroll with a name embossed on each. There were forty chairs in all and, of those forty, only seven were now occupied; that seven represented the entire senior council of Dredgemarsh.

Tancredi sat in his usual seat, next to the now empty seat of the King. Facing him and occupying three seats to his left, were Grunkite, the Marshall of the Royal Household, the monk Jerome and the ambassador Flinch. To the right sat Spline, the sage, Flingthrift the treasurer and old Captain Gastsack, so-called military advisor. Gastsack had, more or less, slept his way through thirty years of council meetings. His only contribution in all that time had been an impassioned plea to provide better heating in the chamber, during one particularly severe winter.

Grunkite was entirely clad in heavy black leather, except for his feet, on which he wore a pair of torn slippers. He suffered from bad feet. They were his curse and daily torment, poor and miserable supports for an otherwise powerful and robust body.

'Come on, come on, get on with it,' he was mumbling to

no one in particular and drumming his fingers on the arms of the chair.

Beside Grunkite sat a tall lean man with short jet-black hair lying flat on a narrow skull. His skin was off-white, and stretched so tight across his face that there seemed to be every danger of his chin or nose perforating the dry tissue of flesh. Spline, for that was his name, was a philosopher. He was staring fixedly at Tancredi. Spline's tiny black eyes were like smudges of soot on each side of a long tapering nose that almost completely hid the tiny slit of his lipless mouth. It was hard to determine if Spline was extremely intelligent or grossly stupid. The only two expressions ever displayed by this razor-faced man were intense concentration or complete blankness. He was a puzzle to everyone because his sporadic utterances sounded profound, though no one ever really understood them. Spline never explained anything he said, no matter how esoteric the pronouncement. Others interpreted his words to suit their own ambitions or to explain current events. Whether his words were the output of a powerful analytical mind or the spontaneous eruptions of an idiot's shattered brain did not really matter, for he always seemed to encapsulate some wisdom that provoked and directed the thought processes of others to some imagined wisdom.

Tancredi's normally pale cheeks were slightly flushed. He stole a nervous glance in the direction of the monk Jerome. As always, there was a palpable tension in the holy man, the feeling of a continual inner struggle to subjugate some fierce passion. This restraint seemed only to emphasise the aura of strength that emanated from him. He was the aesthete and the libertine, the saint and the sinner and all were in awe of him. Tancredi was looking for some clue as to Jerome's state of mind. The monk just sat there glaring at the floor, his bearded chin supported by his fist, his elbow on his knee and his glistening black hair looking like the shiny black oak of Grak's throne. Then slowly, as if sensing Tancredi's glances he raised his head slightly, without removing his chin from his fist, and looked straight at the Chancellor. Their eyes locked for an instant but Tancredi, the politician, the avoider of direct confrontations, quickly disengaged and proceeded to read, or pretended to read a parchment spread out on the small desk beside his chair.

There were two others at that council meeting: the scribes, who sat shoulder to shoulder at a large desk to one side of the King's chair. There was a massive logbook open before them and they were writing simultaneously, each on the opposing pages. Dipslick, the small grizzle-haired man with a comic little paunch and a red nose wrote down every word spoken by Tancredi while his larger stooped companion recorded all the replies and retorts of the council members. This was Havelock. Havelock's skin was of a greyish yellow colour, and despite his large frame he appeared to be endowed with an over-abundance of this same skin. It was wrinkled and folded all over his body, even down to his fingertips which spread like soft putty every time he placed them on a hard surface.

Havelock and Dipslick rarely looked up from their work and communicated only very occasionally with each other and only with Tancredi when it was absolutely necessary, and only then in monosyllables. In the main, they were able to communicate by nudges, nods, winks, grunts and coughs, thus avoiding the effort of articulate speech, which they had long ago abandoned as tiresome and superfluous. Their actual knowledge of the language was, however, staggering for individuals who chose not to speak. They could write with astounding fluidity, recording every utterance of a speaker, no matter how fast he might speak. They were inseparable, working, eating and sleeping together.

Dipslick was the more wayward of this couple and was permanently drunk, a condition he diligently maintained by a constant and dedicated addiction to medovukha. His yellowing companion detested medovukha but surrendered himself to the pleasures of smoking Black Shag every evening when they retired to their quarters.

Tancredi, for whom they worked, knew practically nothing about them because he had simply inherited them when he secured his present office. In his eyes they were nonentities, merely recording machines, useful but otherwise of no consequence. This, of course, suited the scribes perfectly.

'Councillors of Dredgemarsh,' Tancredi finally intoned, 'The news may already have reached your ears that our dear King, Cesare Greyfell, is gravely ill. A cowardly and vicious assault was made this very day on his royal person. He barely clings to life. He is in the care of Surgeon Keenslide. All we can do is pray for a miracle.' He paused for several moments to gauge the effects of his words. Remarkably, Gastsack, the old military adviser was awake, and Flinch the ambassador was nodding his approval.

'Hypocrite,' Gruntkite muttered under his breath.

'But there is work to be done.' Tancredi resumed. 'We must find the perpetrator of this heinous act. Who would possibly wish to kill our King? Why? Is it simply some madman, or are there darker forces attempting to destroy us? Is there an old enemy within our midst? Is it someone we know? Do we have anything to fear from a neighbouring kingdom? Ambassador Flinch, what do you think?'

'Em ... I ... eh, I cannot imagine so, Lord Chancellor.'

'Does that mean you don't know or you are not sure?'

'Well ... what I mean is ... I don't think we have any reason to suspect any of our neighbours. There has been no indication of hostility, but, of course, things may have changed.' The ambassador was sweating profusely. There was silence. Flinch had obviously finished what he had to say, but Tancredi waited, as if more was expected. Flinch looked nervously from side to side, clearly hoping that some other councilor would fill the void. But the unnerving silence was not broken.

'Naturally, of course, in the circumstances it would probably be wise to ... to–' Flinch began to babble.

'Wise to prepare for another round of visits, Ambassador Flinch.' Tancredi curtly cut in. 'I suggest you leave tomorrow. I will see you tomorrow morning and prepare the appropriate letters and seals before you go.'

Tancredi began immediately and pointedly to peruse another document on his desk, making it quite obvious that he was finished with Flinch. The ambassador sat back into his seat with a sigh of relief. No one in that chamber, apart from Jerome, who sat opposite, noticed the faint sardonic smile on the Chancellor's face.

Then slowly, and with the kind of emphasis one reserves for profoundly serious matters, Tancredi intoned the word SECURITY. Instantly Grunkite became attentive and leaned forward in his chair like a roused watchdog. Tancredi nonchalantly turned his gaze towards the bristling Marshall.

'I'm sure, sir,' he said, 'that it has crossed your mind, that this savage attack on our dear King is associated with all the other recent misfortunes; the missing weapons, the slaughter of Thunder, the King's alaunt, his hawk, need I go on? You have been investigating these outrages for some time now; perhaps you might tell us if you have anything to report, anything at all.' He stressed the 'anything.'

'You know well,' Grunkite flung every word towards Tancredi, stabbing the air with his thick forefinger, 'that everything that is humanly possible is being done. There will not be a single bolthole in this city, above or below ground, that will not have been searched by the end of next week. There is no hiding place for the slime polluting this castle.' Grunkite realised he was beginning to shout, and immediately lowered his voice. 'My men are on duty, every one of them, every hour of the day and night. They will remain so until we rid ourselves of the evil amongst us. We will root them out! No one, high or low,' he glared at Tancredi, pausing on the word high, 'will desecrate this kingdom and escape, no one.' He hammered home the last two words and sat defiantly onto his seat.

Tancredi sat impassively throughout this tirade and when it subsided, merely said, 'Yes,' in a most offhand way, paused to browse further through the documents in front of him and then, without raising his eyes, continued, 'Let us hope your prodigious efforts will shortly bear fruit, Marshall Grunkite. I am led to believe that some of your men are somewhat reluctant to search the tunnels. However, in view of what you have told us, I think we can assume that we have been misinformed.'

Grunkite had by now turned a deep red; throbbing veins stood out on his temples. Tancredi continued in a quiet tone of voice. 'One small matter which you might pursue further, Marshall, this em Candlelighter, Vine ... no Verm, Verm Bludvile whose services I have recently dispensed with, he appears to be missing. The foul creature is probably dead.

He is hardly a suspect, but he might just know something. Try to find him, if that is possible.'

Grunkite was, by now, speechless with rage. Tancredi was giving him direct orders, something unprecedented. The Marshal of Dredgemarsh had always taken his orders directly from the King. He lurched out of his chair with as much noise as he could possibly make, and strode as purposefully as his sore feet would allow out of the chamber.

'I would remind the departing councillor that there are protocols on the order in which the King, Chancellor and councillors enter and exit these sacred chambers.' Tancredi called out so that the departing Grunkite could hear him. His face was white as he spoke. 'Tantrums and disrespect for our procedures will not help us,' he continued in a more subdued tone, when Grunkite was gone.

The council meeting finished with a promise from Tancredi to hold another meeting shortly to review all relevant matters, after which he swept out of their presence. The remaining councillors left quickly after him, without a single word or token of acknowledgement to each other. They in turn were followed by Havelock and Dipslick , after the ink had dried on their minutes book, and their writing equipment was cleaned and packed away.

The Griffins were left to smirk in the flickering light of the council chamber and one might well imagine their mocking cackling filling that dreadful timber vault, now deserted by the paltry band of misfits that were the hope and future of Dredgemarsh.

Chapter 12

Never had Dredgemarsh seemed so forlorn. It was subsiding slowly towards extinction, as if in sympathy with its dying King. Once it was a proud, teeming fortress city that had grown and sprawled over the landscape in a fever of shops, cathedrals, inns, palaces and bustling arcades. They were now mostly derelict. On quiet summer evenings, the perpetually flaking masonry was a baleful music that forever assailed the ears of the remaining citizens. It made their sleep uneasy, mesmerising them into a grim acceptance of the inevitable decay of Dredgemarsh.

Surgeon Keenslide, exhaustion etched in every feature, watched with growing dread over his precious patient.

'He grows weaker, Ned. Whatever chance he might have in the infirmary, he has none here.'

' And we can't move him,' Ned sighed.

'I've gone over it a thousand times. Lifting him from his bed onto a litter would probably kill him. We would need to lift the whole bed itself and ... it's just not possible ... even to carry his bed ... the obstacles and steps from here to the infirmary ... it would be a sentence of death to even try it.'

'There has got to be a way, Surgeon Keenslide.'

'I am thinking, Ned, that we should prepare for the inevitable.'

It was night, and the drear castle lay like a great beast under a dense ultramarine sky swimming with stars. The myriad night sounds rose through the sullen air like the song of the locust, and the turgid Yayla River slid like a great python around the western and southern walls of the city. And yet, amidst all that decay, there was still a vital life force, an unquenchable desire for rebirth, burning in the heart of that great colossus.

Signalling that life force, a slowly rotating anemometer in the dome of the university defied the slow sultry air. From a distance it looked like a child's windmill but in reality each of its five hemispherical vanes measured forty feet across, were constructed of iron and mounted on a great shaft that protruded from the dome of the university. Unlike the surrounding structures, the anemometer was maintained in immaculate condition and, despite its massive size, it revolved with an eerie silence. It was primarily used to regulate the airflow to the furnaces buried in the basements of the university. Through an intricate web of chains, cogs and pulleys it regulated the vents on the air tunnels leading to the furnaces and no matter how stormy or calm it might be, the anemometer provided the mechanical feedback to maintain a steady airflow. The inventor of this system was Professor Quickstrain, head of the scientific and astrological faculty and the last professor left in the university. There were no students any more. This did not bother Professor Quickstrain. In fact, it allowed him to devote all his time to scientific research and his many other inventions and ideas.

Quickstrain's more practical work included a sewage system, fresh water supply and mechanical hoists to lift and lower heavy goods, including people, to the many different floor levels within the castle. Water mills were the source of power for most of his machinery, designed into the base of the castle and driven by water channelled through an underground honeycomb of ducts and canals from the Yayla River.

On this particular evening, Quickstrain was seated at his drawing board, where he was making some minor modifications to the design of the Meregloom Dredger. This was one of Quickstrain's larger inventions. It was a floating turf dredger with a chain of interlocking punts. It was designed to scoop turf from the surface of the bog and fill the punts as they travelled on a great semi-circular rail from the interior of the castle to the bog and back into the castle. One of the major constraints on the design was the necessity for the punts to enter and exit the castle environs while still making it impossible for an enemy to use them to infiltrate or escape Dredgemarsh. This was the problem, which was teasing Quickstrain. As yet, he was totally unaware that the life of the young King of Dredgemarsh was flickering towards extinction.

Had he known, he would have been deeply distressed. Cesare was his patron and had always taken a keen interest in his work. Indeed, he was in the habit of discoursing with him on many scientific matters. Quickstrain was always amazed and puzzled at the keenness of Cesare's mind and his ability to comprehend complex scientific theories with apparent ease. If the truth were known, Cesare's mental agility sometimes depressed Quickstrain, when he thought of the relentless studies he pursued to master his subjects. However, his deep respect for the young King and his father before him completely buried such feelings almost before they entered his mind.

Quickstrain was not the only one awake that night. Back down in the little stable yard, off which the temporary sickbay was set up, Surgeon Keenslide paced slowly up and down. The clear starry sky accentuated the shadows where he walked below the great Blue Tower. He found solace in the dark, listening to the occasional whinny and snuffling of the horses and breathing in their pungent, pleasant aroma.

In another small room, deep within the castle, others found their solace in a less subtle but more direct and effective ways. Havelock the scribe was in a state of mental bliss as cloudy and ethereal as the miasma of pipe smoke that enveloped him in a cocoon of happiness. He was barely visible in the dense man-made cloud which he continually replenished by delicate puffs from his soft yellow lips. His eyes were half-closed as he lay back on an armchair in a state of semi-collapse, dressed in a full-length woollen nightshirt and multiple pairs of socks. His companion and fellow scribe, Dipslick, had slithered from the chair where, from all appearances, he had just lately dined, judging from the dirty eating utensils and scraps of food on the table. He lay prostrate and half under the table in an alcoholic coma. A large mazer was still in his grasp, a few drops of medovukha left in the bottom and the rest inside Dipslick, or else spilt on the floor. For this strange pair, it was another uneventful evening with nothing to distinguish it from the hundreds that went before it, and no expectation or wish that it should change for the next hundred.

Unlike his minions, Tancredi was awake and alert. His mind was continually revolving around the events of that day and the implications, possibilities and dangers for the future. It would be true to say that at first, he was shocked by the attack on Cesare, because he could not see Dredgemarsh surviving without the charismatic appeal of the King, and if Dredgemarsh did not survive then his power was gone. He had always considered that his natural place was to rule from behind the throne. There were dangers, of course, in adopting this role, because Cesare was only malleable and well disposed towards Tancredi because of the pledge he had made to his father and his sometimes-careless attitude to his kingly duties. But that might not last because Cesare, though still young and inexperienced, had shown, only too clearly, how much he was his own man when he wished to assert his authority.

Tancredi relished the political arena, and if for some reason Dredgemarsh were free of political intrigue, he, Tancredi, would create it. It was the game itself, and not the goal that completely dominated his every waking hour. Now, late into night, like a grand chess master, he explored the possibilities that that momentous day had brought. He wrote out his priorities for the following day and he turned to his supper of oaten cake and vernage. He took his time eating at a small stone table set in a bay window, which looked out over the northern side of the castle and its surrounding territory. The bright moon etched a stark chessboard of black shadows across the silver domes, spires and rooftops.

He was slightly startled to hear a faint knocking at his door. As he rose and advanced to enquire who was there,

Lucretia's voice, small and attenuated from the other side of the oak door, announced her presence. When he opened the door, she brushed past him without comment. She walked to the bay window, where he had been eating his supper.

'There is an urgent matter relating to the King. I must talk to you,' she said.

He did not answer immediately, but returned to his supper table and sat down. Lucretia remained standing.

'The news is not bad, I hope. I presume you have been attending his majesty.' Tancredi said.

'Keenslide is losing hope, but the King still clings to life.' Her voice trembled.

'And the urgent matter you wanted to discuss, dear cousin?' He directed her to be seated. She declined with a wave of her hand.

'It is the King's security ... another attack ... we don't know ... he can't be moved and ...' Try as she might, her voice was beginning to falter.

'Calm, dear cousin, calm. No one will get close to the King. I have already directed our Marshall and the King's royal guard to be extra vigilant.'

'Good, that is good.'

I'm happy to see that you are as concerned for our King's safety as I.' Tancredi paused to sip from the silver goblet of vernage and continued, 'even as you prepare for your own marriage.' Lucretia was silent. He broke off a small piece of oaten cake and began to eat. 'I know, dear cousin,' he said as he chewed, 'his majesty would be most touched by your loyalty . He does hold you in the highest esteem.'

'Has he said so ... ?' The instant she had spoken the words, a look of regret crossed her features. She turned away from Tancredi and gazed out of the window.

'What a wonderful view, cousin,' she said. Tancredi's eyes narrowed, and a sardonic smile played across his lips. He took another sip of vernage.

Lucretia, her face still hidden from him, bit her bottom lip. She turned and faced him.

'Who did it? How could it have happened? ' Her eyes flashed with anger.

'We don't know. It should never have happened but Grunkite is getting old and inept. We need a new man there.'

'Grunkite cannot be held responsible for what happened outside the castle. You were with the King when --'

'Security in general has been lax. The King has consistently ignored all my warnings regarding this matter.' Tancredi hastily stood up and moved towards his writing table. 'Perhaps good may come of all this. When the King recovers, let us pray he will. When he recovers, he may take my warnings on security more seriously. Yes, maybe this is the very thing we need to tighten up on things in general.' He paused and turned to face Lucretia. 'As to your earlier question, cousin, the answer is yes.'

'Yes? What are you talking about?' Lucretia said nonchalantly.

'Yes, the King did say he held ... holds you in high esteem.'

'I know he holds all his loyal subjects in high esteem.'

'He is a difficult young man to understand, but I know he counts you amongst his close friends.' Tancredi lingered on the word 'close. 'And,' he continued, 'he would not want you to delay your own marriage and happiness on his account.'

'I do my duty, cousin. I will help the King in any way I can. My personal affairs are of no account.' With that, she quickly let herself out. Tancredi smirked at the lavish night sky of Dredgemarsh and raised his goblet to his lips. Before he could drink, the cheek muscles just under his left eye began to spasm and his hand began to tremble.

"S'blood and damnation, not now!' he cried as the goblet fell to the floor.

Chapter 13

A bog jackal sang in the cold morning air. His plaintive melody insinuated itself in and out of the streets, alleyways and terraces of Dredgemarsh. A lone mangy dog, trotting across the Grand Plaza, stopped, listened to his wild cousin; then continued sniffing and pissing as he made his way across the still impressive marble plaza. High in his study overlooking the Plaza, a shaft of morning sunlight picked out, in the gloom, the sleeping Quickstrain. He lay slumped across the latest modified drawings of his turf dredger. He started uneasily at the cry of the jackal but did not waken, nor was he disturbed by the clatter of the kitchen boy as he backed into the laboratory, dragging a trolley after him. Burstboil was making his morning delivery of breakfast to the ageing professor. Unlike most other officials, Quickstrain was given the privilege of having all his meals delivered to his laboratory, so that he might not waste his valuable time visiting the refectory. It was Burstboil's responsibility to see that meals were delivered hot and on time; a chore he carried out carelessly. All too often the meals were cold, spilt and half-missing by the time they reached the professor. Quickstrain, luckily for Burstboil, was not one to pay particular attention to when, what or how much he ate. In fact, eating was a tedious task, just like sleep, which intruded on his time for scientific pursuits.

On this particular morning, Burstboil was so immersed in his own thoughts, a rare occurrence, that the Professor's breakfast, for once, was delivered hot and intact. On entering the laboratory the kitchen boy called out,

'Breakfast is ready, Professor Quickstrain sir.' Unlike other mornings, Burstboil waited for Quickstrain to rouse himself and then set the breakfast tray before him. The startled professor eyed Burstboil with a look of amazement and wonder on his face. Normally this nondescript urchin left the tray anywhere he could find space and departed immediately.

'Em ... oh ... yes ... well thank you em ... eh ... what's your name?'

'Burstboil, Francis Burstboil sir,' he replied with unusual civility and self-possession.

'Well, thank you, Francis, and good morning.'

'Professor, do you know what the latest news is, regarding the King?'

'Latest regarding the King, what do you mean, latest? What do you mean? What are you talking about?'

'He's dying.'

'Who's dying? The King? Is the king dying? What?'

'Yes, Professor.'

'The King ... dying ... well tell me, tell me, boy.' Burstboil, finding himself in the position of being able to inform
a professor of something, was excited with a new feeling of
self-importance.

'I was informed this morning of the terrible things that
have taken place in Grak's Forest. I'm one of the few who
really know where it happened. I know that forest well because I'm responsible for ...'

'Satan's balls! Quit the babbling and tell me what is happening.' Quickstrain's face was getting red. The growing
pride and self-important feeling fizzled from Burstboil's thin
chest like air from a burst balloon.

'He was shot,' he pouted and turned to leave.

'Wait there! Who shot him? Where is he now?'

'Don't know who shot him, no one knows. Surgeon
Keenslide has him in a room by the stables.' With that,
Burstboil almost ran from the study lest Quickstrain should
ask him any more questions.

Seconds after Burstboil had fled the room Quickstrain
followed, breakfast forgotten. He shuffled across the hall
and into the main laboratory of the university. It was a vast
circular space with desks, tables, machines, bottles, demi-
johns, tanks, pendulums, spheres, cones, semi spheres, baths
of acid bubbling and frothing, wheels spinning, and cogs
and pulleys grinding and creaking. In the very centre of this
chaos, the massive shaft of the anemometer revolved silently. The shaft was so big that it seemed the room was revolving around it rather than the other way round. Quickstrain picked his way through the maze of contraptions and
opened a door in a cylindrical cage that reached from the
floor to the ceiling. He stepped onto a platform within the

cage, pulled and jerked at a number of levers and began to vanish into the floor. This was Quickstrain's up and down hoist, which was powered by one of his water compressors. The hoist was the only one of its kind and was in the early stages of development. Only the King knew of this ingenious invention and had encouraged Quickstrain by giving him all the resources he required to complete his research on water compression. As he hurried along, Quickstrain pondered how his whole way of life depended entirely on the King. There was no one else in Dredgemarsh who showed such deep interest in his work. By the time he reached the stables, he was in a state of dreadful apprehension.

'Quickstrain,' Keenslide called to him from the stark morning shadows of the covered walkway in front of the stables, where he had been pacing up and down all night.

'Grak's warts! Tell me, what's happened, how is the King? I just heard about the calamity a short time ago. Why was I not told?' Quickstrain was gulping for air.

'Calm Professor, calm, let us sit over here and I will tell you all.'

They sat close together on a stone bench. Keenslide immediately began to describe all that had happened up to that moment.

'He is a strong man,' said Quickstrain.

'He has survived the night, and that is something. But I cannot see him recovering ... not here.'

As if from nowhere, Chancellor Tancredi suddenly appeared before them.

'Well, surgeon? And what is the news this morning?' As he was speaking, he began to move past Keenslide towards the King's temporary sick room.

'He is not to be disturbed.' Keenslide barked out. Tancredi turned to face the surgeon.

'You're the professional, of course.' He glared at Keenslide, and grimaced when the surgeon casually said, 'That's right,' and turned immediately to Quickstrain to resume the conversation that Tancredi had interrupted.

'If you would be so good as to tell me how the King is.' There was a very noticeable tremor in Tancredi's voice.

'Yes, of course. The King, his majesty, is in a most critical condition. Unless I can move him to the infirmary, there is little hope.' Keenslide turned his back on Tancredi and once more resumed conversation with Quickstrain. The Chancellor scowled and left as suddenly as he had arrived.

'Bloody upstart,' said Keenslide.

Quickstrain nodded, rose, scratched his head and mumbled to himself. 'The infirmary ... that's seven floors up ... as fast as possible ... smooth ... no jolts or shaking ... can't use stairs ... whole bed must be moved ... well this is a tricky one.' Then he turned towards Keenslide and said, 'I'll need a little time, surgeon.'

'Is there a way, professor?' There was the faintest glimmer of hope in Keenslide's eyes.

'Time, I need some time.' Quickstrain scratched his tousled grey head more vigorously.

'There is no time left. If I don't get him to the infirmary shortly, I simply cannot save him.'

'Yes, yes, I understand. I'll be back to you as soon as I can. Must find Grunkite.' Quickstrain shuffled off. Keenslide recommenced his endless pacing before the stable where Cesare Greyfell lay, poised on the brink of eternity.

Dredgemarsh

Chapter 14

There were beads of perspiration on Burstboil's pallid brow. 'He is probably dead now ... Mr. Bludvile ... sir.'

'Probably! Probably! Which is it? Alive! Dead! Which, which?'

'Well, he was alive but he, he ... he is very sick. They have him in the stables below the Blue Tower. They say he will not live.'

'But he is not dead! Still not dead! We'll soon settle that '

Verm had changed his appearance. He wore a military tunic, a leather helmet and cloak. Strapped to his side was a short sword and dagger. His second-in-command and only subordinate, Burstboil, was sporting a sword, belt and long cloak over his kitchen rags. The pair belied their clownish appearance with their deadly intent, or at least Verm Bludvile's deadly intent. He was nursing his psychopathic hatred of the King while Burstboil was vaguely conscious that the dreadful crime which was now to be brought to a successful conclusion would somehow free him from a life of drudgery in the kitchens of Dredgemarsh. He grabbed a blazing torch from their small brazier and trotted behind and to the right of Verm.

Despite the fact that Verm Bludvile was shorter than Burstboil, it was the latter who found it difficult to maintain the walking pace of Bludvile, and had to alternatively walk and skip along just to keep up. Bludvile moved so fast and surely through the dark sombre corridors of lower Dredgemarsh that it seemed as if he needed hardly any light to show him the way. Where they were going, only he knew, while his stumbling torch-bearer trotted obediently behind him, his excitement and fear growing with every step.

Eventually, unable to contain himself any longer, Burstboil blurted out, 'What are we going to do?'

'Finish the son of mongrels ... and anyone who stands in our way.' They rushed onwards. Burstboil was silent for a time till once more his fears bubbled to the surface.

'But there are lots of guards. They'll kill us if we are caught.'

Bludvile halted abruptly, turned on Burstboil and grabbed him by the throat.

'Beware, pot-scrubber, I say what is to be done or not done. We will kill him one way or another, no matter how many guards. I will find a way. There's no turning back.' Burstboil's chin wobbled, but he managed to control himself. He followed his demonic master with growing reluctance.

They were beginning to ascend now. As they did so, the air became cleaner and fresher. It dawned on Burstboil that they had entered a tower because the steps which they ascended were in the form of a spiral. The insipid flame from his smoky torch did not penetrate far into the surrounding penumbra, but on his right, he could see and touch the cold, flinty stonework of the curving tower wall. The stone steps protruded some three feet from the wall. There was no balustrade or rail on the left of the stony stairway, just a straight drop into terrifying darkness. The kitchen boy squeezed himself as tight to the wall as possible and tried not to look left. He was gasping for breath, while Verm appeared to glide up the steps as easily as he had traversed the corridors from whence they had come.

'Leave the light.' Bludvile ordered. Burstboil stood gaping up at Bludvile, not quite comprehending what was required of him.

'Leave the light, idiot, and follow me.'

Burstboil snapped out of his trance, found a rusting sconce in the wall and wedged the rush torch into it. To his great relief, at first, they had to go much slower as they left the range of the torchlight and entered the blackness above. It was now only by following the contours of the wall with his right hand and carefully feeling for each step with his feet and left hand that Burstboil made any progress. He could see nothing of Bludvile, but could hear the swish of his cloak and the odd rattle of his sword. However, even at this slower pace, Bludvile was steadily moving ahead until finally Burstboil could not even hear him.

A growing panic began to close in around the kitchen boy's heart. This turned to raw fear when he suddenly discovered, after a seemingly endless climb, the stone steps ended, to be replaced by iron steps that skewed out and away from the wall, and curved up into the darkness with no supports on either side. With a sob, Burstboil dropped to his knees and began to creep up the metal steps. He inched up-wards, crying and whimpering, afraid to go forward but ter-rified to go back. Flakes of rust broke away from the iron steps and drifted down into the black abyss below. He felt as if something was willing him to drop over the edge; it would be easy, just to float away quietly into the darkness. Then, oh, horror of horrors, the metal steps ended in mid-air, nothing in front and nothing on either side but a sheer drop into the impenetrable blackness. His heart was pounding; a low whine came from somewhere inside him and grew in pitch and intensity till he screamed out.

'Nooooooo.'

Then, just above him, there was a rustling and clanking sound, followed by Verm Bludvile's disembodied voice.

'Up here, idiot, above you.'

'Where, where?' wept Burstboil. 'I can't see anything.' He was not even sure if his eyes were open or closed right then.

'Stand up, idiot.'

With legs like marshmallows, Burstboil attempted to stand, but felt at that moment he was about to topple over.

'I can't, I can't, I'll fall over, please help me.'

'Help you! I'll throw you over the edge if you don't stand up now.'

Burstboil was crying uncontrollably as he raised himself on trembling legs. A hand grabbed him by the hair.

'Grab hold, grab hold,' shouted Verm.

Burstboil slammed into something hard and locked his arms around it. It was the end of a ladder, sticking down from nowhere. He had not discovered it initially because it was about four feet above the last step, hanging in mid air. Somehow, with the little strength left in him, and the aid of the hand pulling him by the hair, he scrambled onto the ladder, and after much swearing and cursing by Bludvile above him, he began to climb once more. With every step, he was now regretting the day he had ever set eyes on Verm Bludvile.

The ladder was quite long, and the climb took some considerable time. As he climbed, Burstboil began to collect his meagre wits. He noticed now that there was a glimmering grey light growing above his head. He also noticed, for the first time, that he had wet his pants. They were beginning to get cold and cling uncomfortably to his inner thighs. This was worse than any nightmare, and he wished more than anything for the warm steamy kitchens. Then at long last, the climb ended as he emerged through a trapdoor into a circular room, dimly illuminated by four narrow windows. Exhausted, he collapsed onto the floor and lay there moaning quietly to himself.

Fortunately for Burstboil, his master was totally absorbed, gazing downwards through one of the narrow windows. He gave a little shout of delight, banging his fist on the dusty windowsill.

'Ha, ha! So that's where he is. Well, that will do nicely. Hey you, pigshit, get over here and keep watch. Quick, quick, get over here.' Burstboil did not move. Bludvile ran across the room and landed a vicious kick into Burstboil's bony side.

The wretched boy crept over to the window to which Bludvile had immediately returned.

'Please don't hurt me,' he said.

Bludvile grabbed him by the back of the neck and shoved

him forward, forcing him to look downwards. Burstboil was now gazing down at a maze of buildings, paths, yards, gardens and streets. He quickly focused in on one area of activity; it was the stables and grooms' quarters, just below them, where the sick King was being presently cared for. It was clear that Grunkite had been very zealous in his security arrangements. Burstboil could see twelve fully armed guards and it was obvious that there were many more hidden from view.

With this discovery, the kitchen boy experienced a great gush of relief. His insides, which had been knotted with panic, relaxed. He was now certain that there was no way they could pursue their objective of finally dispatching the King. This, of course, increased his courage and bravado enormously and with as much vehemence as he could muster he swore.

'Damn those guards. We'll never get past them. Damn them all.' Burstboil waited for confirmation of his assessment of the situation. To his dismay, Bludvile did not acquiesce but had now stepped back from the window and was standing in a thoughtful pose, weighing up the situation, planning his next move. Still confident that their expedition was at an end, Burstboil stood up, assumed his version of a thoughtful pose, scratched his scrawny chin and repeated several times,

'Only for those guards we'd have him.' Bludvile appeared not to hear him and remained rapt in his own thoughts. As time went by, Burstboil began to lose his confidence, and eventually sat down on the floor and fixed his attention on Bludvile, a small dog waiting on its master. The longer he sat there, the dimmer grew his hopes of a suitably uneventful ending to the whole affair.

Burstboil's poor heart sank when Verm roused himself, exclaiming 'Ah, ha, we can still do it.'

'But, but the guards, they are all over the place.' Burstboil reminded him.

'Yes, we can do it. Fire, that's how. Yes. Very fitting. Who better than me to light the torch? Yes. Yes. Yes.' The maniac was stamping up and down, pounding his right fist into the palm of his left hand and gurgling horribly, heedless of the white saliva oozing down both sides of his chin. Silent once more, he dashed to the window and gazed hungrily down towards his prey.

'Like a rat in a trap,' he laughed. 'You! Keep watch. We don't want him gone when we light our little fire, do we? Don't move from this spot and don't take your eyes off that square below. If you fail me I'll leave you here, dunghead!' Burstboil cowered at the window unable to speak, feeling he would never speak again. Reality had turned to a nightmare, and terror into deep shock. He just nodded his head in response to Bludvile, who then departed like a wraith through the open trapdoor in the centre of the floor. Burstboil stared blankly at the stables below where, at that very instant, there was great commotion amongst the guards.

Dredgemarsh

Chapter 15

The cause of the commotion, observed but not comprehended, by the catatonic Burstboil, who sat staring wide-eyed from the narrow window high above in the Blue Tower, was Grunkite. He had arrived suddenly, unannounced, to inspect the guard, and found one of them dozing in the entrance of a stable, just next to the King's sickroom. On seeing the slacker, Grunkite's face turned a deep puce and he began to stalk towards the guard, who was still blissfully unaware of his approach. The unlucky guard's companions watched in horrified fascination as Grunkite reached his victim. As soon as he was within range of the sleeping guard, Grunkite crouched down and delivered a prodigious punch straight to the sleeper's crotch. He would have kicked him, but his feet were particularly tender of late. The unfortunate guard dropped like a stone, clutching at his groin, desperately trying to suck oxygen into a body paralysed with pain. He lay there twitching, grimacing and started to turn blue.

'You worthless cur,' roared Grunkite, who was holding his punching fist under his oxter in pain. 'Get up, or I'll give you more. Useless toad, get up, get up!' The guard was unable to comprehend anything other than the excruciating pain. He continued to twitch and gyrate in agony. Grunkite, his fury somewhat abating, screamed at another guard to remove the 'offal' immediately and throw 'it' into a cell. This done, Grunkite set about inspecting the rest of the guard. Never were they more alert, nor were they ever more uncomfortable as their old cantankerous Marshall eyeballed each and every single one of them.

Grunkite was still smarting from the treatment he had received at the hands of Tancredi during the previous evening's council meeting and he was further incensed by the fruitless searches carried out by his guards that very morning in the north-western section of the castle. The searchers were moving eastwards, led by lymers and their fewterers, while another team of guards were inspecting the eastern perimeter of the fortress wall, with a view to discovering some secret entrance from the mist-covered Meregloom Marsh, which would permit the enemy to come and go at will. Grunkite was working on the assumption that the would-be assassin in Grak's forest and the mischief-maker of previous weeks within the castle were one and the same person or persons. That being so, he felt certain that this enemy must have some means of entering and leaving the castle unseen and unheard. Once found, he would set a trap and capture the transgressor who was causing such havoc.

Having completed his inspection of the guard, Grunkite

walked almost daintily from the courtyard, and up stairs that connected to a narrow walkway leading to the lookout towers on the ramparts.

'I'll be back,' he shouted, without turning round. All the guards visibly relaxed. They glanced furtively at each other for some time, not daring to speak until they were certain that Grunkite was definitely gone. After about five minutes, two guards standing close to each other began to cautiously discuss exactly what they would like to do to their Marshall. Suddenly, someone was heard approaching, and the frightened guards snapped to attention, suspecting that Grunkite had sneaked back to catch them unawares. They were wrong, and soon discovered their mistake when a jabbering Assistant Cook Meister, Ratchet, staggered into view with a large insulated urn of soup which he had carried from the kitchen. He was sweating profusely and gasping for air, while at the same time pleading with someone coming up behind him.

'Please, Cook Meister Clutchbolt, just a moment.'

'Nonsense, Ratchet, stop carrying on, we're almost there.'

'But I'm ready to drop ...'

'Ratchet, the soup will spoil if there are any more delays. If you had more control over that creep of a kitchen boy he would be here to help you. Stop whining and move.'

The creep of a kitchen boy could not hear what they said, but he could see them. For the first time since going into his current state of shock, his traumatised face showed just a flicker of mental activity. He arched his left eyebrow slightly and at the same time, halted and reversed the blossoming of a large drip that was accumulating on the end of his nose by means of a sudden sobbing inhalation. With his eyebrow lowered, he resumed his shallow breathing. The drip reappeared and grew with alacrity till it plopped off the end of his grimy nose onto the window ledge. Without blinking, and too late, Burstboil dragged his sleeve across his nose and succeeded in making his face even grimier than before, what with the tears, snots, cobwebs and dust. He was, of course, long past caring about his appearance.

He continued to stare blankly at the distant courtyard below. How long he sat there, face glued to the narrow window-pane, he could not tell, but somehow, as if waking from a dream, what he was now looking at, filled his already tortured soul with dread. There below, pointing straight up at him was Professor Quickstrain. Gathered round him and also looking up were several guards, carpenters and labourers. Once more, Burstboil wet his trousers and sat frozen, unable to move back from the window.

Quickstrain was indeed pointing at the very window where Burstboil sat, but he had not seen the kitchen boy, nor had any of the others who were gathered around Quickstrain. The professor, in fact, was simply giving instructions on one of the anchorage points for a series of ropes and pulleys which would enable them to very slowly winch the sick King, secured to his pallet, up and back over the stables onto a balcony, from where he could be wheeled a short distance on smooth floors straight to the infirmary. There he could be treated properly and had some chance of survival. There would be the minimum likelihood of jolting or sudden movement, which Keenslide feared so much. The plan was simple and neat and could be effected within hours.

'How do we get inside that tower and to that window?' one of the carpenters asked uneasily.

'Don't worry, security will get you there.' Quickstrain said, looking around for Grunkite, who by now had returned and was very carefully taking note of the exact procedure for moving the King. Keenslide was also present and fully involved in the preparations.

'You'll have two guards to take you to the tower above.' Grunkite beckoned two guards. They approached, glancing nervously at each other. Grunkite moved out from the main group with the pair close by him, and pointing up towards the terror-stricken Burstboil, delivered detailed instructions on exactly what was expected of them. Meanwhile, Quick-strain was making sure that the two workmen who would go up into the tower had all the necessary tools and equipment to execute the job swiftly. The two guards and two work-men then came together briefly, and in unison moved in towards the base of the tower, out of Burstboil's field of view. He knew then, even in his demented state, that these men were coming up through the dark tower towards him. He was certain that they knew he was there and why he was there.

He wanted to run over to the open trapdoor and shout down to them, 'I'm here, I surrender, I'm sorry, I'll never do it again, please help me.' But he could not move and they were coming, sneaking, creeping up the long dark stairway.

'Oh Mistress Crumble, I'm sorry. I'm so sorry.' he began to mumble. He wished himself back in the Dredgemarsh kitchens, scrubbing floors and being ordered about by everyone save the kitchen cat. He longed for the reassurance of a stinging slap across the ear from Bella Crumble. The image was bliss and his mind focused and froze on that image. Thus he remained, only dimly conscious of the shadows that pressed and converged in an ever-tightening circle around him. The puny kitchen boy was suspended in a crucible of terror that promised to shatter his mind like glass. His only means of defence was physical and mental paralysis. Some-where deep within him, these primitive mechanisms were triggered.

Chapter 16

Approaching the stable yard and the King's sickroom, unheard and unseen, Verm hauled his antique barrow filled with jars of torch oil. Within the confines of the dark tunnel through which he moved, the noise of the iron wheels and rattling jars was deafening, but thirty feet above him it was attenuated to the merest whisper. Cesare lay sickly and pale, his breathing shallow and pain-filled. He was struggling for life, while below, death stalked him. Like a putrid disease, Verm's frenzied hate crawled and insinuated its way through the brittle veins of Dredgemarsh. The fiendish din of the maniac as he clattered along through the labyrinth was a physical manifestation of savage hatred that radiated from him. A flickering candle on one of the barrow shafts was the only light by which he navigated.

Having reached that part of the subterranean corridor

which he judged to be directly below his prey, he strung two jars around his neck and began to climb a stone ladder which went straight up the side of the tunnel wall and through the corbelled roof. The opening being so narrow, caused him some difficulty, and he had to remove the jars, push them through and follow after them. He was now in a small chamber, from which further steps led up to a narrow passage within the walls that encircled the old stables and surrounding grooms' and guard rooms. Verm knew exactly where to go. He emptied the jars of oil along a section of the passageway and then returned for two more. It was slow and torturous work, but he did not stop or slow down for an instant.

With just two jars left, he located a set of rising wall brackets within the hidden passage, and climbed once more, until he eventually eased himself out onto the stable roofs, just over the King's sick bay. He looked up towards the tower window where he had left Burstboil, to make sure he had line of sight to his present location. He poured out the oil into a large pool in the roof gully. Moaning in grotesque pleasure, he soaked a long flax rope in the pool of oil, left one end of it in the pool, making sure to wedge it under a corner of flashing, returned down into the oil-soaked passage and laid the other end of the rope carefully along the saturated floor. His handiwork complete, Verm rubbed his oily hands together, grunted in satisfaction and returned back down the tunnel. He was on his way back to the tower, where his petrified accomplice awaited him.

Two guards and two carpenters, were at that very moment ascending the first steps of that same tower. Unlike Verm, the four who had commenced their timorous ascent were well equipped with a basket of torches, with which they illuminated the bleak column as they climbed, inserting a torch every twenty feet in the old rusty sconces designed for that very purpose. They pushed forward nervously into the pitch-blackness above, leaving a rising column of light behind them. An experienced veteran, named Lek, led the group. He was no coward but this eerie tower made his flesh crawl. Then, a chill took hold of him, when he suddenly saw, up above, a flickering light from the single torch that Burstboil had left behind, on his earlier ascent of the tower with Verm.

'Oh no,' he rasped and stopped instantly. Without taking his eyes from the flame above he spoke back to the others in a barely audible whisper.

'There's someone or something up ahead.' They froze, and fear as tangible as the acrid smoke from the reed torches, enveloped them as they huddled together.

'I'm only a bloody carpenter. This is securities business.' The younger carpenter stammered.

'Quiet,' Lek hissed. 'Let me think.' After considering their plight for some time, he finally suggested that he and the two carpenters would remain exactly where they were, while Ham, the younger guard, returned for re-enforcements. Ham, with some relief, agreed immediately, and started down the winding stairway, slipping and missing steps continually in his haste. Those left behind envied his passage back down into the light. He was the lucky one.

But far below them, the illuminated tower was reflected in two pink eyes that glared savagely upwards from the shadows beneath the stairway at ground level. Two ears instantly pricked at the hustle and noise of the rapidly descending Ham. An oily hand slid a short sword from its scabbard and Verm awaited his prey. The instant Ham reached the ground, the maniac, seeing he was alone, darted silently from the shadows, sword poised, ready to plunge it into the hapless young man's heart.

Pure instinct, rather than any physical comprehension, made Ham swing round to face his attacker. What he saw was a devil with pink eyes swooping down upon him. A scream tore itself up and out of his guts and in those few moments, when he saw certain death embrace him, he thought how strange and terrifying was that scream and marvelled that it had come from his own throat. He had entered the time zone of imminent death where he found himself observing, as if from outside his own body, the slaying of Ham. He thought about Grunkite, about his own mother and what she might say and how she would weep when told that he was dead. He wondered why he was not afraid. Verm, with savage haste, plunged his sword straight into Ham's heart; then recoiled back in agony himself, because Ham, in the final throes of death, had unsheathed his dagger and with his last gulp of air, swung it forward and upwards, plunging it into his assassin's thigh. Verm, quivering with pain, grasped the handle of Ham's knife and slowly withdrew the blade. The muscles in his face and neck were stretched to snapping point and perspiration ran into his eyes. The knife finally came away, followed by a gout of red. Verm's yell of rage and pain was magnified in that fearful tower.

Ham's scream, followed by the unearthly yowl from the wounded Verm, riveted Lek and the two carpenters where they sat. Their terror grew with every pounding heartbeat as they realised that they would have to face some unknown evil, whether they ascended or descended the stairway. Both carpenters just stared wide-eyed at Lek, waiting for him to do or say something. Lek swallowed hard, started to speak but could not. He closed his eyes, collected himself and after several seconds attempted to speak again.

'We must go up now. The danger is below us. We know that, but we don't know about ...' He just pointed upward, attempting to suppress the quaver in his voice. 'They will have heard those screams below, and will send some of our lads to investigate. Now hurry.' He looked almost beseechingly at the two below him for some form of support, but they just nodded faintly, with a look of, 'we're only carpenters and this is not our affair.' Even in that fearful situation, Lek almost laughed at how similar they looked when terrified. It was an absurd and comical thought that held at bay the grim reality of their situation for no more than an instant. Without further words, Lek turned and faced upwards.

With cautious haste, he began the ascent, followed by the two who, despite the narrowness of the stairway, were attempting to negotiate it side by side and as close to Lek as possible. This proved difficult and dangerous, but their fear of falling from the stairway was so obliterated by the horror of what might be pursuing them from below, that their performance was quite a spectacular feat of balancing and physical dexterity, as they swung from side to side, teetering on the open edge, gasping and whimpering with every step.

'Shut your damned faces,' hissed Lek, but they seemed not to hear. They passed the Burstboil's torch. After that, Lek proceeded as before, and place a lighted torch in every sconce. As they climbed, they began to hear noises far below them. At first they were barely audible; they only heard them when they stopped for breath or to fix another torch. Gradually, however, the sounds increased in volume, and every few minutes they heard a scraping and banging below them. They began to speed up and discard everything that might slow down their flight upwards. Saws, hammers, ropes and tackle were all flung into the torch-lit gyre below them. Lungs tearing, legs trembling, faces swimming in per-spiration, they reached that part of the stairway where it turned from stone to metal and curving away from the wall, continued upwards in a narrower spiral with no handrails on either side. All three got down on their hands and knees and crept forward, not daring to look to either side.

'Stop pushing, you fools.' Lek had reached the final step, which seemed to simply terminate in mid-air. He felt sick.

Below, the sounds that pursued them drew ever closer. Petrified, they listened and stared wide-eyed down the lighted tower.

'Oh mother, oh dear mother!' One of the carpenters was pointing downwards, his hand shaking uncontrollably.

'The lights, look, the lights! They, they ...' Below them, the lower lights were being extinguished one by one. Every time they heard the scraping sound, another light was extin-guished. It, whatever it was, was coming for them. Lek was the only one to retain any semblance of control. He began to look around to assess their position, and only then no-ticed the iron ladder, some four feet above them, hanging, as it were, in mid-air. He could see it led up and through a trapdoor and realised that it would be easier to ward off who or whatever was coming up from below, from the vant-age point of that trap door.

'We must go up.'

The two carpenters did not hear him, or if they did, they could not comprehend what he meant. Lek kicked one of them in the back and shouted, 'Up, up,' furiously gesticulating towards the iron ladder.

One carpenter, as if in a trance, rose and followed Lek, who had now scaled the first few rungs of the ladder. His companion, without a moment's hesitation or comprehension of what was happening, followed as closely as possible.

Above, in the tower room, Burstboil had not stirred from the window, except to rotate his head towards the trap door, which Lek was now cautiously opening. The tower was too dim for Lek to notice the kitchen boy at first, and it was only when he had raised the trap door sufficiently to introduce his last remaining torch, did he discover with a shock that there was someone in this desolate tower room. After waiting to see the reactions of the recumbent kitchen boy, Lek finally threw the trap door back fully and entered the loft, all the time keeping his eye on Burstboil. The two carpenters then tumbled into the loft almost simultaneously. Lek slammed the trap door shut, stood on top of it and screamed at the two carpenters, who were on all fours, staring stupidly at Burstboil.

'Quick, you idiots, if you value your lives, grab that trestle. Bring it here. We're not safe yet.' The two did not move. Lek lashed out at one and kicked him in the ribs. 'Quick, get that cursed trestle over here, idiots, now! it's coming up, it's coming up.' He pointed frantically down below his feet. The two carpenters scrambled across the floor and began to heave and pull the heavy trestle towards the trap door.

'Move it, move it, quick, quick.' Lek was screaming at them.

Something was trying to lift the trap door on which he was standing. His first instinct was to leap away, but his nerve held, and he stood there screaming all the more vehemently at the two sweating carpenters to hurry. The tip of a dagger was being wedged up through the trap-door edge, and Lek heard a savage hissing and grunting, just below his feet. Inch by painful inch, the trestle was hauled towards the trap door, until with one final effort, the pair of exhausted craftsmen slid it into place. Lek stepped from the trap door but kept his eyes firmly on it to assure himself that it was holding out against the unknown thing below. His face was bathed in perspiration and his breathing sounded like a torn bellows.

'Too old, I'm too old for this. Grunkite should have sent a younger man.' Lek was pacing around the room, shocked and angry. 'Damn Grunkite, damn them all, damn them all!' he shouted, and slumped down on his knees. 'Damn them all,' he now whispered, and covered his face with his shaking hands.

The trestle was holding. Beneath it, Verm raged in a fury. He had broken his nails and lacerated his hands in a frantic effort to force entry. The pain in his wounded thigh goaded and sustained the frenzy in his brain. There appeared to be no sense of personal danger, just an overwhelming anger that he was being twarted from the final triumph of casting flames down on the oil covered stables and engulfing his enemies in an inferno. He would have challenged anything or anyone that stood in his way. He would have attempted to pierce rock or iron, so irrational was his state of mind at that moment. But such convulsions of the mind could not last, and the physical realities slowly began to penetrate his consciousness, until finally, as if emerging from a dream, Verm ceased his futile assault and slumped, exhausted on the ladder. So he remained for some time, attempting to marshal his shattered thoughts.

When some semblance of calm had doused the fire in his

brain, Verm began to assess his predicament, and realised that if the scream from the guard whom he had killed had been heard, and it surely had, then more guards would come and he would be trapped. Quickly, he swung down from the ladder, and with uncanny speed began his descent down the swirling stairs. The pain in his thigh was forgotten as he circled downwards, soundless as a shadow. Then, a shout from below. He froze instantly. Noises began to filter up. More guards were coming. Verm was trapped. He sat and waited. Sounds from below grew in intensity. There were voices, all talking together, unnecessarily loud. Verm leaned out and looked down. Had those below looked straight up above them, they would have seen two small blazing rubies reflecting back the light of their their torches.

There were four guards. They had already discovered their dead comrade, and the discarded tools and materials of the workmen. These they had collected and brought with them, having been charged by Grunkite to secure the cable, as instructed by Quickstrain, no matter what. Their progress up the stairs was slow. The two guards in the centre of the tiny procession carried the equipment, while the other two covered the front and the rear with drawn swords. They were so close together that they were continually jostling and bumping into each other. They talked continually. Verm, who had not moved, could now see them, about forty feet below. As they drew ever nearer he rose silently to his feet and moved so that his back was against the wall and his head was turned to the right, looking down at the nearest turn of the spiral stairs, where the lead guard would shortly appear. He was totally in control again, and knew exactly what he must do. It was not long before he saw the top of the guard's head, and it was only moments later that the same guard spotted this grotesque creature above him, and almost toppled himself and his companions back down the stairs; such was the violence with which he recoiled from the sight.

'Who goes there?' The guard's voice quaked. Verm did not budge.

'Who are you? This is no game, declare yourself!' The guard at the rear was somewhat more courageous in his challenge. Verm stared unblinking from his pink eyes. With swords poised, the guards now inched forward, and still this spectre stood there, staring malevolently at them. They began to wonder if this was just a spectre, a mirage or trick of the imagination. When the first guard's sword was within inches of Verm, the air was rent by a heart-stopping yowl from the demon. Then Verm, like a coiled spring, hurled himself away from the wall and straight over the precipice of the granite stairs. The guards watched in fascinated horror as the shadowy figure soared out into free space, seemed to hover for a moment, then passed from the compass of their torches' illumination into the blackness below. But the instant he disappeared from their view they heard a thud and an angry cry of pain. They knew then that this creature had not plummeted to the bottom of the tower, but had somehow landed below and opposite them on the spiral staircase. They were dumbfounded at the superhuman feat they had just witnessed. Now, from below in the darkness, they could hear the sounds of rapid flight. Their relief was palpable. Without a word, they started upwards once more, their apprehension somewhat diminished, yet still cautious lest there be some other evil awaiting them.

It took some time to reach the summit of swirling stone. When they did, they sat down exhausted, fearful and unsure of exactly what they should do next. No one wished to speak out, lest in so doing, he might have to initiate the next move. Finally, when it became quite obvious that they were all harbouring the same thoughts, the youngest of them whispered into the ear of Guntrum, the eldest, 'Maybe the others are up above, why don't we shout up to them?'

'Right, call out,' said Guntrum in a slightly louder voice, as if it was his idea right from the start.

Hesitantly the young guard called out.

'Anyone up there?' He tapped on the iron ladder with his sword and repeated,

'Anyone up there? It's us. Lek, are you there?'

Just up above them, Lek, who had been kneeling with his ear to the floor, raised himself with an enormous sigh of relief, his arms fell loosely by his side, his eyes closed, his mouth opened and he exhaled slowly. He opened his eyes and in front of him, astride the trestle over the trap door, were the two carpenters who were now staring at him, moon-faced, beseeching, not daring to believe that the terror was over.

'Move it.'

Lek motioned to the trestle beneath them. Their eyes filled with tears. They were saved. They leaped down from their perch and manhandled the trestle aside. With trembling hands they hauled open the trapdoor. Three pairs of relieved eyes looked down on four pairs of anxious and bemused eyes.

'Lek?'

'Guntrum?'

'You all right?'

'Yes.'

Quickly the new team ascended and between them all,

they completed the primary task of securing hawser lines to the window mullions and lowering the ends to the stables below. Burstboil just sat through it all, staring blankly in front of him.

'Right lads, let's get out of here.' Lek did not have to repeat his order and it was not too long before the proud group ushered the catatonic Burstboil into the presence of Tancredi and Grunkite. Their feelings of jubilation were soon dashed.

'It would appear, Marshall,' Tancredi stared at the disconcerted Lek and his companions, while addressing the smouldering Grunkite, 'we have another embarrassing security blunder on our hands. The assassin was trapped, cornered, cornered like a rat! And yet he slips through your hands like smoke. We are left with this miserable wretch. Maybe, just maybe, you might get him to reveal something before we are all murdered in our beds.'

Grunkite was speechless with rage and shame, and before he could utter a word, Tancredi was gone with an imperious swirl of his cloak. The captors of Burstboil stood disconsolate with their prisoner not daring to move or say a word, watching with fearful apprehension as though a volcano were ready to engulf them. Grunkite could find no words or actions to express his anger at that moment, and to the utter amazement of those before him, he spoke quietly.

'Well done men, take this wretch to the guardhouse, I will question him shortly.'

Chapter 17

The moving of the King was smoothly and speedily carried out after these mishaps. By early evening, he was installed in Keenslide's intensive care room with the multitude of medical accoutrements and concoctions that were the tools of the learned surgeon. Although not out of danger, Cesare's condition had not deteriorated, and Keenslide was just beginning to hope. Over the next few days, there was just the faintest hint that the deathly blue of the patient's lips was changing.

Every morning, just after daybreak, Lucretia Beaufort made her way discreetly to the infirmary with a fresh posy of flowers. Consuela, the custorin, would quietly admit Lucretia and leave her to sit with the comatose Cesare. Lucretia would take her place close to him, and sometimes read quietly from her book Ars Amatoria, until the first visit of surgeon Keenslide to check on his patient. After hearing Keeenslide's prognosis, Lucretia would then leave as discreetly as she had arrived.

'Surgeon Keenslide,' she said on her first visit, 'I would prefer that no one be informed of my coming here. It would only cause – '

'No need to explain. You can be sure that no one here will speak of what is not their concern. I will make sure of that. But I beg you, please continue with your visits. I am certain they are as beneficial as my medication.'

It was on the seventh day that Consuela heard Cesare moan, and saw his eyelids flicker. There was jubilation in the infirmary and the following morning,on admitting Lucretia, Consuela could not contain herself.

'Great news, Lady Lucretia. Our patient, at last, shows signs of recovery. Oh, but I should not be speaking of this. Surgeon Keenslide, he will tell you all.'

The blood drained from Lucretia's face.

'Are you not well, my lady?' Consuela asked.

'It's just … I'm so relieved. I'm fine.'

Lucretia, as was her routine now, began to arrange her posy of blue and white gentians in a small vase by his bedside. Her hands shook.

'Good morning, your majesty,' she whispered her greeting to the still unconscious Cesare, and gently stroked his hand. There was the usual look of compassion and longing on her face. But also, this morning, there was a hint of alarm in those exquisite green eyes. In truth, she was terrified at the idea that Cesare might waken at any moment. The idea that she could continue to visit him as he got better was, after all, only a fantasy on her part. Was she not promised to the Brooderstalt, Albrecht Pentrojan, and had not Cesare himself condoned the marriage? She paced up and down, no thought of sitting quietly or reading, as she usually did. When Keenslide arrived, he was shocked to see how agitated she appeared.

'What has happened?' he cried, and rushed to Cesare's bedside.

'Nothing, nothing has happened. Consuela told me that the King will ... will get better, that already he has ...' Her voice wobbled out of control and tears began to flow down her cheeks.

'My dear young lady, be seated. This is a joyous thing. There is no need for tears.' Keenslide gently steered her to the seat beside Cesare's bed. 'Why, I am more than hopeful that he will now make a full recovery. It would not surprise me if he woke from his healing slumber this very morning. He can thank you for that.'

'No! No, you are the healer, Surgeon Keenslide.' Lucretia rose instantly. 'I must go now. Forgive me, but my work here is done.'

'He will want to talk to you, to thank you for all you have done.'

'No. That is not necessary. I have simply done my duty. But thank you for all your kindnesses. I shall not return.' She glanced one last time at Cesare and ran from the room weeping. Keenslide scratched his head. 'There are some things I will never understand,' he turned his attention to his patient.

****

Lucretia, while rejoicing at Cesare's deliverance, felt an extraordinary personal loss. She fled outside the grim and oppressive walls of Dredgemarsh, out along the banks of the Yayla. She walked for hours, going she knew not where. She stumbled through mud, thistle and briar, heedless of the stinging nettle and razor sharp thorns that plucked and tore at her clothes. By late afternoon, without even realising it, she had arrived back at her home.

'Where have you been?' Arnulf Beaufort demanded. 'You have been missing since dawn. Look at the state of you. What has happened?' His voice wavered between anger and concern. Lucretia just stared at him, as if she could not comprehend what he was saying.

'Please, father,' she said, 'please, I wish to go to my room.' Arnulf Beaufort threw his hands up in frustration.

'Go, go. But be back here at table in one hour. We will talk then. And I want explanations ... Celeste! Celeste! See to your mistress.'

Celeste instantly entered the room, rushed forward and enfolded Lucretia in her arms. 'Lucretia, Lucretia what has happened. Are you hurt? I was so frightened. You were missing for so long.'

'My room, I must go to my room now.' Lucretia extricated herself from Celeste's arms and rushed off, followed closely by her loyal companion. Arnulf Beaufort sat down wearily and shook his head.

****

It was only after bathing and putting on fresh clothes, and when Celeste stopped asking her what was wrong, did Lucretia begin to reveal the real cause of her sorrow.

'I am happy that he is out of danger. Of course I am ... it's just that things have not really changed. He will be well again, I am still promised and the past few weeks mean nothing. I have allowed myself to hope when there was no reason for hope.' Her eyes, already red and puffy, filled with fresh tears.

'He will want to thank you for all you have done,' Celeste said.

'I could not bear that, Celeste. The last thing I want is his gratitude. No! Anything but that.' Celeste was rubbing ointment onto the back of Lucretia's hands where she had been stung by nettles.

'I can't bear to see you so unhappy.' She reached out with both arms and embraced her mistress. 'What can I do? Tell me, dearest Lucretia, what can I do.' Lucretia put her arms around Celeste and they remained locked together like two children lost in a wilderness.

It was Lucretia who eventually broke the spell. She stood up abruptly.

'We must leave,' she said. 'There is no other way. We must leave today.'

'Today?' Celeste gasped.

'Quiet, Celeste, anyone could be listening.'

'But today,' Celeste whispered, 'we are not ready. There are so many things to think of and –'

'It is better this way.' Lucretia reached out and took Celeste's hand. 'Dearest Celeste, if you care for me, please do not try to dissuade me. You don't have to come with me but I must leave this place.'

'What? Not go with you? Do you think so little of my friendship?' Celeste was standing with her hands on her hips and and anger in her eyes.

'No, no, it's not that ... it's not fair to ask you to–'

'Fairness does not come into friendship. Just tell me what

you want me to do.'

'It will be dangerous, Celeste, just the two of us travelling alone to Nuvarro, off the main routes, because they ... my father will surely come after us.'

'I am not afraid. What do you want me to do?' Lucretia considered for some moments and then spoke.

'I will go to my father and tell him what he wants to hear. I will also tell him that I am retiring early. We will leave quietly at dusk. With luck, no one will notice our absence until late tomorrow morning. You go now and have our horses made ready. Take them down by the Yayla and tether them in the copse. Pack as much food as you can ... and warm cloaks. Be careful, my dearest Lettie. Come back here when all is ready.'

****

As she prepared the evening meals in the infirmary, the custorin, Consuela, almost dropped a pan when she heard Keenslide yelling.

'Consuela, Consuela, come quickly, come quickly. Sire, Sire, can you hear me?' Cesare's eyelids flickered and opened. Consuela arrived.

'Oh, the saints be praised ... the saints be praised.' She squeezed her hands together under her chin, which was beginning to quiver, and tears welled up in her eyes. 'The saints be praised ... and your healing hands, Surgeon Keenslide.' She threw her arms around the startled Keenslide.

'Now, now, Consuela, let us look after his majesty.' Keenslide disengaged himself from her embrace. 'Your Majesty, you are in the infirmary.' he leaned over Cesare. 'You were badly wounded.' Cesare's brow was furrowed, as if he was trying to remember something. He moved his lips, but made no sound.

'Consuela, water. That's it. Now help raise his majesty. Careful, careful.' Cesare drank and once more attempted to speak, but made no sound. Keenslide and Consuela eased him back onto his pillow and the King grimaced in pain.

'Rest for the moment, your majesty. Don't try to speak. I will give you something to ease the pain.' He beckoned the custorin to the far side of the room and spoke quietly. 'Find Jakob for me.' He returned to the King's bedside. 'Now, your majesty, sip this slowly.' He took a tiny glass beaker of green viscous liquid, from the bedside table, gently tilted Cesare's head forward and put it to his lips. Cesare swallowed with difficulty. He lay back on his pillow and closed his eyes. His breathing was laboured, but once again he attempted to speak. Keenslide bent close to hear.

'Lucretia ... ' Cesare whispered.

'Lucretia, yes, of course, your majesty. Now, please don't try to speak anymore, you are exhausted. We will inform the young lady immediately. Rest now, rest.' Within seconds the King drifted into a quiet sleep as a beaming Jakob arrived with Consuela.

'Shhhh. He sleeps peacefully.' Keenslide put his forefinger to his lips and quietly directed the young squire back out of the room. 'Jakob, inform the Chancellor and Grunkite that the King is back with us. Tell them he sleeps peacefully now, but they may visit him briefly in the morning. But most importantly, find young Lady Beaufort and tell her, impress upon her, that his majesty expressly asked for her. Persuade her to come at noon tomorrow.'

Dredgemarsh

Chapter 18

Arnulf Beaufort clapped his hands together and gave a sigh of satisfaction. 'Well, so be it. St. Sigeberts day it is. We will send word immediately to Albrecht Pentrojan. He will be pleased. A toast, daughter.' He raised his goblet.

'Thank you, father, but it has been an exhausting day and I would like to retire early.'

'But you have not even touched your food.'

'May I go, father?' The door to the dining room half opened and Beaufort's servant stuck his head in and muttered something.

'What, what's that? Speak up, man.' Beaufort barked.

'The King's squire wishes to speak to you, sir.'

'I will leave now, father.' Lucretia rose hastily and made towards the door.

'Show him in, show him in immediately,' said Beaufort. Jakob stepped into the room just as Lucretia attempted to leave it.

'My lady, this matter concerns you directly,' Jakob said.

'Speak to my father. I must go.'

'Lucretia! Come back here. Be seated. Sir, forgive my daughter's ill manners,' said Beaufort. 'Now, what news, young sir? Does it concern his majesty? Is he ... ,'

'Good news, it is good news, sir. His majesty woke briefly this morning. He is out of danger,' said Jakob.

'Wonderful. Wonderful. Do you hear that, Lucretia? The King is out of danger.'

'Yes, father. ' Lucretia was sitting, head bent, staring at her hands .

'When he woke, his majesty made one request.' Jakob looked directly at Lucretia.

'Yes?' said Beaufort, looking alternately at Jakob and then at his daughter.

'His majesty asked to see your daughter, sir,' said Jakob.

'What? Lucretia?' said Beaufort.

'It was the one and only request he made when he woke. He sleeps again, but Surgeon Keenslide has instructed me to request that your daughter attend on the King at noon tomorrow.' It took some time for the astonished Beaufort to reply.

'Well, of course. If that is what the King requested, then, certainly, my daughter will attend on his majesty. Of course she will. Yes. Certainly.' Beaufort looked, with raised eyebrows, at his daughter. Lucretia's cheeks were bright red. Jakob nodded and left.

'Well, well, and what do you think his majesty wants?' said Beaufort.

'I don't know … probably wants to thank me for the small service I rendered on the day he was wounded.'

'Hmmm.' Beaufort frowned. 'We shall know soon enough.'

****

'I got your message.' Celeste was out of breath after climbing the spiral stairway to the Belvedere of Arnulf Beaufort's residence. 'We're not leaving after all?'

'I don't know what to think,' Lucretia said. She was pacing back and forth to the lancet windows that formed an arc of glass and delicately carved masonry, stretching across the whole north wall of the room, giving a panoramic view of the Anselem mountains to the west, the Vildpline and Grak's Forest to the north, and Meregloom Gorge and the mighty Blue Mountain to the east.

'What has happened?' Celeste said.

'Maybe I am just fooling myself. Maybe we should just go as planned.' Lucretia wrung her hands together.

'We can't go now. The horses are re-stabled,' said Celeste. 'But please tell me, what has happened?' Lucretia sat, her back to Celeste, looking out at the darkening sky.

'He asked to see me. When he woke –'

'The King? Is the King recovered?' Celeste asked.

'Yes. When he woke, he asked for me. Only me: no one else. Surgeon Keenslide has asked me to visit at noon to-morrow.' Lucretia turned and looked towards Celeste. 'What shall I do, Lettie? I have already agreed with father on a date for my marriage. What shall I do? I can't think. My mind is in total confusion.'

'Do?' said Celeste. 'What shall you do? Why, obey your

King.' She sat beside Lucretia and took her hand. 'My dearest Lucretia, you have been summoned by your King. You must go.' They sat quietly, hand in hand, and watched as a great cloud of rooks tumbled their way across the darkening sky over the Vildpline. The noisy throng were flying to their roosts in Grak's forest after feasting on the abundance of autumn meadowhawk in Meregloom Swamp. It was only when the rooks had settled in the faraway treetops, and the distant clouds' ruddy reflection of a vanished sun faded to a faint violet, did Celeste say quietly, 'Come, it is time to rest. We have a busy morning ahead of us.'

Chapter 19

Verm moved into the deeper recesses of Dredge-marsh, as teams of guards and fewterers, using ly-mers bred for tracking hart and wild boar, method-ically searched every chamber, nook and hole that might re-veal the assassin. They had started from the western wall of the castle and as they worked their way eastward, they left guards at strategic points to ensure that the quarry did not retreat to those regions already searched. They also refilled the sconces with blazing torches, that illuminated every room and corridor searched. This was the biggest hunt ever undertaken in Dredgemarsh.

Verm's instinctive flight to the lower regions of Dredge-marsh was a mistake, but his natural inclination to delve deeper into those regions, so congenial to him, blinded him to the fact that he was trapping himself. He was finding it progressively more difficult to hide his tracks from his pursuers, because as he moved into the long forgotten eastern region of the castle's subterranean world, he frequently had to hack his way through giant black nettles that somehow managed to grow without light in those oozing tunnels, built in the marshy ground where the castle abutted Meregloom swamp. He was, by this time, covered in slime, and it became harder to walk in the thick muck that covered the tunnel floors. He had not eaten for three days. The wound in his thigh was now festering, and sent hot spasms of pain through his body. His left ankle was badly swollen as a result of his leap in the tower, but he moved relentlessly onwards, as if he were trying to outdistance the pain itself.

His frantic flight was not simply a matter of self-surviva. It was more a pathological passion to avenge himself on Cesare. He had to survive, to wreak his revenge on those who had ruined his life. He stumbled over a large nettle root and fell heavily against the jagged rocks on his right.

'Shite-a-bed! He will pay dearly, he will burn yet.' His wild ranting echoed back and forth within the dark labyrinth. The pain in his body was excruciating but it was still only a flicker of discomfort compared to the fire in his head, that fury that made his eyes burn with untrammelled hatred.

As yet, the pursuers had not glimpsed the assassin. They moved cautiously, but eventually the lymers gave voice: they sensed Verm was close at hand. Shortly after that they began to notice fresh signs of Verm's recent passage. Every now and then, they thought they could hear the faint echo of a yell or strangled curse bubbling up from the pitch blackness, and they grew fearful at the thoughts of the mad creature that they must surely corner very shortly. Inexorably, the net began to close in on Verm. The reluctant pursuers could now hear the splashing of their quarry, frantically smashing his way through the inky quagmire. As ordered, they sent back word to Grunkite to tell him that they were closing in, and the assassin was cornered. They were under strict instructions not to commence the final assault until Grunkite himself was present. He trusted no one. He would not be humiliated again by Tancredi. It took a relay of messengers almost three hours to deliver the good news to him, and he set out immediately on the arduous journey to where he would confront and destroy the fiend, with his bare hands if need be.

Verm could smell the hateful pursuers now, could hear the excited baying of the lymers. He turned sharply right through a small opening in the tunnel wall. There was nowhere else to go. The way forward was blocked by the massive granite blocks of Dredgemarsh's outer wall. He was trapped at last, in a dismal chamber in the very pit of Dredgemarsh. He crouched down in the furthest corner of the room.

Poor Vermie, poor Vermie. He was experiencing an incredible dislocation in time and place. He was a small petrified boy, trying not to cry, not to give himself away and the terrifying unctuous voice saying, poor Vermie, poor Vermie, I'm coming, coming, won't hurt Vermie...be nice to your... no harm, no harm at all...our little secret, Vermie. The smells came back, rich perfume, nauseating, the sweet comfits, and the soft white insistent hands. Verm Bludvile wailed in anguish. His pursuers stopped, appalled by the sound. It was not anger or defiance they heard, but a cry of unfathomable desolation and loss. Then the lymers gave voice again and the spell was broken.

'Let's end this,' one of the pursuers said, and they began

to rapidly converge on the source of that awful cry. At the same time, the baying of the lymers and the sounds of the approaching men brought Verm back to reality.

He began to examine every crevice, every dark seam that might offer an escape route. As the hopelessness of his situation began to register in his tortured mind, he realised, at last, that he was doomed. The hated pursuers were practically outside the chamber now.

But there was something else: another sound that his brain was attempting to decipher. Water, somewhere beneath him was water. A desperate hope flickered in his eyes. On hands and knees, he began to feel his way across every inch of the roughly flagged floor, scrabbling through the layers of muck and filth.

Outside the chamber, with their excited hounds, Grunkite's men realised with some trepidation that, finally, their quarry was at bay. They could hear his frantic movements. They hesitated for some time before venturing to even look through the opening into the chamber. Verm was now crouched low in the middle of the floor, watching as the flickering light of their torches began to illuminate the dingy walls of the tunnel outside. Slowly, a blazing torch was shoved through the entrance of his chamber, and after some moments a head cautiously followed. Two more torches appeared. The room was now dimly but fully illuminated. The head began to slowly scan the interior, past the mound in the centre of the floor, then suddenly jerked back towards it with a low gasp and focused on that heap of slime, from which two blazing red eyes glared.

'Blood of the Christ,' the head spoke and withdrew instantly from the entrance. 'It's him or it or whatever it is. There's no way out, no escape.'

'We'll just wait for the chief. Keep your swords ready lads, hold the dogs back.' It took the fewterer all his strength and authority to hold back the lymers and quell their excited baying.

Verm began to move again, continuing the minute examination of the chamber floor with bleeding hands. A half hour went by. Those on guard were content to stay outside and wait. They could hear the continual sliding movement from within, which reassured them that their prize had not escaped and there was no need to keep visual contact, much to their relief.

'What in thunder is happening in there?' The question was put, more than once, simply to break the silence and ease the tension.

Then something changed; they heard a low moan, almost of pleasure, followed by a groaning, as of great physical exertion, then the sound of gushing water.

'What in the name of ...' The guards cautiously but rapidly gathered in the entrance to the chamber with their torches and swords thrust before them. There in the corner Verm was sliding a massive flagstone aside, leaving a black hole from which spewed the roar of fast flowing water.

'A trapdoor, there's a damned trapdoor, he'll escape again.' There was anguish in the voice. As one they began to move in on Verm.

'We'll finish this nightmare now, once and for all.'

Verm stood at the edge of the trapdoor and looked into the jet blackness below. The water could have been two or forty feet down. It was impossible to see. As the guards closed in to strike he stepped, almost casually, into the roaring abyss. There was no splash. The screaming torrent swept him away instantly, leaving the bewildered guards gaping helplessly into the yowling blackness below them. Now that they could no longer see or hear Verm, they were gripped with fear and the awful feeling that this creature or demon was indestructible. The nightmare was still not over.

When the unfortunate guards had recovered from the shock of losing their prey, the realisation that they would have to shortly face Grunkite began to bear down heavily on them. They huddled together in despair.

'That thing or whatever it was must have drowned,' one guard whispered hopefully. The others nodded, but in their hearts they were not convinced.

'Maybe there's a ledge or something down there,' said another.

'Yes, maybe there is, he could be hiding on a ledge, get all the torches over here.' There was a glimmer of hope once again. All their torches could not penetrate the deep shadows below, so they tied a couple of them to one of the dog leashes and lowered them down. It was clear then that there was only one way the maniac could have gone, and that was straight into the raging torrent below.

'The flow is out through the east wall,' observed one, 'and if that beast is still alive, it's somewhere out there.' He pointed through the fortress wall.

'We must get a search party out there at once.' After some deliberation and a bitter argument they at last decided to leave two men behind while the rest retraced their steps upwards towards more familiar territory, from where they would set out for the eastern wall and the marshlands beyond. One reluctant recruit was chosen to return as fast as possible to intercept Grunkite, who was on his way, under the illusion that the felon was trapped.

'Witch's piss,' he fumed,' the old bastard will skin me.'

The others, comprising five guards and two fewterers, moved off as swiftly as possible, wishing to stay out of Grunkite's way at all costs. They were hoping that in the meantime there might be some hope of finding the drowned carcass of the fugitive in Meregloom swamp. It was an enormous relief to their frayed nerves to move up and out of the putrid air of the tunnels. They emerged into the open, exhausted and breathless, but kept moving till they reached the parapet walkway that ran along the eastern wall. They began to scan Meregloom swamp, leaning far out through the embrasures and working their way along the parapet.

Below them, evil smelling vapours burbled from the ocean of foetid ooze that continually shifted and swayed, like a giant beast in a fitful slumber. Floating on the surface of this shifting sea of mud were dollops of luminescent green moss and weeds of poisonous colours. They watched and waited, hoping, yet half dreading to see the corpse of that awful creature, or man, or whatever. They wanted an end to it. They wanted to return to their homes, their wives, children, sweethearts.

Could he survive under that mud, could he or it or whatever it was, be swimming down there under all that filth, looking at them, taunting them. These thoughts or something akin to them were passing through their collect-ive minds. They shivered at the terrible idea.

Unbelievably, directly below and just out of their field of view, the half-drowned Verm lay wedged between a boulder and the fortress wall, his ashen face barely breaking the sur-face of the slime. He was unconscious. Fortunately for him, the slough was not cold and little energy was expended or body heat lost as he lay suspended in the tepid muck. He could hear nothing of the shouting and talking from the guards way up above him. His eyes were closed, his breathing shallow. He just lay there, embalmed, unmoving.

The shrill cry of the moorhen echoed against the dark lichen-covered walls of the fort, that flared upwards from the immeasurable depths of mud and water. The sky began to darken over the swamp and the motionless body of Verm, while the guards above were still scanning, inch by inch, the bleak vista before them. Night came and they remained on the parapet with lighted torches and glowing braziers. The search would continue. It would never be over until Grunkite beheld the corpse of the assassin and was sure that the threat to his King was no more.

****

The night passed. Verm was tranquil in his shroud of mud, unmoving, unknowing. As the first flinty streaks of morning crept across the endless bogland, a flat-bottomed punt nosed its way through the mist. The grim light of two cressets on long poles fore and aft barely pierced the putrid Meregloom miasma. Grunkite sat morosely at the prow, completely still except for his bloodshot eyes, that continually darted back and forth across the brackish pools. There was a determination, a grim resolve in that small search party that seemed to say, however long, however far, we will continue until we find him. It was not surprising, then, that Grunkite could hardly believe it when, within half an hour of launching the punt onto Meregloom, he spotted Verm's hand locked onto the boulder at the base of the wall.

'There, there,' he shouted. As they approached, in the lambent red glow of the cresset that hung on the pole over the bow of the punt, he began to pick out the contours of the attached body suspended in the murky fluid. He cried out.

'The bastard, the murdering bastard, we have him, we have him.' When he discovered that Verm was still alive, though only just, he was euphoric.

The swollen body was hauled into the punt where it was shackled and quickly transported to a secure cell, below the Four Towers' Square. Three guards were posted to stand permanent watch over the comatose assassin. All this was done under the direct supervision of Grunkite, who then made his way to the refectory.

'Over at last,' a weary but jubilant Grunkite muttered as he slumped down at his own special table in a quiet corner. Mistress Crumble was supervising the first breakfasts of the day.

'Your very best frumenty Bella, braggot and your finest botargo.'

'Nothing but the best for you, Marshal. I heard the good news. You caught the monster. I can sleep easy in my bed again.'

'Yes, we can all sleep easy now Bella ... at last.'

At that very moment, the hairs on the necks of two of Verm's guards stood on end when their companion, on looking through the barred grating of the cell, turned white-faced to them and said in a strangulated whisper, 'What devil's work is here? The monster is awake.'

Dredgemarsh

Chapter 20

Lucretia Beaufort did not sleep easy, nor could she drink the quince cordial or eat the wastel bread, cheese and comfits of sugared caraway seeds that Celeste had prepared for their breakfast. Celeste ate heartily and smiled inwardly at her fidgeting young mistress.

'Well, I suppose we should start and make you even more beautiful than you already are,' said Celeste finally, popping a last comfit between her smiling red lips but not moving from her seat. 'Hmm, they are delicious. Maybe I should have some more.' She looked mischieviously at Lucretia.

'Oh, stop teasing me Lettie. How can you eat when my ... our whole future is poised between ... between ... disaster and ... I can't even imagine?' Celeste, feigning a sorrowful look of sympathy for her companion, could not restrain herself and exploded into laughter, spraying the table with crumbs of the comfit she was chewing. Lucretia's initial frown of disapproval quickly vanished and the pair of them collapsed into uncontrollable laughter.

With so much time in hand before Lucretia's visit to Cesare, they lingered over every detail of of their preparations.

'Try this.' Celeste held out a bliaut with gold embroidery on the hem and sleeves.

'No, it is too formal. Let me see the white one again,' said Lucretia. They whiled away the morning thus, trying every combination of clothes, jewellery and footwear. The whole process was like a languorous ballet. After the clothes were finally chosen, Lucretia bathed in water perfumed with oil of Lydian ambergris. The elegant arch of her neck as Celeste brushed her hair, the delicate tilt of her wrist while her nails were being manicured, manifested the instinctive grace of a young woman conscious of her own beauty. Her eyes, face and body glimmered, as if there was a light inside her. Over a chemise of the most delicate satin she donned a light blue bliaut of silk, tantalisingly revealing the contours of her body.

'You look so incredibly beautiful.' Celeste clasped her hands together under her chin and shook her head from side to side.

'I hope that ... that ... he will ... think so.' Lucretia, normally so self-assured could not control the flutter in her voice. 'Oh Lettie, I sound like a silly young milkmaid.' She blushed.

'Dearest Lucretia, if the King is not instantly cured when he sees you, then nothing will cure him.' Celeste laughed impishly. 'He's only a man, after all.'

'Lettie!' Lucretia said sharply, but could not hide the nascent smile on her face.

'My coat, Lettie, your chatter will have me late.' Celeste took the long ruby samite coat, which she had laid out earlier and helped Lucretia to put it on. Then she carefully rearranged her mistress's dark shimmering tresses, so that they glistened against the elaborate orfrois of the deep collar. The ruby samite cloth of the coat draped tantalisingly over her breasts and was worn open from collar to hem, revealing the delicate blue bliaut underneath.

'Poor man,' Celeste said in a breathy whisper.

****

'Don't stay too long; he is still very weak, but he will relish the good news.' Keenslide quietly opened the door to allow Grunkite into the King's sickroom.

'Sire?' Grunkite said, barely above a whisper.

'Ah, Grunkite, my good sir, you look a great deal happier than you were at our last meeting.' Cesare's voice was weak and as yet, he was unable to sit up. 'Come, come, old friend. Sit and tell me, how goes it.'

'Thank you, Sire. I'll be brief. I don't want to exhaust you, but we have him. We caught him at last.'

'The saints be praised! Nobly done, Grunkite, nobly done. How could I have doubted you, my dear friend?' Grunkite just nodded continuously, as if he could not trust himself to words. 'Take your ease, Grunkite. A goblet for our esteemed Marshall.' Cesare beckoned to Jakob, who was seated quietly in the corner of the room, unnoticed by Grunkite up to that moment. 'But tell me,' Cesare raised his head off the pillow, 'who is he? What is he? Why the attempt on my life?' Cesare's head dropped back onto the pillow and his shallow breathing became laboured.

'Sire, this is too much for you.' Jakob said, proffering a goblet of vernage to Grunkite, who refused it.

'I should go. It is too soon.' Grunkite looked alarmed.

'No, tell me, Grunkite,' Cesare gasped.

'It's the Candle Lighter, Bludvile, Sire.'

'Bludvile ... Bludvile ?'

'Perhaps you never met him sire. Most people hardly know of his existence.'

'If he was in our service, I should have known him. My fault. But why did he attack me?'

'I'm not certain, Sire, but, from what I have been able to piece together, he may have held you responsible for his dismissal.'

'Dismissal? Did I dismiss this candle lighter?' Cesare looked at Jakob.

'It appears, Sire,' Grunkite answered before Jakob could respond, 'that our Chancellor gave the order some weeks ago to dismiss Bludvile from his duties.'

'Tancredi? I see. I am beholden to you, Grunkite. You have served Dredgemarsh well. I have been reflecting on my own stewardship in Dredgemarsh and I find myself,' Cesare gasped for air, 'I find myself wanting.'

'Sire, you must not blame yourself for these things.'

'But I do and must, Grunkite. Things will change, however. Be certain of that. Things will change.'

'Sire, your words fill me with joy, but I must let you rest now. Good day, Squire Jakob.'

There were tears of joy in Grunkite's eyes as he strode away from the royal quarters, totally oblivious to the soreness of his arthritic feet. As he departed, Tancredi came gliding silently in the opposite direction. Grunkite bustled past him. Tancredi turned and called after him.

'I believe, Marshall Grunkite, you may have apprehended the criminal ... finally.'

Grunkite did not stop, but shouted back over his shoulder,

'I've made my report to the King. He may acquaint you with it,' and he strode on, triumphant, unable to hide the grin on his face.

'Your time will come, old man,' Tancredi hissed under his breath. Then, with an effort, he composed himself and knocked lightly on Cesare's door, lifted the latch and walked in.

Cesare glanced up and a frown passed over his face.

'Yes Tancredi, what do you want?'

'Sire ... I, I trust everything is well with you.'

'Everything is just fine, just fine. Is there anything urgent you need to discuss, Chancellor Tancredi?'

'Well, no, Sire. I am simply overjoyed to see you are recovering so well. Now that we have apprehended the culprit we can –'

'Yes, yes, Grunkite has done an excellent job' said Cesare. 'Perhaps we should let him take the matter to its conclusion. Now, if you don't mind, Chancellor, I must rest.' Cesare waved Tancredi from his presence.

'Of course, good day, your majesty.' Tancredi smiled and turned to leave. The smile vanished the instant he turned away from Cesare. He left quickly.

'I think, Sire,' Jakob said with a wry smile, 'our good Chancellor is not very happy.'

'From now on, Jakob, our Chancellor will have to get used to being unhappy, very unhappy.'

Lucretia quietly stepped into the shadow of a deep pillaster and watched as a grim-faced Chancellor Tancredi left
the King's sick room. Seeing him reminded her, once again,
that nothing had really changed; she was still promised to
Pentrojan. Hadn't Tancredi assured her that Cesare was fully
supportive of the union? I am making a complete fool of
myself, she thought. She turned and began to walk away,
dropping the small bunch of gentians she was carrying.

'My dear young lady.' The voice startled Lucretia, and she
half turned to see a figure step from the other side of the
pillaster.

'Surgeon Keenslide. I didn't see you. I –'

'I think you are going in the wrong direction.' He stooped
down and picked up the gentians. 'Do not waste these.' He
handed them to her. Stepping forward, he put his arm
around her shoulder and gently steered her back towards
Cesare's sick room.

'There is no medicine I can give this young man that will
benefit him half as much as a visit from you. Come.'

'But Surgeon Keenslide, you don't understand. It's com-
plicated and –'

'Oh, but I do understand. I understand better than you or
that young man in there think. Trust me.'

Keenslide quietly opened the door. He and Lucretia
stepped into the room. Cesare appeared to be sleeping and
Jakob was gently settling the bed covers. Jakob's eyes were
instantly drawn to the startling presence of Lucretia and he
could not suppress a tiny open-mouthed gasp of appreciation at her beauty. He recovered himself quickly and put
his forefinger to his lips, requesting them not to speak.

'He sleeps,' he soundlessly mouthed the words. Keenslide
nodded to him and quietly led Lucretia towards the bedside.

He and Jakob then left so discreetly that they were gone before Lucretia realised she was alone with the sleeping Cesare.

'Your majesty,' she barely whispered, not wishing to wake him. It was easier this way. She turned to his bedside table and removed the withered gentians that she had left on her last visit and began to arrange the new flowers in the silver vase. Her mind was in total confusion, caught between an overwhelming love for this wounded young man who lay so helplessly before her, and the unbearable thought that he simply wanted to thank her for her services during his illness. She stopped arranging the flowers. I really am a fool, she thought. I should not have listened to Lettie or Surgeon Keenslide. How could this possibly work? In that moment of despair, Cesare Greyfell reached out and took Lucretia's hand.

'Lucretia,' he said. She felt her insides melt and a tingling heat suffused her whole body with dizzying speed. She turned to look in wonder at Cesare, still not believing that what she desired above all else was being offered so simply.

'Sire?' She could barely speak. He released her hand, hesitated for a moment, then reached up under her lustrous hair to gently stroke her neck and cheek. Lucretia took his hand in hers, pressed it fiercely against her lips and, moving aside the rich orfrois collar of her samite coat, she cradled it against her breast and the soft silk of her bliaut.

'I am yours, Sire.'

'I loved you from the first moment we met,' he said. She stooped to him and their lips met.

Dredgemarsh

Chapter 21

Chancellor Tancredi was shouting, as he stormed into Arnulf Beaufort's dining hall. 'Do you think I will allow your daughter to destroy everything I have worked for?'

'What? What are you talking about?' Beaufort, seated alone at his dining table, spluttered, as he tried to swallow a mouthful of doucette, a favourite late afternoon indulgence of his.

'Have you any control over her or is this a plot against me?' Tancredi was white-faced.

'Plot? There is no plot. We have set a day, St. Sigbert's Day! For the marriage. It is all arranged.'

'Arranged, ha! Have you any idea of what your daughter is up to?' Tancredi slammed both hands, palms down, onto the table and leaned across the table so that he was staring directly into Beaufort's face. 'I have been informed by a squire, me, the Chancellor,' spittle was gathering at the corners of his mouth, 'informed by a squire, not the King, a squire informs me that the marriage is not to proceed.'

'No, no, there's some mistake, I've just told you ...'

'No mistake. Your daughter will destroy this kingdom, destroy us all. She made a binding promise. You made a promise. It cannot be broken. Where is she now?'

'Get out, out,' Beaufort snapped at the page boy who was waiting at his shoulder with a jug of braggot. 'She may still be attending his majesty,' he said, avoiding Tancredi's stare.

'What?' Tancredi jerked back from the table and raised his face towards the ceiling. His eyes were shut, and his body trembled like a taut bowstring.

'She was summoned to meet him at noon. She said he probably wanted to thank her for her assistance on the day he was wounded. That's all.'

'Fool, fool. She has made a complete fool of you.'

'What could I do? I could not –'

'Bah!' Tancredi flicked the back of his right hand as if he was batting Beaufort's words away from him. Beaufort sat sullen and red-faced like a chastised schoolboy.

'We must put an end to this madness.' Tancredi began to pace up and down. 'The Brooderstalt will raze this city to the ground.' He was talking to himself rather than addressing the bewildered Beaufort. 'We will all die if we break our word on this marriage. There will be no mercy from the Brooderstalt.'

'Oh, oh,' Beaufort groaned and thumped his forehead with the heel of his hand. 'I sent a messenger, just yesterday, to Pentrojan... to tell him that Lucretia had chosen St Sigbert's day for the marriage. I could send a fast rider to intercept him, if he has not already –'

'No. Leave it stand.' Tancredi said. He had stopped pacing up and down. His head was bent forward now, eyes closed in concentration, while he massaged both temples with his bejewelled fingers. 'Leave it stand. Your daughter will marry Pentrojan. She will do what she promised, what you promised. We will make sure of that.' Head still bent forward, he opened his eyes and stared fiercely at Beaufort. 'Are you with me?' He spoke quietly. Beaufort pushed aside the half-eaten doucette. Little patches of perspiration were clearly visible under his eyes and on the bridge of his nose.

'But what about the King?'

'The King? Forget the King. Wiser heads have to rule now. He will thank us in the future.'

'But, he is still King.' Beaufort's hand shook as he raised his mazer of braggot to his lips, spilling it down the front of his jerkin and lowering it shakily to the table without drinking.

'King?' Tancredi raised his voice. 'He will be King of nothing. Insult Pentrojan and we insult his master Cawdrult. And uncle, it were better to slit your own throat and your daughter's than to make the acquaintance of Cawdrult of Brooderlund.'

'What can we ... what can I do?' Beaufort said.

'If you value life, do nothing for now. Speak to no one about this. Do not confront your daughter. Let her believe what she will. I will speak with you tomorrow.'

'But what if ... '

Tancredi turned and left without another word.

****

As he walked back to his own quarters, Tancredi began to feel calmer. There is always a solution, he thought, always. It was at that very moment, when he thought he had gained control once more, that the twitch under his left eye began. This physical manifestation of something broken inside him was a private and personal humiliation for Tancredi. It had dogged him since childhood.

'A pox on it!' With the palm of his hand pressed tightly to the left side of his face, he quickened his step. Rather than take the direct route to his residence, he dodged through the tiny streets and back alleys of Dredgemarsh, braving the stench of open drains rather than risk meeting anyone of consequence. The sky darkened suddenly. He felt the first few heavy drops of rain that heralded one of those lightning downpours that swept in from the Anselem mountains in late autumn. It began to pour. Within seconds, the gully that ran down the centre of the narrow street filled and widened into a mucky stream. He could barely see a yard ahead of him as the slanting spears of rain assaulted his face and eyes. He tried to shield himself with the light cloak he was wearing, but it was instantly soaked through. Water trickled down inside his tunic, and he felt his feet grow cold as the deluge in the gully washed up around his ankles.

Then, the stench, that awful stench of stale piss from a fulling yard's tanks of wash, violently transported his mind back to a time he thought he had blanked out forever. He dropped his hands to his sides and stood in the foetid gully water, a look of bewilderment on his face. To any of the small tradesmen or their wives, who were busily slamming shut doors and shutters along the narrow street, and who might have caught a glimpse of the Chancellor, all they would have seen was a bedraggled wretch standing in the downpour. They might well have imagined he was crying. And he was.

At that moment in time, he was once again the wretched child who was forced into slavery in a fuller's yard after his father and mother died of plague. He felt again the awful shame of his ragged clothes, impregnated with the wash of piss and fuller's earth. He could hear the jeering of other children; 'piss pot, piss pot, greasy Tancredi's a piss pot.' The muscular spasm under his left eye pulled his face into a grotesque rictus of hatred and he sank to his knees in the foul water.

As suddenly as it had started, the downpour ceased. A door opened and two children, shouting and laughing, dashed onto the muddy street. They stopped and were silent the instant they saw the strange man kneeling in the water of the gully. They stared with wide eyes at him. A young woman with hands dyed red, wearing a long leather apron, rushed out and grabbed them. She bustled the pointing children inside and kicked the door shut. At the sound of the slamming door, Tancredi looked around him as if he hardly knew where he was. He stood up and staggered onwards, dragging his saturated cloak after him through the small river that flowed down the centre of the street.

On entering and locking his door, he went instantly to his bureau. With shaking hands he retrieved a small casket from its recesses. From the casket he took a delicately carved porphyry bottle and a small silver goblet. He uncapped the bottle and with trembling hands he carefully filled the goblet with a thick purple liquid: the addictive Melipsis from Lycia. He retired to the seat by his balcony window. There he sat, water dripping from his saturated clothes, and sipped sparingly till a quietness came over him, and finally all care was dismissed in a heavy-drugged sleep. He slept soundly for almost four hours when he was brusquely awakened by a loud knocking.

'Who's there?' Still slightly dazed from the melipsis, Tancredi was not about to confront anyone in his present state. Had he known, it would not have mattered whether the interrupter of his sleep had seen him howling at the moon or dancing naked on the battlements, for it was none other than Havelock the scribe with his inebriated companion Dipslick. Havelock sighed, and his loose skin drooped more than usual when he heard Tancredi shout, 'who's there?' Not only did it look as if he would have to embark on a speech, which for Havelock was anything more than three words, but he would also be expected to shout. A great wave of apathy rippled through his body and he fixed, in so far as he could fix, his two bulbous eyes on his companion. 'Dipslick,' that look of Havelock's was saying, 'I've knocked at the door, the least you could do is answer the Chancellor.' Dipslick, however, was past that hour of the day when intelligent speech was a faculty at his disposal. He opened his mouth and unleashed an enormous belch straight into Havelock's face. Havelock was not surprised, so he decided to knock at the door once again. If only Tancredi would came to the door, the need for talk would be greatly curtailed, because the Chancellor always communicated with them by asking questions which they could respond to by nodding or shaking their heads, or at the very most uttering a couple of syllables. Havelock, with a sigh, knocked on the door again.

Tancredi knew, when his question was answered by a long delay, followed by further desultory knocking, that it was Havelock and Dipslick .

'Damn you Havelock, go away and return in a couple of hours.' He heard a thud against the door followed by much grunting and shuffling that gradually died away to leave him in peace once more. The thud, in fact, was Dipslick's skull bouncing off the door. He had attempted to rest his head against the door, which, his eyes told him, was only inches away, but in reality was two feet or more. Now in a state of semi-consciousness, he was dragged away by Havelock, whose spirits had been elevated to mere gloominess because he did not have to bother himself with speech for at least another two hours.

****

When the pair of scribes returned two hours later and knocked at his door, a refreshed and confident Tancredi admitted them immediately.

'Well, what of the prisoner, is he conscious?' Tancredi's exuberant tone depressed Havelock, who just about responded to the question with a weak nod of the head. Dipslick nodded in synchronism.

'Good, good, well, you know the procedure for a trial. Prepare the litigation documents and court citations. The charge is outlined here.' Tancredi handed a short scroll to Havelock. 'The trial will take place in five days' time. The prisoner should be ready by then.'

Havelock looked profoundly aggrieved.

'Is that all?' he whispered.

'Yes, yes, that's all Havelock, I'm not asking you to re-write the law books, just a simple trial. Now get on with it.'

The pair of scribes wandered off without another word. Shortly afterwards, the Chancellor emerged from his chambers, and set off with a resolute stride.

Chapter 22

After the deluge of the previous evening, as often happened in Dredgemarsh, an intense sun ravished the dawn sky, and by mid-morning the ancient stones stewed in an unseasonable heat. The stifling air crackled with the sounds of shifting masonry. From the turret of the unused tower, overlooking the north curtain wall, Tancredi, dressed like a common soldier, scanned the fringes of Grak's Forest where it merged with the restless grasslands of the Vildpline. He had paced the tower from first light, and had steadily displayed more and more signs of impatience as the morning wore on.

'A pox on him. Will that idiot ever come?' He was muttering to himself when he spotted in the far distance a tiny plume of dust on the road that snaked down from the forest to the floor of the Vildpline.

'At last, at last,' he said, and hastily descended from the tower. Pulling the capuchon of his rough military cloak well forward so that his face was hidden, he mounted a horse already saddled and bridled since early morning. Discreetly, he walked his mount across the plaza and down the long winding street with towering granite walls that rose like shadowy cliffs on each side. It led onto the weedy yard of the postern gate. Pluck, the gatekeeper, now sober and bilious-looking, winched the gate open without challenging the rider, a carelessness in his duties that Tancredi would normally punish severely. On this occasion, he said nothing and quietly exited the castle. When he emerged onto the castle promenade and the postern gate groaned shut behind him, Tancredi turned and scanned the towers and brattis works of the castle, as if he suspected that someone was watching him. After some minutes he descended the glacis onto the long road that stretched across the great expanse of the Vildpline to Grak's Forest.

Tancredi's suspicion that he was being watched was not groundless. He had been observed for many hours past by Grunkite who was secreted in the upper chamber of a bartizan just east of tower where Tancredi had maintained his long vigil.

'What the devil is he up to?' Grunkite said. He could see that the Chancellor, disguised as a common soldier, was riding out to meet someone approaching Dredgemarsh in the far distance. He settled himself onto some broken masonry, where he could survey the Vildpline through an embrasure without being seen himself.

The rider whom Tancredi was so anxious to intercept was the ambassador Flinch, returning from an official visit to Cawdrult of Brooderlund. Flinch, relieved to be back in his own land, allowed his mount to amble along at a leisurely pace. He paid little heed to the lone rider approaching in the distance, his mind ruminating on the imminent pleasure of eating one of Bella Crumble's renowned breakfasts. He patted his horse on the neck, leaned forward and whispered in his ear.

'Yes, old fellow, I suppose you're looking forward to a fine oat breakfast.' As the two riders got closer to each other, Flinch began to imagine there was something familiar about the approaching soldier. He began to feel anxious, wondering why the rider wore his capuchon up on such a warm morning. As they drew within twenty yards of each other, Tancredi pulled the capuchon back and revealed himself. Flinch's mouth opened in wordless surprise. Perhaps the King is dead, he thought at first but quickly dismissed the idea.

'No, he wouldn't bother to show such courtesy to me. That would be the day,' he spoke quietly to his mount. When they drew abreast, both halted and Flinch inclined his head to Tancredi.

'My Lor ... Lord Chancellor.'

'Well, Ambassador, I trust you have had a successful mission?'

'Why yes, yes ... most successful, sir.' Flinch looked surprised by the friendly salutation. 'Yes indeed, sir, you will be glad to hear that our neighbours are saddened at our troubles and send us their best wishes, and furthermore—' The ambassador's babbling was quickly silenced by a firm but still cordial request that the details of the visit could be related later.

Tancredi turned his mount and both men were now moving slowly in the direction of Dredgemarsh.

'And you, ambassador will be glad to hear that our King is recovering, and we have caught the would-be assassin.'

'Excellent, excellent news, sir; may I ask who is this assassin?'

'Later, Ambassador. You have some letters for me?'

'Yes, I do indeed sir, safe and sound in my saddlebag.' Flinch patted his saddlebag.

A flicker of impatience passed over Tancredi's face.

'Perhaps, Ambassador, I might trouble you for the letters now. It is unlikely I will be in my quarters until very late tonight, and I am sure you will wish to retire early.'

'Now! Here!'

'Yes, here and now, Ambassador. I am not returning to the castle just yet; some pressing matters with the Waldgrave.'

'Ah, Waldgrave Bendict. A most hospitable waldgrave he is. He laid on a very fine supper for me, at Grismald Keep.' Flinch patted his ample stomach and smiled.

'The letters, Ambassador.'

'Oh, yes, yes, of course.' Flinch slowly rolled himself off his mount, and began to rummage through his saddlebags. Tancredi glared at the fumbling ambassador. Then a look of anxiety crossed his face, and the cursed twitch on his left cheek began. He turned his head away from the ambassador and pulled the capuchon up to cover his face once more.

Finally, Flinch produced a small bundle of letters and proffered them to Tancredi, who was now pretending to be casually surveying the landscape around them. He feigned a slight surprise, took the letters in an off-hand way and immediately redirected his attentions to the landscape, dropping the letters into a leather scrip attached to his belt.

'Well, I must leave you now, Ambassador. Affairs of state

call.'

'Sir.' Somehow Flinch did not sound quite as servile as usual. He was not so stupid that he did not understand that he had collaborated in something that, at the very least, was unorthodox. Because of this, the relationship between himself and Tancredi had changed in a subtle but definite way: Tancredi's authority was somehow diminished while Flinch was somewhat emboldened. Tancredi, of course, was instantly aware of this shift in their relationship and cursed inwardly, but there was nothing he could do about it now. He left the roadway and veered off northwest back towards the forest.

'Strange, very strange,' Flinch said, leading his horse aside to a group of boulders on the wayside. With their help, and much grunting, he rolled his great bulk onto the unfortunate animal's back, and resumed his journey to the castle.

Meanwhile, Tancredi, having reached the fringe of Grak's forest, stopped and dismounted. He plucked the letters from his saddle pouch and began to shuffle through them until he found what he had been searching for. He tore open the seal of Cawdrult and began to read.

I knew it. I knew they would support me. He shook the fist holding Cawdrult's letter towards the sky and laughed. But he suppressed the show of triumph almost immediately, as if he was embarrassed by the spontaneous outburst. He began to read once more,; then paused. This foolish boy has forfeited the right to rule, he thought. He puts his own pleasure before duty. It is up to me to save Dredgemarsh and its people. He bit his lower lip and gazed at the letter again. Three days and they will be here. Three days to set matters right. I will make Dredgemarsh great once again. It is my time. He slammed his right fist into his left palm, crushing Cawdrult's letter.

He set out at a leisurely pace, taking a circuitous route through part of Grak's forest and back towards Dredgemarsh, by a goat path deep in Meregloom Gorge that formed the eastern boundary of the Vildpline.

In the meantime, Ambassador Flinch was close enough to Dredgemarsh for Grunkite to recognise who it was that Tancredi had accosted on the north road.

'Curse the sluggard.' Grunkite watched as the ambassador ambled slowly towards Dredgemarsh. When at last Flinch did arrive through the postern gate, Grunkite was waiting for him and immediately escorted him to a disused guardhouse.'Ambassador Flinch, there is something wrong, something afoot. I don't know what or who or where, but this castle and our King is still in danger.'

'But, you have caught the traitor who tried to kill the King. Surely that is the end of the matter.' Flinch said.

'Who told you that?'

'Chancellor Tancredi.'

'Ah, Tancredi! He met you on the road.'

'Yes.'

'And did he tell you anything else?'

'No, we only met briefly. He was off to do business with Waldgrave Benedict … or so he said. Can we discuss this later, please, I'm tired and hungry.' His gut rumbled in confirmation.

'Of course Ambassador, you may go, but you would tell me if there was anything suspicious, anything at all.'

'Of course, of course. Well, come to think of it, there was something, not really suspicious but … unusual.'

'Tell me.'

'Well, the Chancellor asked for the letters from Cawdrult

out there on the road. He seemed anxious to have them. I thought it strange.'

'Something is wrong, I know it,' Grunkite said to no one in particular, and Flinch scurried from the guardhouse, rubbing his hands together in anticipation, at last, of breakfast in the refectory. Grunkite followed immediately after him.

For all his bulk, Grunkite moved quietly through the laneways and streets, not knowing exactly what he was looking for, but certain that some imminent danger lurked somewhere in the shadows. It was most unusual for him to indulge in any long-extended physical activity at this stage of his life, but he could not refrain from his fretful wandering about the castle.

'Curse these damned feet,' he groaned, as he climbed another stone stairway. For hours, he padded his way across dusty floors of long-forgotten halls and endless corridors. He is plotting some evil, thought Grunkite. I am certain of that. The bastard won't sneeze without me knowing. He will make a mistake eventually and when he does, I'll be there. Grunkite decided that he would watch Tancredi's residence all that day.

'Fishing,' he said, when Bella Crumble handed him a neat parcel of wastel bread and botargo and asked where he was off to.

'Fishing?' she said.

'Fishing,' he replied and left.

'He's gone fishing, did you ever hear the likes?' Bella addressed her single customer, Ambassador Flinch, who was ravaging a trencher of nombles at a small table in a cosy corner of the refectory.

'Ummm,' he moaned with pleasure and took a great slurp of braggot. 'Strange fish he's after,' he muttered half aloud.

'What did you say?' said Bella.

'Lovely … dish … lovely.'

As the shadows deepened, Grunkite found himself a dark alcove where he could observe the Chancellor's abode without being seen himself. While he prepared himself for the long wait, the object of his vigil sat in in a small copse by the castle esplanade. The twitch in his face had subsided without the need for melipsis. The only sound was his horse contentedly grazing the sweet grass of the copse. He had already spent several hours just sitting and thinking. It seemed to him now that everything that had happened was pre-ordained. With a twig he spelt out his name in the clay at his feet; Demetrius Triculatus Tancredi and then added King before the name. He smiled.

'King Triculatus Tancredi.' He savoured the sound and then looking around suspiciously, erased the words with his boot.

'My hour has come. Dredgemarsh's hour has come,' he whispered into the night air. 'He must die, for all our sakes. There is no other way.' He mounted and turned towards the castle. Over and over he rehearsed the details of the plan he had been incubating all that day. When it all fell into place, he gave a little gasp of delight at his own cleverness. And, as he approached the portal gate, he felt he could sense the very walls, stones and paths of Dredgemarsh welcoming him, their new master.

Chapter 23

Tancredi re-entered Dredgemarsh, receiving only a cursory glance from a couple of guards, who were busy trying to resuscitate a smoky fire in the night watch brazier. He summoned a stable boy to take his mount, and made his way on foot to his residence. He retired quietly to his own quarters. Outside in a hidden alcove, across from the Chancellor's residence, Grunkite, exhausted from his wanderings that day, slept soundly.

Alone in his solar, Tancredi smiled and rubbed his hands together in satisfaction. Once more, he read through the letter from Cawdrult of Bruderlund and then locked it away in a tiny closet, concealed behind a hanging drape embroidered with a battle scene from the Manchian wars.

Below in the servants' quarters, a mild panic erupted

when the calm hum of domestic chores was abruptly disrupted by a clanging bell.

'It's the Chancellor. He's back. What does he want at this late hour?'

'Calm, calm, Mistress Anna,' said the old cellerer and house servant, Victor.

'It's fine for you, Master Victor, but no doubt he'll want a late supper just when I have everything cleaned and cleared away. When is a decent woman to get any sleep?' Victor had already left the kitchen before she had finished her complaint.

Anna was half right. The Chancellor did want a meal, but it was a special breakfast, he requested, to be prepared for the following morning and not just for himself: it was a breakfast for three. His instructions were to use the very best meats, nombles, pastries, spiced ypocras, cheese and wastel bread. Victor was sent into the night to inform Arnulf Beaufort and a Sergeant Felric that they were invited to attend this breakfast. Refusal was not an option. They were informed that the breakfast would commence at sext. Felric, a sergeant of the Royal Guards and long time protégée of Tancredi, was instructed to arrive an hour before the breakfast.

****

The following morning when Arnulf Beaufort arrived at the Chancellor's residence and was shown into Tancredi's solar by Victor, he exclaimed, on seeing Tancredi in close conversation with Sergeant Felric. 'Excuse me Chancellor, I will wait outside until you are ready.' He turned to leave the solar as he spoke.

'Wait, wait, uncle. Come in. Come in.' Tancredi rose and approached immediately. 'Come drink. I think you know Sergeant Felric. Victor! ' he called out. 'We will eat now.' He handed a goblet to Beaufort and gestured for him to sit opposite Felric at his dining table. Tancredi sat at the head of the table.

'Uncle can I presume you are still totally committed to honouring the commitments made with regard to your daughter and Albrecht Pentrojan?' Beaufort hesitated and looked from Tancredi to Sergeant Felric, and back again to Tancredi.

'The sergeant is completely of one mind with us on this matter. You may speak openly,' said Tancredi.

'I am committed, Chancellor. '

'And your daughter?' Once again, Beaufort hesitated.

'She is headstrong, but she will do her duty when she realises what disaster she may bring on this whole kingdom by breaking her solemn oath. That is not the problem, Chancellor'

'Go on,' Tancredi said, and exchanged a quick glance with Sergeant Felric.

'The King, his majesty ... he, well you know what he thinks, and ... he is the King.'

'He is King, yes, but he is also a very young man and is not above a young man's foolishness. It is our duty to protect him, to save him from his own foolishness.' Beaufort fidgeted uneasily in his seat. 'And,' Tancredi continued, 'of course, our greatest duty is to the kingdom of Dredgemarsh itself ... Ah, good, our food is ready.' The conversation ceased while Victor and two pages carried in steaming croustades of boar meat thickened with goose eggs and milk, trenchers of nombles and a great jug of ypocras.

Arnulf Beaufort took a spoon and, leaning forward, immediately began to ladle the boar meat from the croustade into his mouth.

'Mmmmm ' he purred and closed his eyes tight.

'Eat hearty, today we have a kingdom to save,' said Tancredi, and winked at Sergeant Felric.

****

'I can't wait all afternoon,' Lucretia Beaufort said to Celeste, trying to concentrate on the game of alquerques they were playing. They sat at a small table in the great bay window of the belvedere of her father's residence..

'My lady, be patient, your father has been most agreeable, and simply asks you to wait for the Chancellor. Besides, his majesty is no doubt still resting and dreaming of a beautiful _'

'My dear ladies!' Tancredi was practically beside them before they realised he was present.

'You startled me,' said Lucretia.

'Forgive me, cousin. I did not wish to break your concentration on the game.'

'You wished to speak to me?'

'May I sit?' Lucretia nodded to a third seat in the bay window.

'Lettie, some ypocras for the Chancellor. I will take some quince water.'

'Not for me,' he laughed. 'Your father and I have over-indulged already.'

'It has not dampened your good spirits.'

'Yes, yes indeed cousin, I am in good spirits. The King is improving daily, the villains await their trial and punishment for their abominable crime. That will be the end of it.'

'Yes, a happy ending to the nightmare,' she sighed.

'Indeed. We must look forward now. And of course, the recent events have not been without benefit. The King... yourself...a happy conclusion. You mean so much to him, cousin.' Lucretia began to blush. She rose hastily, and turning her back on Tancredi, gazed out at the Vildpline. 'You know the trial is on tomorrow?' he said.

She turned instantly and stared at him.

'Has something happened?' There was a tremor in her voice.

'Calm yourself, cousin. The reason I bring this unfortunate matter up, is that our dear King is intent on attending the trial. Now, I am certain that would not be good for his health. He is still very weak. He does not realise how sick he has been, or the importance of avoiding any agitation until he is fully recovered.'

Tancredi rose and gazed out through the bay window.

'What a wonderful view.'

'You were saying ... about his majesty.'

'Yes cousin. Keenslide insists that violent emotions could still be extremely detrimental, even fatal, but will he listen? No, he is insistent.' Tancredi paused and continued to stare out the window. Lucretia bit her lower lip. 'However,' he continued, 'if you were to talk to him, cousin, I feel certain he could be persuaded to –'

'To what? What do you suggest?' Tancredi rubbed his forehead and closed his eyes in concentration.

'Yes, yes, that's it,' he said eventually. 'I know the very thing.'

'Yes?' she said.

'Go to the King. Tell him you cannot bear the thought of

him being anywhere near the assassin. Convince him that you are frightened, that you want to ... to be away from the castle tomorrow. Convince him. I know you can.'

'But where; where should we go?'

'Where, yes where?' Tancredi massaged his chin. 'Where?' he mumbled several times. Then, 'I know. Green Valley. To-morrow morning, go with the King to Green Valley. Spend the whole day there. That is what he needs, tranquillity, peace, what you both need.'

Lucretia thought for a while.

'Green Valley ... Yes, I will do it. I will do as you suggest.' She hesitated, 'But is there any danger for him? what if – '

'No, no, you need not fear another attempt. Rest assured, I will have the valley searched at first light and thereafter it will be sealed off. No one will be allowed near the valley. Those guarding it will not impinge on you in any way. In fact, I will arrange it so that you won't even see them.'

'Can you arrange to have a coach and a reliable coachman by tierce tomorrow morning?'

'It will be done.'

'Celeste!' She summoned her maid, 'go to the kitchen; have the Cook Meister prepare a hamper for two; wine, fruit everything, the very best. Have it ready for our departure to-morrow morning. We will be away for the full day. Tell them it is for the King. Everything must be perfect. Go now.'

'Dredgemarsh will be in your debt for this, cousin. I must go now, I have much to do and wish this unpleasant trial over as soon as possible. Tomorrow all things shall be ac-complished.'

Lucretia was not listening to him now. His rapid exit heightened the sense of urgency for the task before her. She left shortly after his departure, determined and resolute.

In the meantime, Celeste was making her way to the steamy world of Clutchbolt's kitchens. She first encountered Miss Nelly Lowslegg, who was mopping out one of the sculleries.

'Nelly, I'm glad it's you. My mistress wants a hamper prepared.'

'I can't, Celeste,' Nelly whispered. 'You'll have to ask Cook Meister Clutchbolt. I'm not allowed.'

'Oh dear, that's the one thing I wanted to avoid. Where is he?'

'Just follow the sound.' Nelly nodded towards the main kitchen.

Celeste reluctantly entered the cauldron of simmering heat. She could barely see through the steam, but could plainly hear a high nasal tenor voice singing,

'Sweet rose of my heart
Bloom only for meeeee ...'

Moments later, she saw the rotund singer of this serenade swaying towards her like a ship looming out of a fog. A flagon of vernage dangled like a anchor at the end of one limp arm while the other arm, held aloft, proffered, as it were, his song to the ceiling. When he noticed her, he immediately glided across the tiles and swept his arm around her waist.

'And what can we do for you, my little pepper pot?'

'Die.'

'Anything for you, my little apple fritter, my dainty puff pastry, as long as I can knead your dough.' Clutchbolt cocked one eyebrow and leered at Celeste. She was overcome, not by his gallant words, but the reek of stale Vernage. He puckered up his wet lips, closed his eyes and lunged in the general direction of her face. Deftly, she ducked out from under his arm and left him kissing the marble column of the door jamb. It took some time for Clutchbolt's insensate lips to signal to their master that the kissee was somewhat hard of feature. By the time he had determined this and opened his eyes for further investigation, Celeste had positioned herself behind the large table in the middle of the kitchen. Ratchet was chopping onions on a wooden counter in one corner, with tears rolling down his cheeks and shrieking like a demented peacock. Bella Crumble glared and tapped her carbuncled foot on the flagged floor, not so much at the carry-on of Clutchbolt but rather at the laughing Ratchet. She hated any emotions displayed by Ratchet that did not include, touch or concern her in some way or other. How dare he be amused at something which she did not find amusing.

Clutchbolt waltzed across the floor in hot pursuit of Celeste.

'Aha, you frisky little parsnip, come to daddy. He'll cook your goose.'

'Go away, you horrid creature, you ... you beast.' Clutchbolt shuddered with pleasure.

'Ohh, ohh, more, more, abuse me, lacerate me, I love it. Your words are paprika, chilli and coriander to my heart. Grill me, roast me, baste me and then my feisty little pomegranate, taste me.'

Ratchet was having serious difficulty sucking enough air into his lungs between convulsed bouts of laughter.

'Cook Meister,' Celeste's voice was an octave higher than normal.

'Yes, speak, speak, my little lamb chop.'

'Cook Meister! The King and my lady require a hamper.

You are to prepare it. It must be ready by tomorrow morning, by tierce. They will require enough food for the whole day and wine of course, and you are to have it delivered straight to the King's coach at the postern gate. I must go. I am expected back immediately. I must go.' Yet she remained where she was, hoping that Clutchbolt would move away, so that she could leave without hindrance. The pickled Cook Meister was still deciphering her message and was in no hurry to release his quarry.

'I know what we can do,' he drooled. 'Now listen. Pay attention. Go to your lady and tell her to prepare a hamper for me, Lord Clutchbolt. Listen, listen, we, you and I, will dine tomorrow, tell her not to forget the cider. Tell her– '

His words were drowned by an unmerciful shriek of laughter that exploded from Ratchet's gullet. Leopold Ratchet was now on his knees, hanging on grimly to the edge of the worktop, his face purple and aching from laughter. Clutchbolt began to bellow in synchronism and immediately afterwards, an uncontrolled tittering trickled in from the scullery, where Miss Lowslegg was scrubbing the floor. Bella Crumble stared thunder at Ratchet.

'Out, out, you little hussy!' she hissed sideways at Celeste. 'The hamper will be ready on time. Go! Out of this at once. Disgraceful carry-on, just disgraceful. Is there no decency left in the world?' She glared at Ratchet, but try as he might, he could do nothing but abandon himself to great body-shaking shrieks of laughter. Bella Crumble stormed out of the kitchen. Celeste darted past Clutchbolt and ran all the way back to her mistress's chambers. Clutchbolt collapsed onto the table like a bag of sand and instantly fell asleep, chuckling to himself between snores. Miss Lowslegg washed the outer scullery for the third time that day.

Elsewhere, Grunkite waited for Tancredi's return, Verm paced his cell like a caged beast and Burstboil stared through the barred window of another prison cell in a catatonic stupor. Cesare kissed the soft pleading lips of Lucretia, and Tancredi, whispered instructions to Sergeant Felric, in a private room at the Slaughtered Horse.

In that same hostelry, long after Tancredi and the sergeant had departed, the proprietor Humbert Fullfare cursed quietly, when Sergeant Felric returned with four men.

'I'll take the same room again. And send her up with your best braggot,' the sergeant ordered, pointing to a young serving girl.

'You go on ahead, sergeant. We will be with you shortly,' said Humbert.

'Oh master, please don't make me go to that room.' The young serving girl twisted the bottom of her apron in her hands. Her eyes were beginning to fill with tears.

'Calm yourself, Hiltrude. I'm sending you home now. You are finished for the day. Go home to your mother, lass.' She reached out shyly, took Humbert's great shovel of a hand and kissed it.

'Thank you, thank you.'

'Get along now, and on your way out, tell Frambert I want him.' Moments after Hiltrude's departure, a brawny young boy carrying a small barrel pushed his way backwards through the inn door.

'Hiltrude said you wanted me, father.'

'Aye, leave the barrel lad, and take a couple of pitchers of braggot and five mazers up to the back room.'

'Yes, father.'

'And Frambert, don't talk to them. Just leave the braggot and go.'

'Yes, father.' Within minutes, Frambert was off to the backroom with his tray neatly laid out. When he walked through the door the conversation ceased and the five men stared at the boy.

'Well, well.' A blotchy red-faced man with rotten teeth spoke first. 'I thought I heard the sergeant order the young wench to serve us.'

'You're right, Shem Sledge,' said a dark, greasy man by his side.

'Course I'm right, Pete.'

'Well lad, where's the wench?' Felric glared at the boy.

'My father sent me,' the boy said, staring back at Felric.

'Well boy, these two beard splitters,' he pointed to the other two men, 'they want the wench to serve them.'

'Any wench,' said the larger of the two.

'So long as it's got a muff in the right place,' the smaller one bellowed, and they all roared laughing. Frambert said nothing, but walked to the table and placed the tray amongst them. He turned to go but the red blotchy-faced one, Shem Sledge, grabbed his arm.

'Hold on, boy. Since your father was so kind as to send you, we won't quibble over a little thing like a muff, will we boys.' The room resonated with their coarse laughter. Frambert tried to pull away, but Shem Sledge began to pull the boy towards him, and puckered up scabby lips as if to kiss him. Frambert drew back his right fist and punched his tormentor in the face. Shem Sledge yowled and clasped his hands to his face. Blood was flowing from his nose.

The door burst open and Humbert Fullfare stormed into the room.

'What's going on here,' shouted Humbert. Shem Sledge, who was looking in disbelief at the blood on his hands jumped to his feet, and turned to face the landlord. Humbert stood erect and imposing, almost a foot taller than him. Frambert stood defiantly beside his father.

'Has anyone laid a hand on you, son?'

'No, father.'

Shem Sledge's face was a mask of blood-streaked fury. 'Are we going to let a poxy innkeeper and his brat away with this?' He roared, and looked around at his companions who remained firmly seated and averted their eyes from him.

'Shut up you cullion, and apologise to the landlord,' said Sergeant Felric.

'But we can't let –'

'Now, right now.' Felric jumped to his feet and grasped the hilt of his sword.

'I apologise, I apologise,' Shem Sledge sat down and glared at his companions.

'Forgive the fool, landlord,' said Felric. 'I'll make sure he pays for his behaviour,' He pulled a coin from his purse and proffered it to Frambert. 'Here, boy.' Frambert did not take the coin.

'Come.' Humbert laid his hand on his son's shoulder, and the pair turned and left the room.

'Curse his impudence.' Felric said, and took his seat. Shem Sledge wiped his hand across his bloodied face and was about to speak.

'Shut your mouth, you clotpole.' Felric pointed his finger directly at Sledge. 'We've more important matters to attend to.'

It was almost an hour later, when Shem Sledge and his greasy companion emerged from the back room. Sledge's blotchy red face had paled to a sickly grey and the pair slunk out of the Slaughtered Horse without a sideways glance.

They were followed minutes later by the second pair of Felric's confidantes, who looked equally subdued and anxious to be gone as quietly as possible.

'Murderin' bastards,' an old man muttered to Humbert, when the pair had left.

'You know them, Stefan?' Humbert asked.

'Aye, I know 'em. The Hatchet brothers; Gross and Jem. Slice your gullet for drink of water. And the pair before them, Shem Sledge and Black Pete, even worse. Strange guests you have, Humbert.'

'Not of my choosing or liking. But I tell you Stefan, they have powerful connections.'

'Something bad is ...'

'Hush, Stefan.'

Felric strode up to the table where Humbert was talking to Stefan and flung a few coins down. He turned and left without a word.

Dredgemarsh

Chapter 24

Shem Sledge hated the early mornings, and only the thought that Felric would have him flayed alive stopped him from turning over and forgetting what he had agreed to do that day. Besides that, Gross Hatchett was kicking him in the ribs and shouting,

'Up, up, you lazy cur.'

Shem Sledge, snarling like a dog, scratched himself all the way to the barracks kitchen service hatch and returned with his breakfast. Black Pete and Jem Hatchett were already up, wolfing down great gobbets of pottage dished out by Stench Harmer, field cook. Stench was cook because he had lost one arm in a brawl over a gambling debt, and cooking was his only choice for staying in the military. He detested the job, but at least, while in barracks, he was only called upon, on the odd occasion, to provide an extra-early morning breakfast. Clutchbolt and his crew supplied all of the main meals in the refectory.

The four conspirators, Jem and Gross Hatchet, Shem Sledge and Black Pete huddled together. The barracks kitchen, at that dismal hour, was empty. They spoke very little.

'What foul work has you cullions up and out of your flea pits at this hour?' Stench Harmer shouted from his serving hatch.

'Not your gut rot pottage, you nosey bladderskate,' Shem Sledge retorted.

'Pig fuckers.' Stench Harmer slammed the service hatch shut.

'I suppose I should be off,' said Black Pete, rising. He looked down at his three companions, as if waiting for a response. There was no answer. Black Pete did not move off, but stood rubbing his hands together.

'I said, I suppose--'

'We heard what you fucking said. Now go and do your bit. We'll do ours,' said Shem Sledge. Black Pete spat on the floor and left.

One hour after the prime bell, Black Pete was ready and waiting with the King's open-topped coach by the postern gate, The sky was clear and bright. He spat on his hands and tried to smooth his hair, then attempted to view the results in the shiny blade of his seax.

'Not bad,' he muttered and began to clean his nails with the point of the seax. His toilet was interrupted by a loud female voice.

'He is no good, Leopold; no sense of responsibility, a drunkard and a womaniser. You ought to assert yourself. You're twice the man he is, twice the man.'

'Yes, Mistress Crumble.'

'Bella, Leopold, Bella. I told you to stop this Mistress Crumble thing. Call me Bella.'

'Yes ... Bella.'

Leopold Ratchet was wheeling an antique trolley piled high with several large baskets, while Bella was carrying a fine leather satchel that was designed specifically for carrying two bottles of wine with a pair of delicately wrought silver goblets. They were in quite a hurry, Ratchet pattering along on spindly legs behind the trolley and Bella gliding like a galleon in full sail beside him.

'He is not fit to be Cook Meister of Dredgemarsh, or any other marsh for that matter. So what if he knows a few special recipes. Does that give him the right to lord it over us? Does it? Well, does it?'

'No ... Bella.'

'And his carry-on with those, those tarts and hussies is despicable. Of course, they are no better. No decent man would look twice at them. Would he? Well would he?'

'No, yes, no, I mean, no.'

The harassed Leopold was struggling past the coach and Black Pete.

'Hey dung head, over here.' Black Pete shouted.

Leopold stopped and looked around.

'Yes you, dung head. Here, the hampers are for here. Put them up on the wagon.'

Leopold, without comment, returned to the wagon, took hold of one side of the first hamper and waited for assistance. Black Pete sat staring at him; not budging an inch and not offering any kind of help.

'Get down at once, you lazy wretch. Assist Mr Ratchet. He is the Assistant Cook Meister of Dredgemarsh.' Bella Crumble glared at Black Pete. He turned slowly towards her and stared menacingly, as if contemplating whether to stamp her into the ground or laugh at her. Bella's angry glare dissolved. She quickly grabbed the other end of the hamper and, without a murmur, hoisted it into the wagon. Much to her discomfort, Black Pete continued to stare intently at her until all the hampers were loaded. When they were finished, she stole a rapid glance at him. His small animal eyes were still fastened upon her. To complete her mortification he lobbed a glob of sputum inches from where she stood. She swallowed hard, turned and retreated as fast as dignity would allow. Ratchet scuttled behind with the empty trolley. Had anyone the slightest interest in observing Ratchet, they would have noticed that there was a lightness in his step and the slightest of wry smiles on his face as he trailed after the now silent Bella Crumble.

It was not long until voices alerted Black Pete of someone else's approach. This time, however, sweet laughter and convivial conversation heralded none other but the King of Dredgemarsh and the Lady Lucretia. Black Pete's self-assurance and cockiness vanished instantly.

The young King, though still pale, had a commanding presence that caused Black Pete to break out in a sweat. Cesare and Lucretia were too absorbed in each other to notice the look of fear in Black Pete's eyes. With the sleeve of his uniform, he trailed an oily streak of dirt across his forehead.

'Well, well, madam,' Cesare smiled at Lucretia, 'I see you have everything planned. It is obvious there is no refusing you, I am at your service. Whatever you say, I will do,'

'Good, I will hold you to that promise.'

'Let us away then, driver! To Green Valley, take your time, we are in no hurry.'

'Yes m'Lord.' Black Pete said in a hoarse whisper. The iron portal gate screeched on its hinges as it was winched open. The coach moved out at an easy pace into a glorious landscape. Lucretia sat with her head leaning lightly on the shoulder of Cesare and the morning, though radiant, was a mere adornment to her glowing beauty. Cesare turned towards her and his lips brushed delicately across her dark hair, that appeared to sparkle in the bright morning air.

Black Pete stared grimly ahead. Beads of sweat continually blossomed on his greasy forehead and trickled down his nose and cheeks. His garments at the neck and around his armpits were becoming visibly saturated with perspiration. It looked as if every moment was an agony for him. Cesare was completely engaged with Lucretia as he talked and pointed out various landmarks and features of historical and personal interest. Neither he nor Lucretia glanced at their petrified driver, during the two hours it took to reach Green Valley. They drove to the eastern edge of the beautiful Lake Tranquil, which lay like a silvery shield in the heart of the valley.

'Stop here.' Cesare ordered. The grinding wheels were instantly silent. The hypnotic beat of the horses' hooves ceased and a breathtaking silence embraced them. It was as though they were sitting in a vast and empty cathedral. From the distant Rim Wood a bird began to sing. Its plain chant echoed across the lake that looked like shimmering crystal covering the valley floor.

'Could anything be more beautiful?' he said.

'I am so happy,' she whispered. Cesare stepped down from the coach and gave Lucretia his hand.

'Be careful,' she said. 'You are far from recovered.'

'I never felt stronger,' he laughed.

Lucretia beckoned to Black Pete.

'Place the baskets under that tree, please. Then you may retire. Do not go too far. Return three hours after noon.' Black Pete did as Lucretia instructed and immediately started back up and out of the Green Valley.

'He was right, you know.' Lucretia smiled, looking all around the valley.

'Who was right, and about what was he right?' Cesare enfolded her in his arms, pulled her close to him, and gazed into her eyes.

'Tancredi was right. You can't see them ... the soldiers ... guarding the valley,' she whispered. Cesare looked all around.

'Well, at least he got that right. They stayed out of sight even as we came through the pass.' He turned back to Lucretia.

'But enough of them, forget they are there, my dear Lucretia.' He kissed her lightly on the cheek. She blushed.

'That's the last I'll see of them,' Black Pete muttered, as he glanced back and saw them embracing.

But his traitorous work was not done. When he emerged from the valley, he set off for Maulin Forest. Having gone through the ordeal of the last few hours, he was now looking buoyant and cocky. He set the horses to a brisk canter.

'Now we'll see what these Brooderstalt are made of. They'll need balls for this day's work.' He was talking out loud. The crude, aggressive language helped to re-establish and re-centre his ugly nature. As he neared Sour Hollow, where he was to collect two of the Brooderstalt men and smuggle them into the castle, a flash of whirring steel sizzled inches in front of his nose and with a sickening thud, buried itself into a beech trunk just beyond him. Black Pete yelped like a kicked dog and hauling on the reins, stopped immediately, afraid to even look around.

'Greetings.' a heavy set soldier with wild black hair and beard stood grinning at the rigid driver.

'I said greetings, my friend, have I sliced your tongue off or are you just stupid?

'No, I'm not stupid.'

'Good, good, well, now that we have established that, can you tell me are you our escort to this Dredgemarsh shitpile? We have a little task to perform there.' He stepped forward with a swagger, followed by a group of grinning soldiers.

'Speak up, man. Are you our escort?' He advanced on Black Pete, who was now aware that he was surrounded by Brooderstalt. They looked like tough, seasoned campaigners, and Black Pete decided right then that the best thing to do was ingratiate himself with these fierce-looking men.

'Yes, my noble sir, I am the one who will help you to get into the castle. I have already carried the King to Green Valley below. He will wait there expecting my return. Lord Tancredi has entrusted me –'

'Enough, enough. I asked a simple question. I expect a simple answer. Are you our escort to Dredgemarsh?'

'Yes.'

'How long will it take?'

'From here, sir, it will take about two hours.'

'Very well, we move out in five minutes.' He addressed two of his officers.

'We move quietly, no talking, two single files each side of this road and under cover of the forest. Do not under any circumstances break cover. Do you all understand?'

'Yes, Captain Pentrojan,' the officers answered.

Black Pete paled when he heard the name Pentrojan. Albrecht Pentrojan was a name feared every bit as much as that of his master Cawdrult , King of Brooderlund. He was amazed at the speed with which the camp was struck, and the fierce-looking warriors were mounted and ready to move out. Pentrojan nodded to Black Pete. They advanced through the forest, weaving left and right as the narrow road swirled and looped around the giant Maulin oaks and beeches. The army of Cawdrult was a deadly snake, sliding invisibly and noiselessly, towards the drowsing old fortress city of Dredgemarsh.

With their approach, the final enactment of Tancredi's master plan moved towards its denouement. Every element of that plan had been rehearsed and tested a thousand times in his mind so that even now, he could mentally imagine the progress of every event with such precision that, had one the capability of comparing his mental picture with the reality, it would have been hard not to believe that Tancredi had some telepathic powers.

It was now well into the morning. Voices arguing, singing, snatches of greetings, oxen moving, stables being swept out, doors slamming, feet running, walking, tools grating and a multitude of waking sounds percolated into the crisp bright air above Dredgemarsh. The breakfast steams and smells wafted out through granite chimneys and down draughty corridors, seeped under doors and out of windows, tickling the noses of the mongrel dogs that congregated each morning and evening by the pig swill vats. These two monstrous rusting containers were filled each morning and evening by means of a screw pump, designed and installed by Professor Quickstrain. The screw was two feet in diameter, made of wood and encased in a wooden pipe that penetrated diagonally downwards into the heart of Dredgemarsh castle. Its

lower extremity rested in another huge vat, in the offal scullery off Clutchbolt's kitchen. It was powered by a water mill
buried deep below the floors of Dredgemarsh, where the
Yayla tumbled through the black watery arteries of the fortress. Each morning and evening, the vat in the offal scullery
was filled with the remainders of previous meals and the offal of animals slaughtered for that day. The screw pump was
then engaged by the water mill drive shaft and the odorous
contents of the full vat pumped up to the feeding vats in the
piggery.

The castle was shaking itself awake like an old dog, while
the deadly viper of Pentrojan's column slid relentlessly nearer the unsuspecting prey. Grunkite, although he was unaware of the events taking place, sensed something was
amiss. Some evil was threatening Dredgemarsh and he was
certain that Tancredi was the instigator of that evil, but he
could not prove or substantiate his suspicions. His night's
vigil outside Tancredi's rooms had been fruitless, except for
the fact that Tancredi's failure to return at all reinforced his
feelings of unease. Dismayed and worried, he abandoned his
post and returned to his own apartment for a brief rest, and
hopefully some inspiration as to the nature of the threat that
he sensed, so ominously close. He decided that, no matter
what, he was resolved to force Tancredi's hand at the council meeting scheduled for later that morning. However, Tancredi was cunning, and Grunkite knew the dangers of
openly accusing him of being a traitor without having sub-
stantial evidence. He was physically exhausted after his long
vigil and found he could not come to grips with the problem. A short sleep, he thought, might refresh him and
maybe clear his mind of confusion. Before retiring, he
ordered an assistant officer called Trudge to wake him in

three hours and on no account was he to be disturbed until then. Among his subordinates, an order given by Grunkite was inviolate and to be carried out to the letter.

Shem Sledge, Jem Hatchett and Gross Hatchett marched brazenly down to the dungeons where Verm was incarcerated. The guards were rostered in threes to provide a permanent round-the-clock watch. It was an unwelcome duty, not simply because of the foul air in these lower regions, but there was not one who did not feel a shiver of fear as he walked past Verm's cell door. A black brooding presence was palpable, an aura enveloping everything, infecting everything like a disease. Those who had the temerity to glance through the cell peephole wished instantly that they had resisted the temptation, because staring from the shadows were two red orbs that seemed to them like devil's eyes, peering from the gates of hell itself.

It was, therefore, with some relief that the three guards heard the boisterous approach of Tancredi's hirelings. The form of the three approaching figures was just discernible in the guttering light. Sledge rasped out something. Verm, listening intently from the interior of the cell, could not decipher the meaning. It was not that his hearing was impaired, but rather the inability of his brain to assemble the sounds into any meaningful form. He silently moved to the door and peered through the tiny peephole. He saw the three guards instantly move as if to depart, but just as they passed the incoming three, they were struck down from behind and their throats sliced open. The murdered guards gyrated, shivered on the cold damp stones, blood gushed and within moments they were still. The red eyes blinked again. Verm's shattered brain tried to make sense of what he had seen, but rational thought was beyond him.

Shem Sledge ripped the cell keys from the belt of one of the slain guards. He held his bloodied falchion poised, ready to strike. His two companions followed suit and the three assassins converged on the door of Verm's cell. Verm retreated with a snarl to the furthest corner. The three outside hesitated; then stopped. Shem Sledge anxiously massaged his chin. He beckoned to the others to draw up closer on each flank. He then entered the key into the lock, turned, kicked open the door and leapt back with his falchion poised to strike. He stumbled, knocking Jem Hatchett to the ground. With a squeal of terror Jem scrambled to his feet and began to slash out blindly in the direction of the cell door. Nothing emerged from the cell except a low eerie growl. Inside, it was pitch black, so that the entrance presented what appeared to be a completely matte surface with no depth, completely absorbing every flicker of light into nothingness. In vain, Shem Sledge strained his eyes to penetrate the blackness. The now barely audible growl became intermittent.

'The knife, the fucking knife, who has it?' Sledge shouted.

'Here, here it is,' said Jem Hatchet, holding out a butcher's long knife. Shem Sledge grabbed it and flung it onto the threshold of the cell door.

'You in there, take the knife, get out, quick. Come on you bastard, this is your chance, you're free, get out.' The three assassins retreated back from the doorway.

'Listen, we've done our bit, let's get out of here.' Gross Hatchet tried to sound casual but could not hide the trembling in his voice.

'No, I'm not turning my back on that monster. Just stay here, stick together, let him pass, then we'll go.' They squashed closer together. The low growling began to grow in volume. In unison, they held their breaths and fastened their bulging eyes on that black opening. Then he stood there, begrimed, tangled hair, eyes blazing with malice. Without releasing them from the baleful beam of those terrible eyes he stooped, snatched the knife from the ground and stood poised, ready to fight. They stumbled backwards a few paces, pressing even closer together until they looked like one three-headed creature. The Shem Sledge part of this composite slowly raised an arm and pointing back from whence they had come said, 'Go.'

The red eyes blinked, the brow furrowed in puzzlement and then in an instant, Verm vanished.

Sledge and the Hatchett brothers recovered slowly and without a word, turned in unison and still tight together, began their ascent from the dungeons. Their retreat, however, in contrast to their entrance, was subdued and hesitant. Gradually, as they approached their final destination, they began to speed up until finally they split asunder and ran like maniacs, shouting alarm, murder and treachery. They burst into the main barracks square, and within minutes were surrounded by a mob of guards.

'What has happened?'

'The murderer, he's escaped.'

'Killed all three guards.'

'Cut their throats.'

'Grunkite will slaughter someone for this.'

Then a roar of anger sliced through the babble. Complete silence, and all heads turned to see Grunkite.

'What's this, what's this?' No one answered.

'Answer. Someone. Answer. Now.'

'He's escaped, chief.' It was Trudge who spoke.

'Bludvile? Not Bludvile? Not Bludvile? Is it? Is it? '

'Yes.'

The blood drained from Gunkite's face.

'Tell me this is untrue.' There was something akin to a childlike pleading in his voice, a kind of hopeless desire that someone could make things right, could say the right thing. Trudge and the others stared at the ground.

Grunkite's insides lurched at the thought of announcing at council that the killer, who had been so difficult to capture, had escaped. He could not bear to think of what Tancredi might say. His heart was thumping violently in his chest. It was difficult to breathe. He could hear the blood gushing and tumbling inside his skull. All kinds of ideas danced unbidden across his mind. If he could only die that instant. If he could disintegrate, vanish, disappear, turn into a rat, a louse, if only he was never born, if only he had executed the killer immediately, if, if, if. The guards dared hardly breathe. They hunched their shoulders involuntarily, as if expecting physical blows were about to rain down upon them. They waited. Then the words came; not in a torrent of rage but painfully, slowly, one by one, every syllable coated in vitriol.

'You ... incompetent ... oafs ... clotpoles ... every last one of you. Stupid ... lazy ... good for nothing ... useless dung maggots. One hour ... one hour is what you have to recapture him. Don't even think of failure. One hour.' He had no more words. He turned, and as if every step was infinitely painful, walked back to the room where he had been resting. The door closed quietly and his rage hung like a pall over the square.

The grey-faced senior officers immediately began to organise search parties. They sent for the lymers and their fewterers once again, to dispatch them below into the dark warrens of Dredgemarsh. In a matter of minutes, the square was completely empty and quiet, as if nothing had happened. Every available man who could walk was taking part in the search. The upper ramparts and battlements were completely deserted. Grunkite sat in his rooms, shutters closed, shocked and aching with a sense of helplessness. Those were the blackest hours of his life. He was without hope and Dredgemarsh, in those few hours, was without its old hoary protector.

How surely and how deftly Tancredi played out the game. In one move, he had confounded his enemy Grunkite, and diverted everyone's attention to the hunt for Verm, leaving the castle defences abandoned.

Pentrojan was now close to the edge of Maulin Forest. Already, he could see Quickstrain's giant anemometer revolving in the gentle morning breeze. The clank of armour and the rattle of horse tackle played counterpoint to the muffled drumming of the horse's hooves. There was a barely suppressed air of excitement amongst the troops. Black Pete trundled ahead in his wagon, still ignorant of the size of the force that followed behind. When he finally reached the edge of Maulin Forest he stopped as bidden: waited, while Pentrojan's men filtered in through the trees to assemble in a wide clearing behind the wagon. Pentrojan leaned forward laconically on his saddle horn, waiting until everyone had arrived. Black Pete's eyes widened in amazement as more and more soldiers came to add to the already milling army of horsemen. They bristled with knives, swords, lances, maces, hatchets and war hammers. The treacherous coach driver shuddered at the thought of the slaughter and mayhem that they would inflict on the soldiers and citizens of Dredgemarsh. Even he felt a twinge of shame, when he thought of the many acquaintances whom he imagined at that time would be idling away the hours, unaware that death stalked the bright morning forest of Maulin. But regret and remorse found scant sustenance in his heart, and with little effort he dismissed the thoughts, or rather smothered them in the contemplation of his own rewards for this evil day's work.

'You,' Pentrojan addressed Black Pete. 'Take four of my men with you into the castle. When you're in safely and in command of the gate, signal with this.' He grabbed a pennant from a young soldier and flung it into the rear of the coach. 'Daltun! Take three with you. You know what to do.' Daltun, a low swarthy soldier, selected three men with a simple nod of the head. They jumped into the coach, lay flat on the floor and pulled a large canvas over themselves. The wagon set out immediately.

'Don't keep us waiting.' Pentrojan shouted after them. 'Pidgin! Keep watch. Dismount,' he called out to his troops.

Pentrojan was the first to dismount, and promptly sprawled himself under an ancient shagbark tree and closed his eyes. The others followed suit, and lay or sat on the springy forest carpet of leaves and twigs, each preparing in his own way for the coming conflict.

It was the simplest of tasks for Black Pete to gain entrance to Dredgemarsh through the postern gate. From there he drove to the deserted Four Towers square and drew the coach up close to the guardhouse of the main gate. Pentrojan's men quickly overpowered and killed the one old gatekeeper, who had been left while all his comrades searched for the escaped murderer. Without anyone noticing, they hoisted the Brooderstalt pennant on the turret flagpole. They then raised the portcullis and swung the massive main gates open. This did attract some curious looks from a couple of canal lads in the vicinity, but there was no sense of alarm.

'They've done it, Captain,' Pidgin shouted from his lookout on the branch of a great oak tree. Without delay, the army was mounted, and advanced at a canter across the sweet undulating meadows of the Vildpline, towards Dredgemarsh Castle. The inhabitants were totally unaware of anything unusual, apart from the spreading news in the Market Square about the escape of the Verm Bludvile the murderer. The possibility of any radical or immediate change in their way of life would have been greeted with amused disbelief. Dredgemarsh never changed. Its daily routines and customs were fixed, immutable as the seasons. The recent failed attempt to extinguish the life of their King, though at the time disturbing, somehow strengthened that feeling of immutability.

Chapter 25

The ingrained sense of duty and adherence to custom amongst the inhabitants of Dredgemarsgh was what Tancredi relied upon to execute his plans. All the council members – even Grunkite – had gathered and were awaiting the Chancellor's arrival who was strolling casually to the Council Chamber in the company of Sergeant Felric.

'You know what to do, Sergeant? You must convince her to come with you. said Tancredi.

'Don't worry, Chancellor, I'll be most convincing. She'll come immediately.'

'And I will ensure your story is no lie. Go now, Sergeant.'

Outside the chamber door, Dipslick and Havelock waited. Protocol dictated that they could only enter the chamber behind the Chancellor. Unlike the councillors within, they showed no signs of impatience at Tancredi's delay.

If one could judge from appearances they would be quite content if he did not arrive at all. When he did arrive, the air of excitement emanating from him was so unusual that even the semi-comatose Dipslick elbowed Havelock and by a deft little nod of the head and wink of the eye, indicated that it was worth taking a second look at the Chancellor. Havelock sluggishly rotated his large eyeballs to focus carefully on Tancredi. It was clear that he agreed with Dipslick, for his eyebrows popped up at least three or four centimetres above normal; sudden movements were most uncharacteristic of any part of Havelock's anatomy. When Tancredi walked slowly into the chamber with the two scribes behind him, Havelock still carried the amazed look on his face. His mind, it must be said, had settled back to its normal state of lassitude, but it took some time for his eyebrows to get the message and slide back to their accustomed place.

No one spoke while the scribes set out their accoutrements and Tancredi settled himself behind the speaker's lectern. He was in no hurry and it became obvious that he was preparing himself for something out of the ordinary. He had replaced his usual dark tunic with a red samite caftan. The elaborate gold embroidery on the collar sparkled, but seemed out of place on Tancredi. It was too opulent, and gave the distinct impression that the wearer was trying to be something he was not.

'Councillors,' Tancredi at last broke the uneasy silence, 'our King is fully recovered, and this morning took advantage of the fair weather to relax and renew his strength. He went to spend the day in Green Valley. However, I must tell you now that I fear for him once more. The murderer Verm Bludvile has escaped, unbelievable as that may seem.'

Grunkite squirmed in his seat.

'I have dispatched a party of soldiers to go to the King's aid immediately. Let us pray it is not too late. Dredgemarsh must continue to function, however. No one is indispensable.' Although Tancredi uttered the latter comment in a low, casual fashion, its impact was like a sledgehammer blow to everyone listening. Tancredi knew without looking at anyone that, with those few casual words, he had stepped irrevocably onto the path of power or extinction.

'Bludvile's escape ...' he was about to continue.

'What? What did you say?' Grunkite erupted. 'Not indispensable! Our King! Our ... King Cesare Greyfell? You dare speak of our beloved King like that. You! Upstart! Peasant! How dare you! How dare you speak of the King like that.' Grunkite's face had turned a deep purple.

'I would remind our Marshall of the Royal Guard that I am in authority at this moment,' Tancredi said. 'I can understand his frustration, given this morning's debacle. Yes, very understandable, but as I was saying, Bludvile has escaped and our security, our ability to protect ourselves and our King, has been shown to be entirely inadequate. Our very status as an independent kingdom has been in jeopardy these past few years. Our name is not as great as it once was. Our influence is not as it should be. We owe it to our people to raise this kingdom to its past glory. It is my intention to pursue these aims relentlessly, no matter what.'

'His intention!' Grunkite could barely speak. 'Who is he to have intentions? What of our King. Has he already put him in the grave? Oh, I fear for our king's safety, and not from the lunatic Bludvile but from him, that traitor.' Grunkite was pointing a quivering finger at Tancredi.

'Traitor? You call me traitor when you, through your gross incompetence, or maybe something more sinister, have twice endangered the King's life? Twice you have put us all in jeopardy.' Tancredi spread his arms wide, as if inviting the judgment of all present. 'Who is the traitor here?'

Grunkite was frothing at the mouth. He looked around at his fellow councillors.

'Jerome? You understand. Ambassador Flinch, I know you have your doubts.' Flinch looked away and mumbled something about normal legitimate concerns and the need for calm discussion. Jerome said nothing. His glittering eyes were focused on Tancredi, like a wolf sizing up its prey. Tancredi glanced at the monk, but instantly averted his eyes from that relentless stare.

'Even if the worst comes to pass,' Tancredi's voice wobbled for an instant before he regained his composure, 'and I pray it does not, there will be great changes.' He raised his voice. 'I trust that our loyalty will be to Dredgemarsh and its future glory. We must not allow personal likes and preferences rule over our better judgement.' At that precise moment, the clatter of arms and the sounds of marching feet could be plainly heard approaching the council chambers. Tancredi stepped out from behind the speaker's lectern. 'Because of the extraordinary recent events, and the knowledge that there is a canker growing in our midst,' he stared at Grunkite. 'I have taken steps to guarantee our future. In view of the failure of our own security, whether by accident or intent, I have secured the services of a friendly neighbour. I'm sure you will all co-operate with this temporary arrangement until I have cleansed our beloved Dredgemarsh of the evil that flourishes in our midst, and,' he paused for a moment, 'and,' his voice rose, 'I regret, here in this very chamber.'

The marching feet had by this time reached the chamber

doors, and with little ceremony they were thrown open. Albrecht Pentrojan stood there with ten fully armed men close behind and Black Pete at his side, pointing towards Tancredi.

'Chancellor Tancredi, I presume.' Pentrojan advanced into the chamber while his men remained blocking the entrance. 'I am Albrecht Pentrojan. The castle is secured. I await your instructions.'

'Captain Pentrojan, we welcome your assistance, in this, our hour of need. I hope we can reciprocate in the future,' said Tancredi. 'I have explained the situation to my fellow councillors. I think we all understand the danger that threatens us.' Tancredi turned to face the councillors. 'For the time being I must insist, good councillors, that you all remain in chambers until I return. I must confer with our friend and ally, Captain Pentrojan. Please be patient, I will return shortly.' Tancredi left the council chamber, followed by Pentrojan, who whispered some instructions to his men on the way out. Immediately four of the ten stepped inside the main chamber doors and closed them, while the rest remained on guard outside. Tancredi immediately took Pentrojan aside.

'Captain Pentrojan! I presume all went well.'

'It could not have been easier. A few resisted. The rest threw down their weapons. We're gathering them together in the square.'

'We'll deal with them later. But first, I want twelve of your best fighters to ride out immediately to Green Valley. See to it that our boy King is dispatched. Throw the carcass in the lake. He,' Tancredi pointed to Shem Sledge, 'will show your men precisely where to find the quarry.'

'How many men guard him?' asked Pentrojan.

'None, Captain.' Tancredi pursed his lips in a half smile. 'You will find him completely on his own.'

'Consider it done, Chancellor. I'm surprised you needed our help for such a simple task.'

'A simple task indeed, Captain Pentrojan, but you will be needed here, in the aftermath to, shall we say, quell any anxieties that might arise.'

'You expect a revolt, Chancellor?' said Pentrojan.

'No, not at all.' There was a hint of irritation in Tancredi's voice. 'But there are always a few troublemakers, Captain. In the meantime, I have some family business to attend to. Report back when all is done.' As Tancredi turned to go, Pentrojan reached out and touched his arm.

'A moment, Chancellor; speaking of families, when will I meet this beauty, Lucretia Beaufort, your cousin, my future wife?' Tancredi looked down at Pentrojan's hand touching his sleeve. Pentrojan drew it back but not immediately, and when he did, he gestured in the direction in which Tancredi was walking as if to indicate, 'you may proceed.'

'Tomorrow, Captain, tomorrow. Business first.' Tancredi walked away without looking at Pentrojan.

Chapter 26

It was some time before Grunkite could speak, but when he did the words were barely coherent. 'Are we just go-ing to sit here and do nothing? Do we allow this scum, this vile traitor to take over? The devil's piss! I have had– ' Without warning, Jerome leaped to his feet, grabbed a bardiche from the array of weapons that decorated the chamber walls, and swept down upon the startled guards. His strokes were accurate and lethal, and before Grunkite could follow his example, the four Brooderstalt guards lay dead or wounded on the floor. The remaining guards out-side burst through the chamber doors. Grunkite, who, by then, had armed himself with a falchion from a dead Brooderstalt, dispatched the first one and Jerome, with al-most disdainful nonchalance, cut down two more. Old Gastsack joined in. He was brandishing a mace and shouting

'To arms, to arms.' The remaining Brooderstalt turned and ran, screaming for reinforcements.

'To the stables, we must warn the King, follow me'. Grunkite said. He re-entered the council chamber, pulled back one of the full length wall hangings behind the main lectern. Behind it was a small door.

'Go,' shouted Gastsack. Grunkite and Jerome made their escape. Gastsack pulled the wall hanging back into place, and sat down in his usual chair amidst his stunned fellow councillors.

'Stay close,' Grunkite said. He led the way through a labyrinth of narrow passages and stone stairways built within the thickness of the Dredgemarsh walls. At intervals, tiny openings onto interior galleries or the outside provided just enough light for them to keep their bearings. As they passed each tiny opening they could hear the swell of sounds - angry voices, swearing, orders given, running feet, the clatter of armour - advancing, retreating.

'At last,' gasped Grunkite, pushing open a door into a huge room with rows of paliasses against each wall and running down the centre. A thick layer of dust lay like a carpet of ash over everything.

'Where are we?' said Jerome, brushing cobwebs from his face and hair.

'Dortour for ostlers, fewterers, farriers. I remember seeing it full in King Philip's time. Glorious days ... what a pass we've come to,' said Grunkite. For a few moments, as he gazed at the ghostly room, it almost appeared that he had forgotten why he was there. But the brief trance passed. 'That traitor ... but enough of that for now,' he said. 'The stables are close by. Follow me.' He led the way down an iron stairway.

The stables were quiet, apart from the contented munching of the horses. They selected two fine coursers, saddled them up, and walked them from the stables. Positioning themselves between the two horses, they led them across the Four Towers Square towards the main gate, which was still open after Pentrojan's entrance.

'The cursed treacherous swine, look!' Grunkite pointed to the Brooderstalt flag flying over the barbican. Jerome did not reply. His whole attention was focused on the grim scenes around them. Brooderstalt soldiers were securing all buildings surrounding the main square. Scattered here and there were bodies in the Dredgemarsh colours. Other disarmed Dredgemarsh soldiers were being kicked and beaten into a long line and marched into one of the stable yards, which was heavily guarded by Broodestalt foot soldiers.

'Christ's blood! This is beyond endurance.' Grunkite pulled the purloined falchion from his belt. Jerome reached out and grasped him hard by the shoulder.

'Endure it! Think of the King. We must find him.' Grunkite jerked his shoulder back, in an effort to dislodge Jerome's hand, but the monk held him in an unshakable grip. 'The King, think of the King,' he said once again. Grunkite, his face a mask of helpless anger, closed his eyes and breathed deeply.

'The King ... yes, the King,' he said, and the pair moved forward.

When they were well into the centre of the square, they mounted the horses and continued to walk them towards the main gate.

'You two! Off those horses! Off! Now!' A sergeant in Pentrojan's army was screaming at them. They paid him no heed.

'Prepare yourself,' Jerome whispered, as three mounted soldiers appeared as if from nowhere, to cut off their escape route.

'Surrender or die,' bellowed the Brooderstalt sergeant. They ignored him, and continued to walk their mounts forward, Grunkite drawing his falchion and Jerome finding the balance point of the bardiche in his right hand.

'They're all yours,' the sergeant shouted to the three horse soldiers. They spurred their horses into a gallop and bore down on the strange pair who still ambled towards them. When the soldiers were almost upon them, Jerome and Grunkite surged forward. In one great sweep of his bardiche, Jerome, riding straight between a pair of the attackers, almost severed the raised sword arm of the one on his right and sliced into the thigh of the rider on the left. Grunkite, with flailing falchion, barged straight into the third rider and his mount. The Brooderstalt's startled horse tumbled onto the cobbled square. The distinct crack of bone was immediately followed by a scream of pain from the Brooderstalt, whose leg was pinned under the fallen animal.

'Close the gate, close the gate!' the sergeant was bellowing at the top of his voice and to the dismay of Jerome and Grunkite, two guardsmen, whom they had not seen untill then, ran towards the gate winch and began to wind frantically.

'Ride, ride,' shouted Jerome.

'Curses, it's too late. We'll never make it.' Grunkite was gasping for breath. Just then, a bedraggled Dredgemarsh soldier lurched out from behind the guardhouse.

'Dungheads,' he shouted. 'Leave my gate alone.' It was Pluck, the drunkard. He staggered over to the winch and sliced through the ropes that pulled the great main gate into place. With the sudden release of pressure, the winch wheel spun backwards, the two soldiers were flung to the ground and Pluck stumbled off behind the guardhouse with surprising speed. The whole episode lasted only a few seconds. Jerome and Grunkite spurred their mounts forward and in single file, raced through the half-closed gate and turned westwards for Green Valley.

****

'So that's what you were studying all those years in Anselem: stones.' Lucretia took the small golden coloured rock that Cesare handed to her, their fingers touching, lingering for an instant.

'Nephryte, a remarkable substance. Do you feel how warm it is?' he said.

'Yes, it has been warmed by the sun, like all the stones,' she pointed to the pebbles along the shore of the lake where they sat.

'True, like all the stones, it has stored up the heat of the sun, but this one,' he took the stone from her hand again, 'this one is special.'

'Like you?' she said. Cesare looked at her, looked into her faultless eyes and for a moment, seemed to forget what he had been saying.

'You are not really listening, are you?' He said in mock anger.

'Yes, yes, I am,' she laughed. 'Please tell me why that stone is so special?' She took his hand, the one holding the golden stone, and held it to her cheek. 'Tell me about the stone,' she whispered.

'It stores the light of the sun,' he said.

'Stores light?' She took the stone again and gazed in wonder at it. 'I don't understand.'

'No one does, but that is exactly what I was studying under the renowned Brother Peregrinus of Anselem.' Cesare held the stone up before him like an offering to the sun. 'If we could control and direct the release of that stored light, there are limitless possibilities, limitless.'

As he gazed skywards, a falcon crossed his line of vision.

'Look, look, a noble hunter,' he said, pointing up at the distant bird, but Lucretia gazed only at him.

'You are happy, Sire?'

'Happy?' he said. 'Lucretia,' he reached out and took her hand, 'I cannot begin to explain how happy I feel at this moment.'

'What do you wish for?' He thought for a moment.

'That you and I will never be apart, from this day forward. That you will,' he stared into her lustrous dark green eyes, 'that you will love me always.'

'I will, I will love you always ... always.' In the swooning warmth of the mid-day sun their lips met.

High in the blue vault of the sky, the falcon balanced on the rising air currents. On this clearest of clear days, he could see all the doings of men below. On the western road from Dredgemarsh, a band of armed riders, in the purple tunics of Brooderlund, galloped towards Green Valley. Two other riders, slightly ahead but hidden by Hazel Wood, raced in the same direction along the banks of the Yayla.

Far ahead of them, where Rim Wood opened onto Green Vally through a sloping defile called Grak's Gullet, a lone rider, with a spare horse in tow, began a rapid descent towards the lakeside where the couple lay together. From the arch of heaven all this activity was a minor distraction for the sky stalker.

The lone rider with the spare horse was Sergeant Felric. When he got within hailing distance of the spot where he knew Cesare and Lucretia were, he began to call out; 'Halloo! Halloo! Your Highness, Lady Lucretia. I am Sergeant Felric. I bring urgent news, urgent news.' Lucretia was instantly on her feet. Cesare sat up stiffly and massaged his left shoulder. Slowly, he raised himself into a standing position.

'What brings you in such haste, sergeant?' Cesare called out.

'A thousand pardons, your majesty,' Felric replied, 'but I have the most awful news for Lady Lucretia.' Felric dismounted and dropped to one knee.

'What, what is it?' Lucretia's face paled and her eyes widened in fear.

'Your father, dear lady. The maniac escaped ... we don't know how, but he—'

'My father, you said my father, what has happened to him?' Lucretia's lips were trembling.

'The maniac ... I'm afraid ... your father is most seriously wounded.' Lucretia appeared to fold in on herself and began to collapse. Cesare immediately grabbed hold of her and grimaced in pain with the effort.

'Help me,' he said. Felric rushed to support Lucretia. Between them they sat her down gently. 'Get water, water,' Cesare pointed to a beaker where he and Lucretia had dined so recently. The cold water that Felric scooped from the lake revived her. For a moment she gazed at Cesare, perplexed, as if she did not know how she came to be sitting there.

'Lucretia, you must go to your father immediately,' he said.

'That is why I brought a second horse, Sire,' Felric said. 'Your coach and escort will be here shortly. The Chancellor was adamant that you should not risk riding.' A dazed Lucretia was assisted to mount the spare horse. Cesare, with his good arm, handed the reins to her and squeezed her hand.

'Go now,' he said. 'I will follow immediately. Go, go.' As he watched Felric and Lucretia gallop away towards Grak's Gullet and back to Dredgemarsh, he reached up to massage his left shoulder and almost instantly drew back his hand. It was covered in blood. His wound had opened.

****

The closer Grunkite and Jerome got to Green Valley, the more their path began to converge on the troop of Brooderstalt horsemen on the West Road.

There were thirteen Booderstalt and Shem Sledge riding to Green Valley. At their head was a giant of a man on a black cob. There was something obscene about him, a grotesque disproportion between a massive trunk, short legs and long powerful arms. It was as if nature had spiralled out of control and disgorged this creature meant for another world. From a distance, one might have thought the riders were a group of boys riding behind an adult.

The Brooderstalt task was an easy one: to execute an unarmed man. Yet, there was a niggling uneasiness within their ranks. Even the meanest and most vicious could not dismiss the fact that it was a king they hunted. But blood had already been spilt that day. It was no time to be squeamish. It was death or glory, and glory was almost assured. They galloped along grimly, without talking. Within the hour it would all be over.

Within half a league of Grak's Gullet, Shem Sledge called out.

'Captain Spoorblut, riders are approaching.' Spoorblut, that was the giant's name, slowed to a canter.

'They ride fast. Who are they?' Spoorblut's cavernous voice did not sound as if it came from a human throat.

'It's Sergeant Felric and that is the Beaufort girl with him.' Spoorblut and his troops reined in their mounts and waited. Less than two hundred yards away, Grunkite and Jerome dismounted quietly and watched the Brooderstalt troops from the cover of Hazel Wood.

'What are they stopping for?' Grunkite whispered.

'Listen,' Jerome held a finger to his lips. 'Someone approaches from Green Valley.'

'We had better warn them, it could be the King himself.' Grunkite was about to turn and mount his horse.

'Wait, wait.' Jerome laid a restraining hand on Grunkite's shoulder. 'It's the young lady Lucretia, and that is not the King with her.'

'Felric, a creature of Tancredi's and look, look, that accursed Shem Sledge amongst them. But what is Lady Lucretia doing with such scum?' They were too far away to hear what was being said, but they could see that Felric, Sledge and the giant were in animated discussion with Lucretia.

'I don't believe what I'm seeing,' Grunkite gasped as they watched Lucretia turn and point back towards Green Valley. 'She's directing them to the King?'

'No time to lose,' said Jerome. 'We must get to the King before they do. To the road. Come.' Jerome leaped onto his horse and held Grunkite's mount while the older man heaved himself into the saddle. The pair set off at full gallop, cutting through the underbrush and taking a course that would see them emerge onto the West Road ahead of the Brooderstalt assassins. Hiding was of no concern to them now. It was a matter of outpacing the Brooderstalt.

'Ho! a little practice up front before the main event.' Shem Sledge shouted when the two riders broke from Hazel Wood onto the road and galloped off towards Green Valley. The thirteen assassins immediately spurred their horses in pursuit of the fleeing pair, leaving Felric and Lucretia in a shower of flying muck and pebbles.

'What's happening? What did he mean by, main event? Is the King safe?' Lucretia demanded of Sergeant Felric.

'Have no fear mistress. Those men have been enlisted by Chancellor Tancredi to protect the King from all traitors. They are friends of Dredgemarsh and will make short work of our enemies. They will take care of the King. Now come, your father needs you.'

Shem Sledge and the Brooderstalt urged their mounts forward and began to draw up to the two ahead. Jerome spurred his mount forward. Grunkite was left trailing. He was too heavy, and too long out of the saddle to match the speed of his pursuers. Inexorably, the hooting and shouting soldiers closed the distance between themselves and the burly Grunkite. By this time Shem Sledge, recognising Grunkite, began to howl his name in derision.

'Here we come, Grunkite, here we come piggy. We're going to stick the piggy with a big sharp lance, come on piggy, piggy.'

In their frenzy of excitement, no one had noticed that, up ahead where the road narrowed into a small gorge before the descent into Grak's Gullet, Jerome had turned and sat motionless, waiting, sword poised. Sledge was now standing in the stirrups, lance at the ready, preparing to impale the large bouncing figure in front of him. For an instant before launching his weapon, Sledge looked beyond Grunkite's broad back. The vicious laugh on his lips froze. His eyes widened in disbelief. He rode straight into the swinging arc of Jerome's sword and was instantly decapitated. Grunkite dashed onwards.

'Get the spare horse and ride on,' Jerome called to him. Sledge's horse galloped after Grunkite with the headless rider slowly slipping sideways from the saddle, arms swinging loosely like a rag doll. The soldiers who were following Sledge hauled their mounts to a slithering halt before reaching the monk, who remained in position with his sword once more poised to strike. It took some time to settle their horses before advancing cautiously, two abreast with drawn swords. Jerome sat immobile, positioned so that they would have to approach him from his sword-arm side. Slowly they advanced until they were within a few yards of him. Then they charged. One of them raised his shield to deflect Jerome's first blow while the other swept his sword down at an angle, striking for the back of the neck. Almost lazily Jerome swung his body sideways just inches from the sweep of the sword while at the same time swinging his own blade backwards to meet the oncoming arm. With a shriek of pain the wounded soldier jerked his horse back from the fray, his sword arm dangling uselessly. His companion, not quite sure what had happened, lowered his shield and instantly received the full force of Jerome's steel across his temple. He fell like a stone from his horse, which scrambled back in panic after its retreating companion.

'Move aside, let me at him.' The voice was startling in its coarseness. It sounded as if came from some animal rather than a human. At first, Jerome could not see the author of this hoarse bellow. 'Out of my way, move aside 'til I swat this gnat.' Spoorblut barged and pushed his way from the rear of the horse soldiers, and without a moment's hesitation, spurred his great black cob straight for Jerome. He disdained to even size up his opponent before attacking. When he was within a few yards of his target, he unleashed a great star-shaped mace that came whistling for Jerome's head. Jerome ducked the blow and retreated. Spoorblut came on with the mace orbiting around his head and swung it once more for the temple of his opponent. Once more, Jerome just managed to slide below the deadly spiked ball.

'Try this,' Spoorblut roared and suddenly swung the mace out of its horizontal orbit into the vertical one, aiming directly for the top of Jerome's head. Jerome hauled his mount sideways. He saved his own life, but the bone-crushing blow ploughed into the lower spine of his horse and lodged there. The poor creature sank back on paralysed legs and then slowly collapsed onto its side, trembling in its death throes. Jerome leapt clear, rolled over once and instantly regained his feet. He had no sword. Spoorblut was momentarily off balance, and was attempting to pull the mace from the ruptured hindquarters of the stricken horse. The monk dived forward, grabbed Spoorblut's ankle with one hand, his wrist with the other and jerked him clean out of his saddle. An astonished Spoorblut landed with a thudding crash onto his back. He scrambled to his feet to face Jerome. Neither had a weapon. Spoorblut, snarling like a wounded bear, charged. Jerome easily side-stepped and delivered a crunching blow with his fist to the side of Spoorblut's neck. The giant, grimacing in pain sank slowly to the ground, gasping for air. His companions watched in utter amazement. They waited, expecting their fearsome champion to rise and prove that what had happened was simply an accident, a lucky blow by the strange monk. This gave Jerome the opportunity to regain his sword, vault onto Spoorblut's cob and gallop after Grunkite.

No one gave chase. They just stood there staring at the fallen Spoorblut, who was beginning to regain consciousness. He scrambled to his feet and stumbled around trying to get his bearings. His comrades in arms waited, mute and fascinated. It did not take long for the giant to regain the full use of his faculties and with that, the uncomfortable and humiliating realisation that he had been vanquished in a one-to-one combat in the presence of those whom he had bullied and scorned. The enraged Spoorblut dragged the nearest man from his mount and took his place in the saddle. The unfortunate animal sagged under the weight.

'I'll have that bastard's gizzards.' Spoorblut shouted and slapped the hindquarters of his mount. The assassins, now reduced to nine, set off in pursuit of Jerome and Grunkite.

****

The blood from the reopened wound in Cesare's chest spread like a great crimson blossom over the front of his jerkin. He shook his head to dispel the sudden fatigue that enveloped him and tried to focus on the two horsemen who were galloping down the green slopes towards him.

'It's Grunkite.' Cesare spoke out loud. Grunkite was shouting something, but he could not make sense of the words. It was only when Grunkite, with a spare horse in tow, came to a slithering halt yards from where he had propped himself against a large lakeside boulder, did the full import of the warning cries begin to penetrate.

'Assassins, assassins, Sire, mount quickly.'

Cesare snapped out of his trance and with a grimace of pain, mounted the spare horse proffered by Grunkite. Jerome swept in behind them on the great black cob stolen from Spoorblut.

'Lucretia, have you seen Lucretia?' Cesare asked.

'Sire, we must go now.'

'Have you seen her?'

Despite the faintness that had come over him, Cesare was aware of the delay in answering his question.

'What, what has happened. Tell me.'

'She's safe, I swear it, Sire,' said Grunkite. Cesare looked to Jerome.

'It's true. She is safe. We must go now,' said Jerome.

After a moment's hesitation, they swung into a gallop along the shoreline of Lake Tranquil, closely followed by the Brooderstalt.

Because of the unaccustomed weight and awkwardness of the rider on its back, Spoorblut's new mount struggled to maintain speed. The remaining Brooderstalt could easily have ridden ahead but they chose to stay behind their leader. It was clear that no one wanted to be the first to catch up with the fearsome monk. Within half an hour, Cesare and his rescuers had completely outdistanced the reluctant pursuers. They rode out of Green Valley and entered the foot-hills of the Anselem mountains. Jerome's and Grunkite's concern now focused on Cesare, who had slumped forward in his saddle and was no longer responding to them. In a small copse they gently took Cesare from his saddle and laid him on the ground, with his head cradled in the distraught Grunkite's lap.

'He cannot die, Jerome, he cannot.' The old warrior's eyes were filled with tears.

Jerome began to cut his own surplice into strips. He removed Cesare's blood-soaked jerkin and shirt, placed a pad of cloth on the reopened wound and with Cesare's arms locked close to his sides, he bound the whole upper chest area as tightly as possible. They then lifted Cesare onto the cob. Jerome sat up behind him, and holding the unconscious young King between his arms he began to weave his way up through the Anselem foothills that he knew so well.

Dredgemarsh

Chapter 27

Tancredi's face went ashen when Pentrojan spoke quietly in his ear. They were in the map room of the chancellery, where Havelock and Dipslick were preparing a new proclamation under the instruction of the Chancellor.

'Out, out,' Tancredi shouted at the pair of scribes. Havelock and Dipslick began to tidy away their writing utensils and paraphernalia.

'Leave everything. Just go. Go!' The lugubrious Havelock, normally impervious to every activity around him, stared at Tancredi as if he had just seen him for the first time in his life. The Chancellor, even in his state of uncharacteristic agitation, momentarily hesitated, as if he himself recognised some new level of awareness in Havelock. The moment passed, and the scribes shuffled out of the map room and into the adjoining scriptorium. Tancredi turned instantly to Pentrojan.

'What foul treachery is this?' His body was trembling and his fists were clenched as he squared up to the burly figure of Pentrojan. 'You said ... you swore you could take care of this. You said it was a simple ...'

'Your King, Chancellor, has more friends than you implied,' said Pentrojan.

'Friends? What friends?'

'A monk and your Marshal ...'

'A monk, a single monk and an old man.' Tancredi spat the words in Pentrojan's face, then turned away and laughed. 'Two against twelve of your invincible Brooderstalt. Hah!' He spun round again to face Pentrojan. He spread his arms out and upwards as in supplication to the heavens. 'How can this be? He should be dead. You have failed miserably.' The veins were standing out on his neck and temple and there was froth on his lips. Pentrojan's initial look of discomfiture changed to anger. He laid his hand on the hilt of his falchion.

'Have a care, Chancellor. Have a care!' Tancredi turned away from him and strode to the far end of the map room, where an oriel window looked out over the chancellery square and beyond it, an endless vista of rooftops, towers and spires. The campanile rising out of this grey ocean glistened a deep gold in the dying rays of an autumn sun. Neither man spoke for a long time. Finally Tancredi broke the silence.

'Who knows of this?' Pentrojan considered the question for some time before answering.

'No one. My men are sworn to secrecy.'

'And you trust them? ' Tancredi laughed scornfully.

'Fear, Chancellor, mortal fear will keep their mouths shut. If word gets out, each and every man will beg for death before I am finished with him. I have already demonstrated how it's done with one of them.' Once again, silence fell over the pair. Tancredi sat down wearily on a window seat and watched as the shadows crept up from the darkness below and began to swallow the golden campanile. His fury, so palpable that the air bristled with it, began to slowly dissipate and fade. Pentrojan sat and waited.

The plaintive clang of a chapel bell, calling what few bedraggled holy men, who still lived in Dredgemarsh to vespers, shattered the silence in the map room.

'Anselem,' said Tancredi. His voice was quiet, controlled.

'What?' Pentrojan said.

'Anselem, they have gone to Anselem.' The Chancellor rose from his seat at the window and strode to the other end of the map room.

'There! That's where they are, Anselem monastery.' He grabbed a long willow rod pointer and jabbed at a spot on the map that covered the whole end wall of the room. Pentrojan joined him.

'I have heard of this Anselem. They say it is impregnable.'

'And so it is,' said Tancredi. 'But that is no matter. We will seal it off from Dredgemarsh. Look here.' He moved the pointer. 'The only way to enter Dredgemarsh from the Anselem mountains is through Boar's Tusk. There is a long-abandoned keep there.'

'If we hold that, he is as good as dead,' said Pentrojan.

It was getting darker in the map room. Tancredi, full of purpose, now strode across to the door leading to the Scriptorium,

'Scribes, back in here. Bring–' he called out as he flung the door open and was about to step through. He almost crashed into Havelock, who was standing right in front of him with a lighted taper. For the second time that evening, Tancredi had the feeling that somewhere within this sombre creature, whom he had always relegated to no more than a useful slave, lay a calculating brain. A tiny flutter of unease trembled somewhere deep within him as he looked into the mournful eyes of Havelock.

Chapter 28

A light drizzle began to fall as the Campanile bell began to ring prime. Already, there was a hint of winter in the air and a pallid moon defied the onset of morning. Celeste pulled her capuchon well forward so that her face and hair were hidden. She slipped into the shadow of a doorway and shivered as a troop of sullen Brooderstalt rode by, their horses' hooves shattering the morning silence. When they passed, she hurried on to the refectory. Bella Crumble and Nellie Lowslegg did not look happy. They were carrying bowls of steamimg polenta to crowds of Brooderstalt soldiers, some seated and some standing. Leopold Ratchet was in a lather of sweat as he ladled out the polenta from a great vat.

'Hurry, hurry, don't keep them waiting,' his voice warbled into a high falsetto.

'I'm goin' as fast as I can,' the refectory scullion, Squint, whined as he filled beaker after beaker from a huge puncheon of braggot.

Celeste pulled the capuchon even further over her face and turned quickly to leave, but in her haste, and with her capuchon limiting her field of vision, she bumped into a Brooderstalt, who was at that moment slurping hot polenta straight from a bowl.

'Aaargh,' the Brooderstalt roared as the bowl smashed onto the floor. He reached out a claw-like hand and grabbed Celeste by the shoulder. With his other hand he ripped the capuchon back off her head, and Celeste's profusion of auburn tresses blossomed like a fire around her terrified face. The Brooderstalt's eyes widened and his speechless mouth opened. His companions, like a pack of curious wolves, immediately began to surround him and Celeste. But before they could completely encircle the pair, Bella Crumble barged her way past them and shoved a steaming bowl of polenta into the chest of Celeste's captor. His immediate reaction was to grasp the bowl with both hands. Bella grabbed Celeste, and before the bemused Brooderstalt could utter a word, she whisked the terrified girl away and out of sight, into the buttery.

'Oh thank you Bella, thank you, thank you,' Celeste said.

'Never mind that now. Have you heard?'

'Heard what? What is going on?'

'Where is Lady Lucretia?' Bella asked.

'She has not left her father's side since she came back yesterday. That's where I am going now, I came here to get some comfits and quince cordial to bring to her.

'Oh the poor child, the poor child. She will not have heard.' The tears began to well up in Bella's eyes.

'Please, Bella! Tell me what's happened.' Bella cupped her hand over her own mouth as if to prevent the words coming out.

'He's dead. The King. He's ... he's dead.'

'What, the King's what?' Celeste said. Bella removed her hand from her mouth.

'Dead. He's dead. They killed him after all.'

'No, that's not possible.' Celeste was shaking her head from side to side. 'No, it can't be ... he was just ... just yesterday ... King Cesare ... dead?'

'They have been posting notices since before dawn. Leopold picked this up at the fish market.' Bella took a crumpled parchment from her apron pocket and handed it to Celeste.

'It says that Marshall Grunkite,' Celeste began to read, 'that he and Jerome, the monk, are part of a conspiracy.'

'Yes,' said Bella, 'they escaped yesterday, but I still don't believe it. I just can't believe ... Oh, but you look so unwell, my dear. You've had such a shock.'

'It's not me I'm worried about,' said Celeste. 'It's Lucretia. This will break her heart. How can I possibly tell her this?'

Bella Crumble shook her head slowly from side to side. 'The poor darling, the poor darling,' she said. At that moment, Leopold Ratchet rushed into the buttery.

'Ah, there you are. We need you out here, Bella.'

'Can't you see we're busy? Now shoo, shoo. I'll be out later. Now, my young lady,' Bella addressed Celeste, 'let me have your satchel. Make her drink some of this. Mix it in with the cordial.' Bella took a bottle of amber liquid from a shelf and put it in the satchel. She then left the buttery and returned with a small basket covered in muslin.

Celeste left the refectory through a back door of a scullery which led unto a narrow alleyway. She was accompanied, at Bella Crumble's insistence, and despite the complaints of Assistant Cook Meister Ratchet, by Squint, the old kitchen boy, who knew every back lane and street in Dredgemarsh.

****

'Come in, my dear. You look cold. I'm so glad you're here.' Consuela, the custorin, ushered Celeste into the atrium of the infirmary.

'Is she awake?' Celeste said.

'Awake, asleep, awake. She has not stirred from her father's side. I've tried to make her comfortable. Perhaps you can persuade her to lie down for a while. Come.'

'You have not heard?' Celeste did not move.

'Heard?' Consuela looked intently at Celeste and her eyes widened in apprehension. 'You look so pale my dear. What has happened?'

'It's just, it's awful. I can't, I don't know how to ...' Celeste clasped her hand tightly over her own mouth, but the low wail of anguish would not be silenced.

'Hush, hush.' Consuela extended her open arms to embrace Celeste. 'It's not that bad. She will be fine again, once her father regains his senses. And he will, he will.' Celeste stepped back from the embrace, pulled the crumpled parchment from her scrip and proffered it to Consuela, turning her own face away.

'Oh Jesu Christe, Jesu Christe ...' Consuela exclaimed as she read the notice. Her cheerful ruddy features turned a sickly grey. 'What foul wickedness has been loosed among us?'

Chapter 29

Clutchbolt had not been drinking when he declaimed to his startled kitchen staff, 'I wouldn't serve him cat's shit. It might nourish him,.' nor was he under the dark cloud of one of his deep depressions. No, he was just plain furious. All that day he had brooded and puzzled over the bewildering happenings in Dredgemarsh; the rumours of Tancredi's bid for power; the arrival of Pentrojan's army; the beatings and imprisonment of so many; the sudden departure of Grunkite and Jerome, branded as traitors; but most devastating of all, the announcement of King Cesare's death.

Now Tancredi, the sly Chancellor, whom he detested, was demanding a sumptuous feast for Pentrojan and his senior officers; a feast fit for a King, at which Tancredi himself would preside. It was Havelock, with his faithful companion

Dipslick, who had, on Tancredi's instructions, come to the kitchens to order the feast.

'I'm sure of it now. That bastard, bollix and his poxy friends are the murderous traitors. Serve them the best from my kitchens? They've murdered him. I just know it, and now like vultures they want everything. Not me. Not me. They can't have me.' He slammed a meat cleaver onto the oak chopping table, cleaving a gutted hare in half. 'I serve the kings of Dredgemarsh, not treacherous scum. Do you see that, and that?' Clutchbolt was half-dragging Havelock around the kitchen and pointing to the emblem of the hawk embossed on pans, pots, ladles, oven doors and even the tiniest teaspoon. 'These are for kings! These serve kings! I serve kings; my staff serves kings, not bloody serfs, not killers, not his killers ...'

What noble hearts lurk within the most unlikely breasts. This unshaven, irascible Cook Meister was transformed, in the eyes of all who saw and heard him, into something grand and bright. Yes, wonder of wonders. Bella Crumble's great pastry of a chin was wobbling and dimpling on the verge of oceanic sobs? Miss Nelly Lowslegg and Leopold Ratchet were weeping openly?

'He's not dead,' Havelock said.

'Yes, not dead,' Dipslick nodded his small nut of a head vigorously.

'What? Who's not dead?' Bella Crumble asked.

'What are they saying?' said Nellie Lowslegg.

'Not dead, what are you saying, you old fools, it was announced.'

'He's not dead,' Havelock said once again.

'The King? You mean the King, our King is not dead?' Clutchbolt scrutinised Havelock's mournful features. Havelock nodded and Dipslick nodded.

'Not dead. We heard. Not dead. Escaped.' they spoke in unison. The kitchen which only moments before reverberated with Clutchbolt's heart-rending outburst was deathly quiet and all eyes turned to the Cook Meister.

With that outburst, Clutchbolt had a visceral feeling that he had unleashed something deadly within himself. He discovered an inner truth that both frightened and thrilled him. He had a decision to make, a momentous decision, and he had to make it now. He could continue down the way of oblivion, the cycle of depression and drunken binges, the mundane but comfortable daily routine that would require the surrender of a lifetime's loyalty and everything he believed in or he could totally break the mould of his life, abandon the well-known cosy patterns, and choose glory with every possibility of death. His heart quickened. An incredible joy filled him, surged up inside him and he thought I will, I will. Clutchbolt wondered if everyone could hear the pounding in his breast because they all stood transfixed, waiting for him to speak again.

'Havelock, are you sure?' he asked.

'Yes, the new one ... Pentrojan ... heard him telling Tancredi. They tried to kill the King but Jerome and Grunkite saved him.' Havelock responded with one of the longest speeches he had made in many a year.

'I knew it. I knew it. I said I didn't believe that Grunkite and Jerome were traitors. I said it. Didn't I say it?' Bella Crumble was blubbering through her tears.

'Where is the King now?' Clutchbolt asked Havelock.

'Anselem.' Havelock tapped the side of his large nose knowingly.

Clutchbolt grabbed the startled Havelock and hustled him

into his own small closet of a room off the kitchen. The rest just stood staring, puzzled. Clutchbolt's head re-appeared around the door.

'Well, don't just stand there like sheep, get in here.' Without a word they shuffled into Clutchbolt's tiny room. With much maneuvering and shoving, Ratchet managed to squeeze the door shut behind Bella Crumble's expansive bottom. Then Ratchet, Lowslegg, Dipslick and Havelock forced themselves between the side wall and a rough narrow table that filled most of the room, while Bella Crumble more than filled the one free space at the end of the table. On the opposite side of the same table was Clutchbolt's bunk, where he now sat and with much effort managed to wriggle his two stout legs between the bunk and the table.

'As long as the King lives, there is hope. Dredgemarsh can and will be saved.' Clutchbolt opened proceedings. 'But first, if there is anyone here in this room who has any doubts about where their loyalty lies, then let them leave now.'

There was much coughing, clearing of throats, snuffling of noses and shuffling of feet while Clutchbolt waited.

'Good! We're all in it together.' Clutchbolt slammed his hand down on the table and the whole assembly jumped in unison with the shock. 'Together we will fight or die, are you with me?' Clutchbolt had lowered his voice to a dramatic stage whisper.

'Yes, of course, yes, we're with you, Cook Meister Clutchbolt, we're with you every step of the way.' Ratchet's voice rose in pitch like a violin string being tuned until finally it warbled out of control.

Bella Crumble was nodding approvingly at Ratchet's words.

'Yes,' she boomed. We're ready for anything. Just tell us, that's all. Those scoundrels will not get away with it. That poor man, bless him, just out of his sickbed. Oh, the low scoundrels, how could they? That poor, poor man ...' Bella Crumble had talked herself into tears once more.

'Thank you, Mistress Crumble.' It must have been the first time that Clutchbolt had ever spoken to Bella Crumble with even a hint of affection or appreciation. She began to sob. Nothing could stop her. All they could do was wait until she had cried herself out, terminating with a massive nose blast into a tiny lace handkerchief.

Not long after that, the door of Clutchbolt's room opened. The occupants tumbled out and instantly went about the business of preparing a meal for Tancredi and Pentrojan. Havelock and Dipslick left without a word. Never before had the kitchen staff worked with such efficiency. Every minor instruction, every suggestion of Clutchbolt's was carried out immediately. All personal dislikes and irritations were discarded. Clutchbolt became the focus and guide of their every action. Every now and then they would steal quick glances at their leader, to see if there was anything he required doing. Clutchbolt thrilled inside at this new-found power.

'Yes,' he thought, 'this is how it should be, this is what I was meant to do.' He felt a pride and confidence that he had somehow misplaced years ago. Those barren decades when his spirit was smothered in the unending drudgery of the kitchens fell from him like magic. It felt now as if he had been only masquerading as a Cook Meister. The last traumatic hour had awoken the real Clutchbolt, the leader, the man of action.

In no time at all, a magnificent meal was prepared and delivered to Tancredi and his guests. Clutchbolt made sure that every last detail of the feast was perfect, including the most exquisite Lydian vernage. Tancredi was so impressed by the meal that he sent Havelock and Dipslick to the kitchens with his compliments. Clutchbolt and his staff exchanged conspiratorial smiles when Tancredi's message of congratulations was delivered.

'Good, good,' said Clutchbolt, rubbing his hands together. 'Lord Tancredi will find us truly loyal subjects of Dredgemarsh. Now, my good friends, let us clean up, off to bed, we have an early start and a busy day ahead of us.' He had hardly finished speaking when Ratchet, Lowslegg and Crumble set about the task as bidden.

For the next two weeks, the kitchen ran as smooth as the lard on Clutchbolt's pan. Even Tancredi felt obliged to make a brief personal call to his catering staff. But if, during his visit, he had decided to inspect the kitchen pantries, he would have been more than a little surprised to find them packed with every conceivable weapon imaginable. Havelock and Dipslick were the couriers who ferried these weapons and armour down to the kitchens. They had access to the main armoury and were completely beyond suspicion or even notice. Indeed, a stray dog would arouse more interest than either of the scribes. Dipslick almost did reveal their subterfuge when he staggered into a buttress on his way out of the armoury, loudly rattling several broadswords, which he had concealed under his cloak. Luckily the guard on duty was rather dim-witted and ignored the odd event. Besides, the new regime had no suspicion that there was any serious threat of resistance or rebellion amongst the inhabitants of Dredgemarsh. Those who were considered likely to resist were behind bars and would be held there until Tancredi had completely consolidated his position. The failure to kill Cesare of course made things considerably more difficult, and would mean a change in strategy for Tancredi, but he was confident that he could cope with all eventualities. In his wildest, most paranoid moments he could not have imagined that Dipslick and Havelock presented any kind of threat, and certainly not the eccentric Cook Meister Clutchbolt, and his motley crew of sweaty minions.

Clutchbolt was well aware of Tancredi's strategy and realised that he could not delay too long, because with every day that passed, Tancredi became more entrenched in his position as the new master of Dredgemarsh. With this in mind, Clutchbolt called another meeting in the main kitchen. It was two hours past midnight when they assembled. By now, his band of followers had grown to include a couple of stable lads, Surgeon Keenslide, Keenslide's assistant Ned Clinker, and Quickstrain the scientist and a fiery young squire called Klip. Clutchbolt strode into the centre of the kitchen when everyone was present and seated.

'Loyal friends,' he said, 'the time is almost at hand. We cannot delay much longer. The viper must be destroyed soon.'

Dredgemarsh

.

Chapter 30

He looked ill again, the young King of Dredgemarsh, standing in the oriel window of the austere guest chamber of the monastery. He was staring into the cold dawn mists that rolled amongst the peaks of Anselem. There were deep shadows like wounds of sorrow under his sleepless eyes. It was three weeks since Jerome had carried him, almost dead, through the gates of Anselem. Under the expert care of the infirmerer, Brother Nicolas, and his miraculous embrocations, Cesare's reopened wound had healed rapidly. But his mind was in torment.

In all, there were almost three hundred souls in the monastery, which was perched precariously amid the flinty crags of the mountains. They lived an austere life, dedicating themselves to the pursuit of spiritual and physical perfection. Each morning they rose before sunset and spent one hour chanting in the grey stony vault of their chapel. The hypnotic singing mingled with the early morning symphony of birdsong that soared up from the breathtaking valleys far below.

Even that glorious harmony made no impact on the brooding young King. He reviled himself for the wasted years when he neglected his kingdom. All the countless times he ignored and put aside the affairs of Dredgemarsh were now stark accusations against him. He remembered Tancredi's constant exhortations to leave the trivial business of state to him, and he recalled with shame how readily he acquiesced.

And Lucretia, what of Lucretia? It defied belief that she was the instrument of his downfall, and yet, and yet; it was Lucretia who had insisted on their trip to Green Valley; it was Lucretia who had left him alone – did she contrive the excuse of a sick father? It was Lucretia who had met and talked to the Brooderstalt murderers who were on their way to kill him. Grunkite and Jerome had seen her with their own eyes. How could this possibly be? How could this exquisite girl, whose radiant image, even now, filled him with desire, how could she have betrayed him? Love and loathing drove him to the edge of insanity He could feel the ghosts of his dear father and his ancestors rebuking him for his weakness.

'Sire.' It was Brother Nicholas who had quietly entered the chamber. Without response, Cesare turned, took a seat by a small table close to the window and undid the loose shirt he wore, revealing his bandaged shoulder. Nicholas laid the tray he was carrying on the table and set to work at once. He undid the bandage expertly.

'Ahh, good,' he said, 'we can leave the bandages off now,

Sire. You have remarkable healing power. An unguent to suppress any further irritation will suffice.' He took a small pot of sweet-smelling cream from his tray and began to knead it very gently onto the angry cicatrix of raised flesh where Bludvile's bolt had ripped through Cesare's shoulder.

'Sire, Abbot Sigismund has asked once again if he may speak with you.' Cesare groaned.

'I am just a simple healer of bodies, Sire.' Nicholas continued quietly. 'There is nothing more I can do.'

'Simple? Brother Nicholas. No, you are not simple. I am the simpleton, the fool. You heal and comfort the sick. I have done nothing; less than nothing. Betrayed my own. I have nothing to give, nothing to say.'

'You are a King!' Cesare looked up in surprise at Nicholas's sudden sharp tone. 'You cannot change who you are, no more than you can erase that.' Nicholas pointed to the half moon shaped birthmark just above the wound on Cesare's shoulder. 'That is the mark of the Greyfells; kings of Dredgemarsh. Your father had it; your grandfather had it, and they had their sorrows and hardships but they persevered.' The sudden outburst of anger subsided as quickly as it had erupted. 'Forgive me, Sire, forgive me. I have spoken out of turn. It's unpardonable.' Nicholas stepped back and cupped his anguished face in his two palms. 'I will leave immediately and report my foolish outburst to the abbot.' He picked up his tray of medication and turned to leave.

'Wait, Brother Nicholas. You will not report this to Sigismund.'

'Your majesty, I had no right --'

'You had every right, Brother Nicholas. The only message you will deliver to Sigismund is that I will speak with him immediately.'

'As you wish, Sire.' Brother Nicholas left as quietly as he had entered.

****

Grunkite pushed the barely touched trencher of nombles aside.

'Not hungry, Marshall?' Jerome asked. Grunkite did not answer. He was staring blankly at the boisterous young novices who were piling into the long seats at the trestle tables.

"S'blood, take it easy, take it easy,' an elderly monk was shouting at them. The twinkle in his eyes belied the apparent irritation in his voice. 'If you prayed with as much zeal as you practiced sword work, we'd be well nigh in heaven,' he said, and the young monks laughed with good humour.

Grunkite and Jerome sat at a small table in a raised alcove where they could look down on the refectory main floor. Abbot Sigismund had entered the refectory. It seemed as if his presence was sensed even before he was seen and the normal hubbub of mealtime in the refectory diminished to a respectful whispering. He made his way to a simple lectern at the end of the refectory and began to read from The Anselem Book of Prayer.

Sancte Michael Archangele, defende nos in proelio; contra nequitiam et insidias diaboli esto praesidium
...

Almost immediately after the second or third word of the prayer, a frisson of excitement filled the room. The cellerer and his helpers for that day, who had commenced serving out food to the gathering, stopped and looked towards their abbot, mouths open. All heads turned towards the lectern. Jerome very quietly laid down his goblet. The excitement was palpable. A puzzled Grunkite could not restrain himself and leaned close to Jerome.

'What is it?'

The normally taciturn Jerome was smiling.

'What is it?' Grunkite raised his voice and a couple of the more senior monks looked up towards the alcove, one putting his forefinger to his lips. Jerome held up his hand, palm towards Grunkite and concentrated on the words of the abbot. The deep resonant voice continued:

Satanam aliosque spiritus malignos, qui ad perditionem animarum pervagantur in mundo, divina virtute in infernum detrude. Amen.

As quietly and as quickly as he had entered the refectory, the abbot left. A crescendo of voices filled the room. Jerome turned to his frustrated companion Grunkite, but before he could utter a word, a breathless young monk dashed up the short stairs to where they sat and blurted out,

'Abbot Sigismund wants you to go to the Chapter House at once.'

'Will someone tell me what is happening?' Grunkite slammed his fist onto the table.

'The prayer, Sigismund's prayer; it is our prayer before battle. We are going to war, Marshall,' said Jerome.

'War! We're going to war?' The look of anger on Grunkite's face changed rapidly to one of disbelief and then joy. 'The King must be ... he must be ready.' Grunkite gave a great laugh. 'The King is ready, Jerome. He's ready at last. What are we waiting for? The Chapter House you say, young man?' Grunkite rose and placed a friendly hand on the shoulder of the startled young monk.

'Yes, yes, Marshall.' The young novice nodded vigorously

When they entered the Chapter House, Grunkite and Jerome were greeted by Sigismund. The only other person present was Cesare. Though he looked pale, there was determination and purpose in his expression. The four men sat in a close circle.

'Marshall Grunkite, Jerome, I thank you for your patience with me. I have not served you well.' Cesare paused.

'Sire,' Grunkite spoke very quietly, 'you have nothing ...' his protest was silenced by a gesture from Cesare.

'I know you mean to be kind, Marshall, but I have had time to consider my stewardship. I am not proud of it.'

'But you were so young ...' Grunkite looked more distressed than Cesare.

'Please, Marshall,' Cesare raised his hand once more, 'let me continue. With the help of Abbot Sigismund and his very wise infirmerer, who heals more than wounded bodies, I am resolved to become what I never have been; King of Dredgemarsh.'

'Bravo, bravo.' Grunkite could not suppress his joy.

'Sire,' even Jerome could not contain himself, 'your father would rejoice at your words. The Knights of Anselem will be by your side.' Jerome looked towards Sigismund, who nodded and added,

'To the last man.'

'And not just the knights of Anselem, Sire,' said Grunkite, 'there are those in Dredgemarsh who know you are alive–'

'Alive?' said Cesare. 'Am I presumed dead, Marshall?'

'Tancredi has announced your death, even held a burial service ... but not everyone believes that and –'

'The vile traitor,' Cesare cried out. 'My father trusted him and I ... I have been such a fool.'

'Sire,' Jerome spoke, 'Tancredi has fastened his grip on Dredgemarsh. He would be King. He has enlisted the help of Cawdrult of Brooderlund. Three hundred Brooderstalt soldiers, under a Captain Pentrojan, hold Dredgemarsh in their grip.' Cesare gasped and shook his head. Jerome continued, 'Tancredi plays a deadly game consorting with these men, Sire. Very few of our own people support him, but they feel powerless. They grieve for their lost King.' Cesare leaned forward, closed his eyes and cradled his head in his open palms.

'But there are those who are planning insurrection in support of you,' Grunkite said. 'Their leader is Cook Meister Clutchbolt.'

'Clutchbolt!' Cesare raised his head instantly. 'Clutchbolt?'

'Yes Sire, Clutchbolt. We have secret communications from him. He has gathered a group of supporters around him. He is ready for action once we give the word.'

Cesare sighed. 'Those from whom we expect little ...' he grimaced as if in sudden pain, 'and those from whom we expect most, trust most ...' He struck the arm of his chair with a closed fist and rose suddenly, turning his face away from his companions.

'My friends, don't doubt my resolution. All traitors, be they man,' he paused 'or woman, they will pay dearly.'

Dredgemarsh

Chapter 31

The inhabitants of Dredgemarsh, despite their abhorrence of Tancredi, nevertheless resumed their normal day-to-day activities as best they could. Surprisingly, Pentrojan's army, after their initial brutal assault, refrained from harrasing the citizens further. Already, Pentrojan had publicly hanged one of his own men for raping the daughter of a wool trader. It was not out of concern for the populace that he restrained his men. He and his King, Cawdrult, had plans for Dredgemarsh which did not include Tancredi. So Pentrojan was careful to distance himself from Tancredi and the atrocities he visited on some of his own people. Tancredi's insufferable arrogance and cruelty would ensure that, once removed, the citizens would gladly give their support to Pentrojan and swear allegiance to Cawdrult.

In the meantime, Tancredi's hubris blossomed, nourished by a band of sycophants and charlatans who formed his retinue. He had ceased to worry about Cesare or, at least, had pushed all thoughts of him to the deeper recesses of his mind. It was only in the hours between half-waking and half-sleeping that the shadow of his former King preyed upon him. He quickly submerged these unwelcome feelings in the swirl of daily activities. He had decided to restructure and renew every aspect of the city. Every trace of the old regime would be erased. A new crest, banners and uniforms for his soldiers were in the making. The Dredgemarshian calendar was being re-written with new ceremonial days and events designed specifically to promote and glorify himself. He had even embellished and added to his own family tree to retrospectively legitimise his new exalted position.

The inhabitants endured all the changes with sullen resignation, but Tancredi could not change their hearts. He knew this, and despised them for their grudging support. Despite it, he had commenced to restructure education within Dredgemarsh so that at least he would gain control over the minds of the children. His days were filled with endless meetings. Every administrator and petty official was summoned before him. In most cases the sole purpose of the interview was to demonstrate that the new master was in total control of every aspect of life in Dredgemarsh.

He snapped out orders, perused lists, signed letters, dictated letters, dictated edicts, issued bulletins, posted posters, summoned meetings and sat at in on all council committees. He seemed to be everywhere at once. He was a veritable whirlwind of activity, with flatterers and hangers-on at every turn to maintain the illusion of shared opinions and objectives, pretending to participate in the charade. Those who

could not bring themselves to play the game had to somehow retire into the background and wait. For them, the
frenetic turmoil was unreal, something passing, a fever that
would abate and burn itself out. The new regime had
emerged too quickly; it had no roots, no philosophy, beliefs
or history. It would expire of its own accord, or so they
wished and hoped.

During this time, the memory of King Cesare was cher-
ished. Even those who had sometimes grumbled over some
trivial hurt or perceived indifference, which they had attrib-
uted, often correctly, to Cesare, now looked back with regret
at his passing. All those who yearned for the demise of Tancredi's hateful rule were filled with anxiety and desperation.
Though Tancredi had announced that a second assassination attempt on Cesare had been successful, and that he had
been unfortunately killed in Green Valley, there were still
some lingering doubts in the minds of the populace. After a
very perfunctory and hasty burial service for the assassinated
King, Tancredi promised a more fitting ceremony later
when urgent security matters, which he could not divulge as
yet, were seen to. The small band of the faithful, led by
Clutchbolt, had not divulged the truth about Cesare's escape
to anyone outside their circle. Any premature talk on their
part might initiate a vicious repression by Tancredi, and
frustrate their preparations for the return of their King.

There were some signs that should have, at the very least,
stimulated Tancredi's curiosity, a turn of events that might
have forewarned him of some profound changes taking
place. Havelock and Dipslick had transformed themselves.
Dipslick was sober and Havelock was beginning to look as if
he was actually thinking of something. From all appearances,
it was a painful and excruciating transformation for

Dipslick. He had lost his usual warm, contented alcoholic glow. His face bore the strain of one suffering a permanent, monumental hangover. His eyes were no longer dead marbles, but tiny cinders of concentrated pain in his mottled face. His partner Havelock's eyes had also changed. Those morose yellow orbs had a new spark, a brightness in them that suggested that the owner had decided to reactivate his brain after years of almost total slumber. At times there was even a hint of some facial muscle activity, and perhaps the tiniest trace of a furrow in his soft buttery forehead. But Tancredi, for once, did not notice or if he did, he ascribed no significance to the changes; indeed, he may have even flattered himself that his new regime had somehow rehabilitated these lowly scribes. However, Pentrojan was of another mind.

Chapter 32

The wily Captain of the Brooderstalt was suspicious. He began to sense that the two apparently insignificant scribes, Havelock and Dipslick, who had access to a great deal of sensitive information, were not completely indifferent to what was happening around them. He resolved to observe them more closely, and assigned one of his personal aides to watch them. Up to then, no one had discovered anything really suspicious, except that the scribes visited the kitchens very frequently, which Pentrojan ascribed to their fondness for food and drink. It took no great insight to see that Dipslick's life revolved around alcohol, and it was this obvious failing that somewhat curtailed Pentrojan's suspicions and saved them from a more intensive scrutiny.

But their luck finally deserted them on one of their trips from the armoury with purloined weapons under their cloaks. They were summoned by Pentrojan's aide to accompany him directly to the Captain's quarters.

The reluctant Havelock and Dipslick were ushered into Pentrojan's presence and requested to seat themselves at a writing table where pens and parchment were laid out in readiness for them. Pentrojan sat at his own small table, eating a hot croustade with relish and washing it down with a large tankard of braggot. The old pair just stared blankly at Pentrojan, although some tiny spark of interest momentarily lit up Dipslick's small muddy eyes, when Pentrojan raised the tankard of braggot to his lips.

'Well, sit, sit.I want you to draw up some documents,' Pentrojan said, wiping the back of his hand across his mouth.

'We must get our own writing materials.' said Havelock.

'Yes, it is not possible to transcribe without our own pens and parchment,' added Dipslick.

'It's the law, Captain, only embossed Dredgemarsh parchment can be used for official business,' Havelock continued. He had never had to think and talk as fast as he did now. Pentrojan was both bemused and suspicious at this sudden outburst from the old man who had, up to then, confined himself to a few perfunctory words when asked anything. He considered the situation for several minutes and then spoke.

'Well, we can't have you flaunt the law, my good sirs. You must get what you need.' The pair turned immediately and began to walk towards the door with more than usual haste.

'Wait!' Pentrojan called out. 'One of you will remain here with me.'

Slowly, the two old comrades turned to face each other. Pentrojan watched, fascinated, as he sensed the mounting tension between them. Neither Havelock or Dipslick spoke, yet Pentrojan was sure that they were in intimate communication with each other. They stood motionless, Havelock looking down into the pained eyes of his friend. They gazed thus for some time, seemingly oblivious to the world around them. At last, Havelock turned his lugubrious eyes towards Pentrojan. Dipslick continued to stare fixedly at Havelock.

'Thank you, Captain,' said Havelock, 'I shall return presently.' There was a strange tremor in his voice. Was it simply old age and was that tearful eye simply the sign of too many years spent reading and writing the documents and history of Dredgemarsh? Pentrojan was not sure. Turning once more to Dipslick, Havelock, with the greatest tenderness reached out, placed both his hands on Dipslick's shoulders, then leaning forwards and downwards he placed a delicate kiss on the grey and mottled forehead of his companion. He turned and hurried from the room.

It took Havelock some fifteen minutes to reach the kitchens. He brushed past Ratchet who had raised his hand in greeting, and went straight to Clutchbolt, who was kneading a large cake of dough. He tugged at Clutchbolt's sleeve. The Cook Meister spun round at this uncustomary contact and was immediately confronted by the extraordinary sight of Havelock crying uncontrollably, his old yellow face distorted and blotched.

'My dear friend,' Clutchbolt escorted Havelock to the nearest chair.

'Mistress Crumble! Medovukha, medovukha, immediately.'

Ratchet and Lowslegg were gazing in absolute horror and

shock at the amazing spectacle. Something terrible had happened. Had the hour of reckoning arrived, unplanned, unexpected? Bella Crumble rushed back from the cellar with a goblet half full of medovukha. She handed it to Clutchbolt, who was stooping over the weeping Havelock. He put one arm behind Havelock's shoulders and with the other, raised the goblet to his trembling lips.

'Drink. Drink.' The medovukha poured down Havelock's chin, down his front as he tried to swallow between great sobs until eventually he was quiet. He looked small and shrivelled.

'What is it, Havelock?' Clutchbolt gently shook the old man's shoulder. 'What is it? Where's Dips?'

At the mention of Dipslick, Havelock gave a great sob and blurted out

'They have him. Caught ... with weapons ... Dips ... they have him. He won't say a word. No matter what they do, Dips won't talk. He'll die first.' The enormity of what Havelock was saying stunned everyone into shocked silence.

'That's it.' Clutchbolt broke the silence. 'Sooner than we wanted, but no matter. Havelock, you must vanish right now; Mistress Crumble, get him a torch. You can go to the Hall of Echoes. Wait there.' All the while he was barking out these orders he was wrapping a parcel of food, which he then thrust into Havelock's limp hands.

'Now go, there is serious work to be done.' He ushered Havelock to the small door through which Burstboil had so recently stepped into a world of shadows. Bella Crumble handed him a lighted torch as he passed and Havelock entered the interior of Dredgemarsh, without his companion of three score years.

'Poor man, it's breaking his heart,' Bella Crumble

blubbered.

'Well my worthies, we go into action sooner than planned. Let us hope that Havelock is right about Dips not talking.' Clutchbolt sounded strangely elated. The small band of conspirators snatched a few moments of silence, as if bracing themselves, before exploding into action.

'Mr Ratchet, take this.' Clutchbolt hastily scribbled a postscript to an already prepared letter and handed it to the Assistant Cook Meister. 'Get that young squire, Klip, to take this to Anselem. He can't go tonight. All gates are locked and manned, but as soon as the postern gate is opened for the mercers in the morning, he must find a way to get out. The letter is to be put into the King's hands and only the King. He must ride like the wind, all our lives depend on it and Mr Ratchet, if you are apprehended, eat the letter. Tell Klip the same. Mistress Crumble, Miss Lowslegg ... remember what we planned: every water barrel, every beer keg and every morsel of food.' All the while he was giving orders, Clutchbolt was divesting himself of his Cook Meister's regalia. Hat, white neckerchief, apron, jacket, shirt and shoes made a trail to the door of his own private room, through which he was now hopping on his fat left leg while trying to extricate the other from his pantaloons. Moments after he disappeared from view there was a loud crash from the room.

'Bollocks!' This heartfelt expletive from Clutchbolt was followed by a veritable symphony of rummaging, clattering, sliding drawers, opening presses, panting, grunting and much swearing until at last the door was flung open, and Clutchbolt strode out in full military attire and a splendid cloak flung nonchalantly over his shoulder.

'Cook Meister Clutchbolt, you look magnificent,' gushed

Bella Crumble.

Clutchbolt slyly checked himself out in the reflection of a large copper vat and was inclined to agree with Bella Crumble.

'Do not flinch, my friends,' he had never called them friends before, 'tomorrow's breakfast, for our good friends from Brooderlund, will be the most famous breakfast in the history of Dredgemarsh.' They all laughed. 'Our King is returning. Long live the King.' As he swept from the room, Miss Lowslegg said, barely above a whisper;

'Long live the King.'

'Bless his great heart,' sobbed Crumble, pointing to the departing Clutchbolt.

'Bless him,' said Lowslegg .

Blast him, thought Ratchet for an instant, but quickly buried the ungenerous thought. 'Bless him,' he said.

'Mr Ratchet.' Clutchbolt stuck his head round the jamb of the door and said politely, 'The letter, Mr Ratchet , now, please.'

'Oh right away, Cook Meister ... sir...' Ratchet awkwardly saluted before rushing away.

Chapter 33

Professor Quickstrain was not very surprised to hear an urgent knocking at his door. Clutchbolt had been a frequent visitor to his laboratory over the last couple of weeks.

'Coming, coming.' When he opened the door, he stepped back in surprise and then moved forward again to scrutinise his visitor.

'Clutchbolt, Cook Meister Clutchbolt? Grak's warts, come in, come in.' As the visitor passed him, Quickstrain leaned out into the dark corridor and rapidly swivelled his head left and right.

'All's clear.' He closed the door and turned to follow Clutchbolt, all the while looking back as if expecting it to burst open at any moment. He stumbled straight into the voluminous folds of Clutchbolt's cloak.

'Agh, curses, get me out of this.' Quickstrain gingerly extricated himself. He stepped back and eyed Clutchbolt up and down.

'Should I call you Cook Meister or General ?'

'Never mind that, our plans have to be moved forward. Tomorrow morning we start.'

'But that's much too soon, we will not be ready...I...how, why tomorrow?'

'We've no choice. The Brooderstalt Captain has caught Dipslick with weapons; he'll be onto us soon enough. If we wait, we could all end up in the dungeons.' Clutchbolt paused and waited for Quickstrain's response. The professor collapsed onto a chair and clasped his bowed head in his palms.

'Don't give up now, professor!'

'Who said I'm giving up?' Quickstrain snapped. 'Let me think, let me think.'

'Whatever you need Professor, I'll get; men, materials, anything.'

'Yes, yes, yes.' Quickstrain began to scrabble through the pile of paper on a long bench and unrolled a large drawing.

'Now, let's see.' He swept the bench clear with his forearm and set the drawing down.

'What is it?' Clutchbolt asked.

'The Turf Dredger.' Quickstrain stood back and gave a little sigh. 'Ah, those were the days. One of my best projects.' He began to examine the drawing, all the while mumbling to himself. 'Clever ... oh ... yes ... ha ... half a day ... thought we'd never ... yes, nothing like ...'

'Professor, professor, we don't have time ...' Clutchbolt was beginning to redden around the neck.

'Keep your breeches on. I'm working.'

For a full thirty minutes Quickstrain sketched and wrote furiously, totally oblivious to the increasingly impatient Clutchbolt. The study was like the inside of a giant clock. Machines and gadgets ticked and whirred in every conceivable corner, shelf and worktop. The old professor scribbled, Clutchbolt paced, scribble, tick, pace, whirr, scribble tick, pace, whirr, on and on, as if it would never stop. The fiery Cook Meister began to breathe hard.

'Right!' said Quickstrain.

'What!' snapped Clutchbolt, before Quickstrain had even finished that one word.

'This is the best we can do at such short notice. Not as elegant as my original plan, but it will work.'

'Bugger elegance, just explain it and I'll get things moving.'

'Patience, patience, man. Now look here, by tomorrow noon, as many of Pentrojan's men and our own despicable traitors should be down here in the Dredger Hall, quelling what they think is a serious uprising. You must keep them there. You retreat towards here.' Quickstrain was pointing out the relevant locations on a map of lower Dredgemarsh.

'We have got to time this manoeuvre perfectly. Here's my plan.'

Clutchbolt and Quickstrain spent the next two hours going over every detail of the plan.

Eventually Clutchbolt seemed satisfied, and commenced rolling up the hastily prepared sheets of paper containing the plan's essential elements.

'Professor, you are a genius. I will send some reliable men to help you complete these modifications tonight. At noon tomorrow be ready to proceed with your part when you hear our signal; a single horn blast. I will take care of the rest. Good luck.' Clutchbolt shook the Professor's hand firmly and departed into the darkening Dredgemarsh evening. He delayed his return to the kitchens in order to get everything straight in his own mind. The confident and ebullient Clutchbolt was suddenly feeling the strain. He was fearful, and it was only in solitude that he could allow the fear to surface. Keeping to the shadows, lest anyone should recognise or confront him in his military attire, he picked his way through the small back streets and allyways to the kitchen gardens. The cool evening air helped to dissipate the natural but unwelcome emotions, before he finally marched confidently into the presence of his kitchen staff. He was in complete control again, and ready for the intensive preparations that would see him and his compatriots busy late into the night.

Chapter 34

Despite getting only a couple of hours of restless sleep, Bella Crumble, Leopold Ratchet and Nellie Lowslegg never prepared breakfast with more diligence than on the morning following Dipslick's arrest. It was Bella Crumble's job to dole out the breakfast rations in the refectory. Nellie Lowslegg assisted her. The rations consisted of two ladles of gruel, a blob of treacle, a square of polenta bread and a beaker of watered milk. The soldiers filed up one side of the refectory with their wooden plates and beakers. Bella Crumble and Miss Lowslegg dished out their rations and they returned to the long wooden trestle tables. These soldiers ate anything on offer; they had known too many harsh and hungry campaigns to be choosy about food. But food was not the only thing rationed in their lives; the company and sight of women, any women, was also in scarce supply. So they winked and made obscene remarks and gestures at Bella Crumble and Nellie Lowslegg . Amongst them, two of Tancredi's men, Shem Sledge and Black Pete, had insinuated themselves and they talked the loudest, made the crudest jokes and out-swore everyone.

On this particular morning, Bella Crumble, with a coquettish little flourish, gave them both a double helping of treacle.

'That lot should perk you up, boys.' She pursed her lips.

'Wehaaay,' they bellowed in unison.

'Get along boys, you won't know yourselves when you get that lot inside you.'

'What would you like inside of you Bella; I've a length of bartago in me pouch, Hey hey! ' roared Shem Sledge, so that everyone could hear him and the place exploded in raucous laughter. Nellie Lowslegg tittered nervously. Bella and Nellie were extra generous to all the soldiers that morning and piled the food onto their plates, filled their cups to the brim and even offered second helpings to anyone who wanted it.

'If you boys are satisfied, Miss Lowslegg and I will leave you now,' Bella called out, and without waiting for a reply, she and Nellie left the boisterous gathering.

One hour after that breakfast, Shem Sledge began to feel a bubbling sensation in the pit of his stomach; his vision became blurred and he began to lose concentration. He was playing a game of dice with Black Pete at the time. It became obvious fairly quickly that he was not the only one losing interest in the game. By mid-morning, the latrines were jammed with green-faced soldiers vomiting and shitting without cease. A chorus of belching, farting, moaning and regurgitating filled the foetid air of the military barracks.

Pentrojan, on his way to morning inspection of his troops

with two of his sergeants, was furiously remonstrating with a grotesque, one-eyed man wearing a blood-spattered leather apron over his uniform.

'The old drunk won't talk, Captain,' One-eye said.

'Make him. Smash every bone in his body if you have to.'

'He will die before talking. I know the type, Captain.' As the small group turned into the barracks square they saw what, at first, looked like the aftermath of a battle. Brooder-stalt soldiers were spread out all across the square in total disarray: some were kneeling and vomiting; others were doubled up, holding their bellies and groaning; some were staggering to where a great melée had broken out amongst the groaning mass of soldiers trying to force their way into the latrines. Still more just lay on the ground, crying out in pain.

'What! What's going on here?' Pentrojan gulped as his lungs were assaulted by the stench. He covered his mouth and nose with his cloak and strode in amongst the reeling masses. 'What has happened?' Pentrojan shouted. 'You!' He addressed three guards who appeared unaffected by whatever illness the others had succumbed to. 'What has happened? Why are you not like the rest of them?'

'Captain, we were on duty ... on our way to the refectory for breakfast.' .

'Breakfast. The refectory.' Pentrojan said and paused for a moment. His face reddened. 'The swine' he snarled, 'the filty swine have befouled the food.' You two,' Pentrojan pointed to one of his sergeants and to One-eye, 'get every last man out into the square. I want them in formation. Get up, you dog!' He kicked a prostrate soldier in the ribs. 'And you, Sergeant Borac.' he addressed his other sergeant, 'gather a dozen men, go to the kitchens and bring back every last man and woman to me now. If they resist, butcher them on the spot. By the Gods, they will pay dearly for this. Are we to be defeated by the scullery staff of this pox-ridden place?' His face had now turned a blotchy white. 'To the centre of the square; no one is exempt.' He turned and strode out to the centre of the square facing the barracks, leaving his sergeant and One-eye to sort out the debacle behind him. They swore, shouted, kicked and beat the sorry mess of fighting men who wobbled and staggered into some semblance of formation, gulping for air and groaning in agony. Finally order was imposed and the lines of green-grey faces looked woefully towards the grim-faced Pentrojan.

'Not one man goes sick on this day, not one single man. Prepare for action, all weapons to hand. Report to our surgeon instantly, he'll give you something to sort out your guts and get back here immediately. Go, go.'

Pentrojan turned to his sergeant. 'Those still on night duty will not have eaten yet. Warn them instantly. Be ready for anything and get the damned Chancellor here now.' Pentrojan was stamping up and down, opening and closing his fists.

'By the Gods, they will suffer,' he snarled. 'Damn that Borac, he should be back by now with those scum.' Much to his amazement, just as he uttered those words, Borac staggered into view. He was holding his hand to his forehead, a stream of blood oozing out through his fingers.

'They're armed sir. Killed two of ours. Armed to the teeth. All the prisoners are out and armed also.'

Tancredi came rushing into view, his face pinched and drawn.

'What in the devil's name, has happened here?' He flung the words at Pentrojan.

'What has happened, Chancellor, is that your people, your traitors have poisoned my men. The bastards are loose down below in this mouldering pile of shit, armed and fighting. You,' he pointed to the bleeding Borac, and the second sergeant, 'set up a table here. Get chairs, paper, pens, the usual. Go! Now! Now!' Then turning towards Tancredi he said, 'And you, Lord Tancredi, will stay right here by my side until we have their guts waving on our lances. I want to know every orifice to the bowels of this putrid heap of rubble.'

Dredgemarsh

Chapter 35

An old, pockmarked and rusting helmet was perched at a rakish angle on top of Bella Crumble's large head. Equally inadequately, two iron breastplates were lashed to her monumental bosom with twine and rope. She stood guard at the main kitchen entrance, behind an up-turned table and squinted into the gloom beyond, her eight-foot lance poised and ready. Beside her was Miss Lowslegg, engulfed in a leather suit, also with lance and helmet, look-ing equally as determined as Bella Crumble, though consid-erably less frightening. These Amazons of the sculleries were shouting at Ratchet to hurry up. He was frantically pil-ing up pots, tables, chairs and anything else he could carry to barricade the main kitchen entrance, which they were guard-ing.

'Just a little while longer ... Cook Meister Clutchbolt told us he'll be here in time. Oh but do hurry up, Leopold; those vile soldiers may attack any minute. Miss Lowslegg, help him carry that vat over here.' Despite Leopold Ratchet's official position as assistant to Clutchbolt, it was Bella Crumble who always took command in the absence of Cook Meister Clutchbolt, or perhaps more appropriately now, General Clutchbolt.

Clutchbolt, along with Surgeon Keenslide, was at that very moment approaching the prison where all those loyal to King Cesare were incarcerated. The six prison guards who had eaten heartily of the ample breakfast, delivered to them first thing that morning by Ratchet, were in a state of near collapse. Systematically, Clutchbolt and Keenslide overcame each guard and began to unlock the cells. By the time they were finished they had a small force of forty men, along with some bemused and delighted long-term criminals who readily threw their lot in with their unexpected deliverers. Clutchbolt, standing on a table amongst the detritus of the prison guards' lethal breakfast, called for silence.

'Loyal men of Dredgemarsh, your King is alive! This very day, our King returns to Dredgemarsh,' The men cheered and Clutchbolt signalled for silence again. 'He returns with the Knights of Anselem to crush the viper Tancredi and his Brooderstalt curs.' More cheering. 'Meanwhile, we will strike at their underbelly. We will gut them and our King will behead them.' The men began to chant, 'Gut them, kill them.'

'Your weapons await you,' Clutchbolt shouted above the chanting. 'Follow me, do everything I say, and we will free Dredgemarsh before the sun sets.' The Cook Meister then, despite his bulk, jumped from the table and led the men out of the prisons. They went directly to one of the cooling larders, where every class of weapon, along with all sizes of brigandines and helmets, smuggled there by Havelock and Dipslick, were quickly distributed. With Clutchbolt at their head, they marched towards the main kitchens.

Their arrival was timely. The retreating kitchen staff were throwing plates, knives, pans, bottles and anything else throwable at a band of Brooderstalt soldiers, who were dismantling Ratchet's barricade at the main door.

'Bella, don't, there are too many of them, move back.' Ratchet was pleading with Bella Crumble, who had dashed forward in a fury to beat one of Pentrojan's men off the ever-diminishing barricade.

'Those curs will not desecrate my kitchen.' To Bella Crumble's surprise and astonishment, Pentrojan's men retreated instantly. Unknown to her, Clutchbolt and his fresh recruits had charged the attackers from behind. Only one, Borac, their sergeant, escaped the frenzied attack to bring the news of their ignominious defeat to Pentrojan.

'Mistress Crumble, you've done it. Look, Miss Lowslegg, she's beaten them.' Ratchet could not believe his eyes.

'You can't best a Crumble when her blood is up.' Bella trumpeted from atop the hill of kitchen paraphernalia where she stood like a statue of Boadicea, her lance held proudly aloft. Moments later, Clutchbolt and his men scrambled over the same mound and into the kitchen.

'Has anyone been hurt?'

'No, Cook Meister Clutchbolt, Mistress Crumble has defeated them all and they ran away,' Miss Lowslegg laughed.

'Oh, well ... yes, good, good, excellent, well done Mistress Crumble. Now gather around everyone, we have not much time. Everything is going according to plan, but this day will test us all to the limits of endurance.'

****

Despite his mounting fury, Pentrojan set to the business of containing the revolt in a rational and decisive manner. The analysis of how things had gotten so out of control would come later, and those found remiss or negligent in their duties would be lucky if they were given a quick death. For now, his sole aim was to re-assert control.

'Now, you say there are no other entrances other than these.' he was pointing to a map on the table, as he addressed Tancredi, more in the tone of an interrogator than a collaborator. Tancredi, keenly aware of Pentrojan's presumption of authority, looked most unhappy to be in such a defensive position.

'In as far as the Lord Chancellor can be expected to know such details, I believe these are the only ones.' Tancredi did not disguise the resentment in his voice.

'You will be Lord Chancellor of nothing if we don't stop this now. If I am to risk my men further in this affair, I will have nothing but wholehearted, unconditional co-operation. Now can we start again? Are these the only entrances?' He rapped the map impatiently with his knuckles.

'These are the only ones.' Tancredi replied through clenched teeth.

'Good, now you take these men,' Pentrojan pointed to a group of about thirty soldiers, 'and take this entrance here. Go straight in, these men will not hesitate. I want no delays and no hostages.' Tancredi complied without response and set out to circumvent the Dredgemarsh kitchens.

'Proudflax!' Pentrojan was snapping out the orders. 'You take this entrance and Spoorblut, you have an opportunity to redeem yourself. Take the main entrance. They cannot escape. Corner them and destroy them. No questions, no quarter!' In all, there was now a force of at least one hundred Brooderstalt approaching the kitchens.

Pentrojan remained at his temporary command post in the middle of the square and to all appearances, now looked more relaxed and happy. Things were under control again. It was simply a matter of time and the revolt would be crushed. It was not long when to his surprise, he saw Tancredi returning.

'Back so soon?'

'They are retreating into the corridors, there is no way out for them.'

'I'm surprised you did not stay for the kill.'

'Nothing can go wrong. They are completely outnumbered. Besides, I have more important matters to attend to than watch your men butcher a bunch of menials.'

'Dismissing them so lightly was very nearly our undoing.'

'Perhaps we can all learn some lessons then, Captain.'

Tancredi was now nonchalantly scrutinising the map set out before Pentrojan.

'Yes, they are well and truly trapped. It will take a few hours, but it is all over. If you'll excuse me, Captain, I will leave you to finalise matters.'

Just then, they heard a shout. A soldier came running up behind them.

'Captain, Captain, we have caught a young squire attempting to escape with this.' He trust a letter triumphantly into Pentrojan's outstretched hand. When the Captain had finished reading he handed the letter to Tancredi.

'It would appear that your ex-King has some intentions of returning. Let us see this young spy and see if he can be persuaded to tell us where the hawk has nested. Come.'

'Captain, you won't be able to question him for a while, ' the soldier said.

'Why?'

'He was unconscious when I left him. He fell from his horse when we stopped him; bumped his head. I will take you to him. It's not far.' Minutes later, they stood in a stable next to where Cesare had lain after the assassination attempt. The squire Klip lay unconscious on the floor.

'I'm afraid Captain, he is still unconscious.'

'Shit! Bring him to me when he wakes,' said Pentrojan.

'Wait! Where was the letter?' Tancredi queried the soldier.

'In his saddlebag.'

'And this squire was knocked unconscious before you searched his saddle bags?'

'Yes.'

'So, he does not know you have discovered the letter?'

'Well...no...of course not, he was unconscious ...'

'Well, well, well. Perhaps, Captain, we can get the hawk to come to us.'

'What are you talking about?' Pentrojan was becoming irritated with Tancredi.

'Captain, don't you think this brave squire could escape and deliver this letter? He would never realise that we had read it.'

'What ? Explain yourself' demanded Pentrojan.

'Wait.' Tancredi put his finger to his lips and whispered, 'Let us go next door, in case he does wake up.' They quickly retired to the very room where not long before, Cesare had lain so close to death.

'Now, Captain Pentrojan,' Tancredi had a smirk on his face, 'no one can hear us now. Let me explain.' But Tancredi was mistaken; they could be heard. Just yards from them, within the hollow rear wall, Verm Bludvile had returned like a hunting dog, to the last location where his hated prey had lain. He was listening intently.

'It's really quite simple, Captain. All we have to do is put the letter back in his saddlebag and let the squire think he has escaped us. He will go straight to the King, if one could call him that, and his highness will walk straight back into our arms, straight into this very square. We will let the plan proceed exactly as this Clutchbolt traitor has laid out in the letter. It's so simple.' Tancredi was jubilant.

'By all the gods and demons, you are devious.' Pentrojan was beginning to chuckle. 'Yes indeed, I'll give you that, Chancellor, you are devious. I like it, I like your plan.'

'It is not the first time this week that a prisoner has escaped. You remember that maniac Bludvile.' Tancredi smiled slyly at Pentrojan.

'You arranged that?'

'But of course, he is my security, my scapegoat. I can blame him for anything and everything; I've already announced that he has killed the King. The demented fool doesn't know it, but he is working for me, the very one who stripped him of his job in the first place. As I said, Captain, I am a politician.' Tancredi was beginning to feel superior once more.

'Well so be it, let's proceed.' Pentrojan called in the senior officer on guard duty. They spent some time discussing the details of the plan and about an hour later, a dazed squire managed to force the door of the stall where he was held, mount his horse, which was conveniently still saddled, and race through the open gateway to freedom. He was pursued by a group of Pentrojan's men, who gave up a lacklustre chase after five or ten minutes. Klip was jubilant and proud of his daring escape, and rode gallantly to deliver Clutch-bolt's letter to the real and only King of Dredgemarsh.

Chapter 36

Verm Bludvile's legs buckled, and he slumped to the floor of that dark hidden wall cavity. He lay there rocking himself back and forth, whispering to the black stones.

'It wasn't the King, it wasn't the King.' He was a child again, crying in the darkness, chanting words as if their meaning would only manifest itself by endless repetition. His plaintive song seeped into the flinty fabric where he sat entombed and melded with the endless murmuring and sighing of the ancient fortress city. Then the raucous laughter of Pentrojan and Tancredi burst in on his cocoon of shadows and whispers.

'It worked, by heavens, it worked. I'll give you that, Chancellor. The triumph on the fool's face. We'll prepare a hot reception for this tiresome King of yours.'

'Yes indeed Captain, and I will be here in this very spot to witness the happy event.' They both laughed loudly.

The fire in Verm's eyes was quenched. He shambled listlessly through the umbra, stumbling through dusty corridors that he, only hours before, traversed with unconscious sure footedness. He arrived in the Great Hall of Echoes and stared into its vastness as if he had never seen it before.

'Clutchbolt, is that you? ' a lugubrious voice called from the shadows.

'What?'

'Is that you, Clutchbolt?'

'It wasn't the King, it wasn't the King, not the King. I was wrong.'

Havelock's face, illuminated only by the lamp he held below his own chin, emerged from behind a pillar. Verm walked over to the grotesque mask and repeated,

'It wasn't the King.'

'What, what wasn't the King, what are you talking about, is Clutchbolt coming yet?' Havelock, who had now raised the lamp above his own head stepped back from Verm.

'It wasn't the King. The King...'

'You, I know you, Stay away. Stay away, murderer!' Havelock began to back away rapidly. 'Clutchbolt,' he called out, 'Clutchbolt.' There was no answer. 'What do you want?'

'He didn't dismiss me.'

'What?'

'The King did not dismiss me. Not the King.'

'No, Tancredi did. I wrote the order. What do you --'

'Tancredi, it was Tancredi.' Verm's voice grew harsh and deep; within the listless eyes, an ember of fire began to glow once more. Havelock moved further away.

'Bugger you. Dips is locked up because of you.'

'Tancredi is going to kill the King.'

'No, you're wrong. The King escaped, he's safe, I know.'

'They're waiting for him. They know he is coming. Tancredi is waiting.'

'No, no the King is safe, the King...' Havelock's words were submerged in a great swirl of sound that burst forth from one of the corridors that led into the Hall of Echoes. There was frenzied shouting and the clatter of arms.

'It's them, at last. Wait here. You explain to Clutchbolt.' As Havelock uttered the last words, Verm melted into the shadows and was gone. The noise rolled like a thunderous wave out of the mouth of the corridor and washed into the Hall of Echoes. Following close in its wake, Clutchbolt's ragged followers tumbled forth from that same black gullet. The last of them into the hall was Clutchbolt himself.

'Come on you rat's turds, whore mongers, you'll never take us, this way. Come on, come and get it.' Clutchbolt was brandishing a bloodied cleaver over his head.

A hail of arrows, spears and knives spewed up out of the mouth of the corridor in response to the taunts. Those missiles that found their target bounced harmlessly off the Cook Meister's heavy armour and shield.

'Hold them for as long as possible.' Clutchbolt shouted.

'There's no way out of here, Cook Meister. We're trapped.' The man who spoke had skin the colour of faded parchment. There was no hint of fear in his pale, almost colourless eyes. The heavy bardiche he carried with ease was bloodied from shaft to gleaming head.

'You know these parts?' Clutchbolt moved out of the direct line of fire of the Brooderstalt advancing towards the mouth of the corridor.

'I've slaved like a beast for fifteen years in the Dredger

Hall.'

'That's where we are bound.'

'Then, that's where we die. There is no way out. But so be it.' They could now clearly hear the marching feet of the Brooderstalt.

'Your name?' asked Clutchbolt.

'Forty Three .. no ... no ... Ragus of Mancia.'

'Well Ragus of Mancia, I don't intend to die today. Delay those dogs as much as possible; there is someone I must find. Havelock, Havelock.' he shouted.

'Here, I'm over here.' The tremulous voice weaved its way through the frenzy of sounds that catapulted and spun all over the Hall of Echoes and found Clutchbolt's ear. Immediately the Cook Meister picked out Havelock's flickering lantern in the shadows. The scribe's first words when Clutchbolt came gasping into his presence was, 'Where's Dips?'

'He'll recover. He, along with Ratchet and Keenslide hid, while we lured Pentrojan's lot down here. They have gone back to assist Quickstrain.' Clutchbolt was sweating profusely. 'Now listen, we must hold out here for another while. Then we will retreat to the Dredger Hall. After that, it's up to Quickstrain and the King. He will be here by then. It's all got to do with timing, like roasting a peacock.'

'The Lamplighter was here, he said they were waiting for the King, that they were going to kill him.'

'That bastard is going to try again – '

'No, no, not the Lamplighter. It's Tancredi and the others. The Lamplighter said they were waiting for the King, to kill him.'

'No ... no. Not after all this. It can't ... they must have ... no ... how could they? If the King is coming then Klip got through. So how could they know that? They couldn't know.' Clutchbolt's face had turned white.

'If the Lamplighter knows then they could know,' Havelock reasoned.

'We can't warn him. There is no way back now.' Clutchbolt turned away as if to hide his face from Havelock.

'We must play this out to the bitter end,' he spoke quietly into the darkness and then turned to face Havelock once more. 'Pray to the sacred blood of Christ for our King's safety.'

'We must save the King, we must save ...' a voice trailed off into the darkness.

'It's the Lamplighter.' Havelock said.

'Curse his foul guts.' said Clutchbolt.

Dredgemarsh

Chapter 37

Ambrose the choir master rapped his knuckles on the lectern.

'Brother Dominic, if we might have your attention!' A lean young monk, who had been staring over the curtained rails of the choir gallery turned to face the frowning choir master.

'Sorry, Brother Ambrose, it's just—'

'Just nothing, Brother Dominic. It's not the first time a King has attended prime in this chapel. Psalm XII.' Ambrose began to beat out a rhythm with his raised right hand and arm and mouthed the words unus, duo, tres. On the fourth beat he flung out his left arm and pointed directly at the organist, Brother Leo, whose gnarled hands were poised over the keyboard while his legs moved vigorously up and down, under his scapula, as he worked the organ pedals. With the first notes, Ambrose closed his eyes, his right arm movement became more fluid and less exaggerated. His left hand, still extended towards the organ, was now making tiny circular movements, coaxing every note into the cool morning air of the little chapel. After a long organ introduction, Ambrose opened his eyes and looked at the ten choristers in front of him, once again mouthing the words unus, duo, tres. On the fourth beat, the small choir began, 'Quoniam novit Dominus viam iustorum.' Ambrose raised his face heavenwards and closed his eyes again, both hands now moving in that circular motion, fanning the very notes out of the air and into his own breast. He did not hear the chapel door opening, the sound of hurried feet on the bare flagstones or the urgent whispering that followed. Dominic glanced in the direction of Ambrose, whose eyes were still closed, and then ventured to look over the choir gallery railings once more. The sounds from the chapel floor were increasing in intensity and the other choristers began to take frequent glances at Dominic, who had now stopped singing and was totally absorbed with the commotion below him. An almost imperceptible raggedness began to manifest itself in the singing. Ambrose opened his eyes wide and scanned the choir, finally settling his gaze on Dominic, who was now leaning over the rails.

'Stop, stop, stop!' Ambrose ceased beating out the time. 'Brother Dominic, how many times do I have to tell you? '

'But Brother Ambrose, something serious is happening.'

'Back into position this instant.' Ambrose said. 'Brother Leo, continue to play. Quiet.' He tapped his forefinger against pursed lips. 'I will see what is happening.' Ambrose grasped the rail of the narrow spiral staircase and very slowly began his descent from the gallery. As soon as his head had disappeared from view, the whole choir rushed to the gallery railings.

A young man in muddied riding boots was standing before Cesare in the main aisle of the chapel. As the choristers watched, the bald pate of their own choir master appeared below them. Abbot Sigismund, who was standing with Jerome on the other side of King and listening intently to the conversation between the King and the young man, saw the approaching Ambrose and stepped forward to meet him. He laid his hand on Ambrose's shoulder and spoke quietly into his ear. Ambrose turned and made his way back towards the choir gallery. The choristers now in unison, fixed their gaze on the head of the spiral staircase. They could hear the slow tread of Ambrose ascending and then the laboured breathing as he appeared into view.

'The knights of Anselem ride within the hour,' he gasped when he finally reached the head of the stairway. Dominic grinned and clenched his two fists, punching the air surreptitiously behind the back of one of his fellow choristers. 'Go now and prepare immediately. May God protect you.' By the time they reached the floor of the chapel, the King had already departed. Abbot Sigismund had remained in the chapel.

'Hurry, hurry.' He called out to the choristers. 'Brother Jonathan, the bells, sound the bells. You, brother,' he addressed one of the choristers, 'take this young man, klip, to the refectory and see he is fed.'

****

Grunkite cursed the clanging bell that disturbed the fitful

morning slumber that had at last brought some relief to his anxious heart.

'The devil take them.' he flung back the ox-hair blanket, rolled himself from the low palliasse and clambered to his feet. He shuffled across the plain timber floor of his private chamber, just off the main dormitory and squinted out through the the tiny window that looked down on the main quadrangle. The sound of the bell increased in tempo. Then he saw Cesare and Jerome in the grey morning light, surrounded by monks, striding across the quadrangle towards the Chapter House.

'Bugger it!' He stumbled back to the palliasse and began to frantically dress himself. There was a loud knocking at his door. 'Come in, come,' Grunkite shouted. A young monk stepped inside.

'Sir,' he said, 'the King requests your presence immediately.'

'What's all the commotion about?'

'We are leaving for Dredgemarsh, sir.'

'Go. Tell his majesty, I will be with him instantly.'

When Grunkite finally stepped unto the quadrangle, still trying to fasten a reluctant fibula on his mantle, he was engulfed in a frenzy of knights, horses and excited young novices, all in the final stages of preparation for war. Grunkite barged his way through the melée and entered the Chapter House. Gasping for breath, he half-walked, half-ran to the main hall of the Chapter House and practically fell through the main door into the hall.

'Welcome, Marshall.' The King looked up from the table, where he was examining a map with Jerome and Sigismund.

'Sire, what is happening?'

Cesare looked down at the map once more.

'We cannot delay. We will take the most direct route through Boar's Tusk.'

'Sire,' Grunkite advanced, 'does this mean we –'

'It means we leave immediately for Dredgemarsh.'

'The armourer is ready, Sire,' said Sigismund, folding the map and handing it to Jerome.

As Cesare left the main hall of the Chapter House, Grunkite immediately fell in behind him and with obvious discomfort from his arthritic feet, danced daintily in his wake.

'Sire, ahhh, Sire, what's the, oow, news.'

'Here, read.' Cesare reached into his jerkin and proffered Clutchbolt's letter over his shoulder, without adjusting his stride. Grunkite, who was beginning to drop behind, had to put on a little spurt to catch up with Cesare and with a grimace of pain, grabbed the letter.

'I'll follow you in a moment, Sire, ' said Grunkite who had stopped, and with a sigh of relief sat into a nearby window seat. He held the letter just inches from his squinting eyes and twisted around to get the full benefit of the light from the window. He spoke each word under his breath like an old crone at prayer. The bells of Anselem stopped ringing.

'Aha, yes, yes.' Grunkite shouted. 'Clutchbolt, you gem, you prince of men. We are going home. Tancredi. Oh yesssss, Tancredi, I can't wait. Sire, my King, I am coming.' Grunkite began to chase after Cesare, who had vanished from sight. The old man followed in an erratic pulsating manner, because each alternate step with his less arthritic right leg pushed him bravely forward to be immediately followed by a painful, tear-inducing hop on his left. Fast, slow, quick, slow quick.

'Wait, wait, I am ... ouch ... coming my ... my King.' By

the time Grunkite had caught up with him, Cesare was fastening his buckler in place while his horse was being saddled and likewise prepared for battle. The knights of Anselem had responded instantly to the bells and were all mounted and ready and for departure. Despite the dents and marks of many battles, their armour and weapons were maintained in immaculate condition. Each knight wore a surcoat bearing the royal insignia of the Dredgemarsh Hawk. Cesare wore the exact same armour and surcoat as the rest of the knights, apart from a black ribbon that encircled his left arm. The same symbol adorned a pennant, which Cesare handed to one of the younger men to carry before them.

'Come along Grunkite, we will enter Dredgemarsh together.'

'Yes Sire, and we will crush the snake. Boy, you there, bring my armour.'

'It's here, sir.' After much squeezing and hauling Grunkite was encased in a thick leather suit and a shirt of chain mail that was supposed to hang down to mid thigh but instead flapped over the proud protuberance of his stomach like a baby's short vest.

'Now hold the bloody nag's head, boy, while I mount.' Grunkite raised his left foot to engage the stirrup and the thick leather hide of his war pants creaked and gave out a loud fart sound. The horse instantly danced sideways and Grunkite hanging grimly onto the saddle was dragged, toes scraping, across the cobbles.

'Stop pushing that horse around the yard, Grunkite.' Klip said in a loud whisper and even Cesare laughed. The horse, Grunkite and the stable lad holding the horse disappeared from view behind the shoeing yard wall.

'You little pig's prick, you did that on purpose.' Though unseen, Grunkite could be heard clearly.

'Bring the monster over here ... beside this ... hold him there ... no ... no, here, I'll have your guts for catapult slings, that's it, now, yes.' There was a cessation of the commotion from the shoeing yard and Grunkite, after a few moments re-appeared on horseback.

'Are we quite ready, Grunkite?' said Cesare and a few of the younger knights laughed. Grunkite glared at the knights.

'I am ready, sire. My bones may creak but I am as ready as any man here.'

'I do not doubt it, Marshall. Only for you and Jerome we would not be here on this fateful morning.'

Cesare turned to the small band of knights.

'My friends, brothers, you honour me. You have nurtured me and comforted me. You have healed my body and my soul in this oasis of tranquillity. And what do I offer you for these gifts? Blood, war, death, and without dissent you have accepted. With joy you have accepted. I am humbled beyond measure, beyond words.'

'Sire,' Jerome spoke up, 'it is we who are honoured.'

'This black ribbon,' Cesare held his left arm aloft to display the ribbon, 'is a symbol of my failures. With your help, I will cast it off this day.'

'Yes, yes,' said Grunkite, 'but begging your pardon, Sire, our loyal friend Clutchbolt would appreciate our presence as soon as possible.'

'You're right, Grunkite. Lead them out.'

As they rode out from the hill monastery, the bells began to ring out once again, and the pennant with the hawk of Dredgemarsh fluttered gaily in the brisk mountain breeze. Grunkite smiled ecstatically beside his King, at the head of that small but formidable band of knights.

Chapter 38

Through the clerestory stained glass windows, spears of multicoloured light from the setting sun sliced through the the dense shadows of the infirmary chapel. A monk, whose white hair glistened in the beams, was setting out a few hymnals for vespers on the chancel seats. His slow, deliberate movements suggested a ritual practiced for many years. He moved to the centre of the chancel and began to polish the famous silver reliquary of St Ita of Dredgemarsh. For an instant, he glanced into the nave of the chapel and stopped polishing. He leaned forward and stared into the shadows.

'Oh,' he said, and turned as if to leave. He hesitated and then picked up one of the hymnals, turned again and quietly made his way to the nave. As he moved into the shadows, the slanting rays from the windows above illuminated a diminishing top half of him until he disappeared into the gloom.

'Young lady,' he said, and proffered the hymnal to Lucretia Beaufort, whose pale face glimmered in defiance of the dark shadows, where she sat still as a statue. She made no response. 'Young lady,' the monk stooped down towards her, still holding out the hymnal. She tilted her head upwards and looked at him but said nothing.

'The hymns for vespers; you might like ...' He placed the small leatherbound book into unresisting hands.

'God keep you safe,' he said, and withdrew.

When the monk and three of his brethren returned quietly and took their seats in the chancel, the light from the clerestory windows had diminished to a dull glow. Each monk carried a lighted candle which he placed in a candle-holder behind the chancel seats. The white-haired monk looked towards the nave. Lucretia was still seated exactly as he had left her. They began to chant.

> LUCIS Creator optime
> lucem dierum proferens,
>
> O BLEST Creator of the light,
> Who mak'st the day with radiance bright,

Lucretia Beaufort wept. She did not notice the cowled figure that silently moved from the rear of the chapel and sat beside her.

'Lucretia, my dear Lucretia.' Celeste moved the cowl back from her face. She reached out and took the hymnal from limp fingers, laid it aside and firmly grasped Lucretia's hands. 'Courage,' she said. 'Courage.' Lucretia turned towards her dearest and only friend. Her face was a mask of despair.

'Why?' She could barely articulate the word. Celeste shook her head and put her arm around Lucretia. The monks sang on.

> primordis lucis novae,
> mundi parans originem:

> and o'er the forming world didst call
> the light from chaos first of all:

'Lucretia, you have visitors,' Celeste whispered. Lucretia just stared at the small choir, now silhouetted against the lighted candles behind them. 'They are with your father now, the Chancellor and the Brooderstalt Captain.'

'What ... visitors ... is my father not well?'

'It is the Chancellor and Captain Pentrojan, the one you are betrothed to.'

'Oh no, I can't ... not now.'

'Your poor father looks so upset, Lucretia.'

****

'At last,' said Pentrojan, who was pacing up and down, when the door opened and Lucretia Beaufort stepped into the room followed by Celeste.

'Father?' Lucretia, without looking at either Pentrojan or Tancredi, moved to the side of her father's bed. Arnulf Beaufort would not look at his daughter.

'They,' he began. Tancredi cleared his throat noisily and Beaufort raised his eyes momentarily in the direction of the

Chancellor. 'We,' he said, 'wish the marriage to proceed straight away.'

'Father?' Lucretia said again.

'Your father is right,' Tancredi said, 'the marriage should proceed immediately. There is a certain anxiety amongst our people. The marriage will calm them, reassure them that all is well.' Albrecht Pentrojan had not taken his eyes off Lucretia from the moment she had entered the room. There was something primal in his fearsome attention, like a wolf stalking its prey. Lucretia turned and looked directly at him. The fierce concentration in his face faltered for a moment. He turned away from her hurt gaze and addressed Tancredi.

'The portrait you sent to me, Chancellor, does a grave injustice to this young beauty. The artist should have his eyes gouged out.' He stepped forward and took Lucretia's hand, tiny in his broad, hair-covered fist. 'I am honoured that you have pledged yourself to be my wife. Like the Chancellor, I would wish to proceed as soon as possible; in two days' time, after we have quelled our little uprising.'

'So soon?' It was Celeste who cried out and turned towards Arnulf Beaufort.

'Uprising, what uprising?' Lucretia addressed Tancredi. Pentrojan released her hand and it dropped listlessly to her side. A frown creased his swarthy features.

'No need for anyone to be alarmed,' said Tancredi. 'It would seem there has been sedition growing in our very midst for some time. We have flushed out the conspirators and they are being dealt with as we speak. I must insist that you stay here until the matter is dealt with. I have placed a curfew on all movement of civilians within the city. There is tight security around the infirmary. I trust this will not be an inconvenience.'

'Conspirators? Who are these conspirators you talk about?' said Arnulf Beaufort. Tancredi waved the question aside.

'There is no danger, the whole matter will be over by to-morrow. Then we can concentrate on happier events. In the meantime, no one can come or go from this infirmary. If there is any pressing matter, ask the guards to contact me. Captain, shall we?' He turned and gestured towards the door. Pentrojan moved to join Tancredi, but continued to look at Lucretia as he did so, lascivious eyes slowly inspecting her body from foot to head, lingering insolently on her breasts.

'I look forward to our union, madam.' The words sounded obscene on his lips.

The unwelcome guests departed, leaving the door ajar. Celeste strode across the room and slammed it shut. She turned back towards Lucretia, whose whole body seemed as if it was about to collapse in on itself. Her arms were spread wide before her, palms upwards in supplication, her face suffused with anguish.

'We are prisoners, nothing more than prisoners,' she cried.

'Courage, Lucretia, courage.' Celeste rushed forward and enclosed her young mistress in her arms. They both sank to their knees in the centre of the room, clinging to each other as if they were drowning.

'No, No! Enough. No more! No more!' Arnulf Beaufort flung back the blankets from his sick bed and painfully swung his legs onto the floor. He stood, trembling, his face ablaze with anger. The two distraught girls stared at him in incomprehension.

'No, no, this monster will not lay a finger on my daughter.

Forgive me, Lucretia; forgive this stupid, vain old man.'

'Father, oh father,' Lucretia scrambled to her feet and rushed to embrace him.

'What have I done?' Beaufort stroked her hair. 'What have I done?' He gently lifted his daughter's head from his shoulder and cupped her tear-stained face in his hands. 'Lucretia, we must leave here at once.'

'But sir,' Celeste said, 'you are unwell. 'There is a curfew and the infirmary is being guarded. They will let no one in or out.'

'Be damned with the curfew, girl. Go find Brother Eugene at once.'

Chapter 39

Clutchbolt's band of misfit insurgents tumbled into the Hall of Echoes and fought their pursuers inch by inch across that cavernous space of sound and granite. The noise was so all-engulfing that each and every man was swept along as if in a sea storm. Strewn all over the centre of the hall were the discarded wooden crates that once held Verm's candles.

'Grab as many crates as you can. Use them as shields and bring as many as you can with you,' Clutchbolt shouted the order repeatedly.

His men were scattered out all over that cauldron of sound but now, as they approached the opposite side of the hall, there was only one passage through which they could exit. They began to bunch around it. Then as quickly and as abruptly as they had burst into the great hall, Clutchbolt's crew were sucked out of it and into another black tunnel.

'Pile the crates here, here.' Clutchbolt flung the two crates he carried into the entrance of the tunnel. His men followed suit, and within seconds the entrance was blocked.

'Every inch you will buy with blood.' Clutchbolt was shouting at Pentrojan's warriors. He grabbed a torch from its sconce and flung it into the pile of crates. The fire took hold instantly and the Brooderstalt moved back from the conflagration.

But the flames would not deter them for long. They were doughty and relentless fighters; it was only a matter of time until the inferno subsided and the insurgents would crumble before their sustained onslaught and superior numbers. Clutchbolt shouted to his men.

'One more hour, men, that's all, give me one more hour.' But he thought with dread of what Verm had said to Havelock, about them killing the King. How could they know he is coming, he thought for the thousandth time. No, no, it's only the ranting of a madman. He consoled himself with this thought.

'We have almost done our part, just one more hour,' he shouted out once more. Then, under his breath, 'Quickstrain, our lives are in your hands.'

But at that very moment Quickstrain was in the hands of two of Pentrojan's soldiers.

'What does anyone want with me? Why don't you leave me alone, you scoundrels, I'm an old man.'

'Old man, even old women are dangerous in this shithole,' one of the soldiers spat on the ground. 'Hurry up.'

'Where are you taking me, at least answer me that?'

'Not far, you old goat, we're just going to tether you for a while to keep you out of mischief.'

'Look at me, you oafs, how could I make mischief? Let me go back to my laboratory, that's all I want to do, I will bother no one.'

'Shut up!' One of his captors punched Quickstrain in the back of the head, making him stagger. With a look of dismay, the old professor went with them.

'I'm sorry Clutchbolt, I'm so sorry,' he mumbled under his breath.

'Scuse me.' Quickstrain was as startled as his two guards to hear the voice suddenly behind them.

'Scuse me, where are you taking the professor?' Dipslick had stepped out defiantly from a narrow side passage.

'It's another one of these old bastards. You! Come here.'

'Fuck off, you pig's pizzle.'

'Hold this one. I'll get him.' The soldier moved quickly towards Dipslick, who turned and began to run as fast as a sober alcoholic of seventy-odd years could run.

'Come back, you old bugger or I'll ...' He never finished that sentence, because he ran straight into a kitchen cleaver that swung out of the shadows on the end of Leopold Ratchet's puny arm.

'I did it, I did it.' Ratchet jumped out from his hiding place and looked incredulously from the cleaver in his hand to the fallen soldier.

'I did it, I really did it.'

The second soldier guarding Quickstrain instantly charged towards the jubilant Ratchet, unsheathing his sword at the same time. He raised his arm to strike and paused because, to his amazement, Ratchet, in his excitement, turned towards him and, seemingly oblivious to the mortal danger he was in, said, 'Look, I did it. Me, Leopold Ratchet .' That moment's hesitation saved Ratchet's life. Surgeon Keenslide stepped from the shadows and plunged a short blade into the bemused soldier's jugular.

'Professor, are you all right?' Keenslide asked the astonished Quickstrain.

'Yes, yes. Keenslide that is the neatest bit of surgery I've seen in many a year. Ratchet, I never thought you had it in you, and Dips, you can run for an old buzzard. But what are you all doing here, you should be with Clutchbolt.'

'Clutchbolt thought you might need our help.' Keenslide chuckled.

'That man amazes me, how did he guess.'

'So we doubled back when we got the opportunity. Clutchbolt was still holding out when we left him. He'll make it to the Dredger Hall. I've never seen a man more determined. But Professor, I must admit, I am puzzled; what exactly can we do up here to help Clutchbolt and the others down there?' Keenslide pointed to the ground.

'Aha, physics, energy, water, timing.' Quickstrain winked at his bemused companions. 'Come, my friends, we must hurry, can't keep Clutchbolt waiting.'

The gang of four hurried away to the professor's laboratory on the top floor of the university building.

****

Clutchbolt, with a belligerent Bella Crumble, Nellie Lowslegg, Havelock the scribe and his remaining exhausted comrades had reached the Dredger Hall. Despite having lost about ten men, their hatred of those who had so brutally disrupted their lives sustained them and they fought on savagely.

'One last effort, men, hold the bastards. Crumble, Lowslegg, you too Havelock, move back.' The fighting was fiercer than ever. Both sides knew that this was the final on-slaught.

'There's no way out, the rats are trapped.' It was Proud-flax, who was now spurring his men on. 'Let's exterminate the vermin once and for all.'

He was right, there was no way out. They had reached the eastern perimeter wall of Dredgemarsh. There were only three openings in the hall; the narrow corridor through which they had just entered, and two shallow canal ports in the end wall, through which the chain of dredger punts de-signed by Quickstrain entered and exited to the boglands beyond. These openings were just big enough for the pas-sage of the punts, which were locked close together in a daisy chain and looped around a great rusting conglomera-tion of wheels, spigots and gears that stood sombrely like a great organ in the centre of the hall. This tower of ma-chinery, although not operating just then, creaked and groaned ceaselessly, as it had done since the time it was built, and even more so now as the fighters scrambled like ants through its intricate works, hacking and hewing at each other in desperation.

'There is no way out,' Bella Crumble shouted to Clutch-bolt.

'No way out,' echoed Miss Lowslegg.

'We can't go through there.' She was pointing at the wall ports for the dredger, which were snugly sealed off by the punts themselves, leaving a gap barely big enough for a mouse to pass.

'Oh, yes, we can, Mistress Crumble, now come with me,' and Clutchbolt dodged and weaved through the maelstrom of fighting men with Bella Crumble and her shadow Miss

Lowslegg trotting behind.

'Here it is, here it is.' Clutchbolt approached a massive turf drying furnace.

'Now Mistress Crumble, hold this furnace door open and watch my back.'

'Cook Meister Clutchbolt, you're not going to get in ...'

'Just hold the poxy door, Crumble.'

'Well of all the ...'

'Do it Mistress Crumble, please ... please.'

'Well, that's better.'

Clutchbolt removed a bugle from inside his leather jacket, inflated his lungs, placed the bugle to his lips and stuck his head inside the furnace door. Bella Crumble looked on, totally bewildered, and did not notice the soldier rushing towards them. It was Proudflax who, on reaching them, sank his boot into Clutchbolt's well-padded gut. The bugle sounded a strangled little BEEP rather than a full-throated blast, which Clutchbolt had intended. Clutchbolt, minus bugle leaped backward banging his head on the furnace door. He turned to parry a swiping sword blow from Proudflax and at the same time shouted to Bella Crumble.

'Crumble, the bugle ... get it ... and blow for all your worth into the furnace.'

He parried another blow and leaped in to grapple with Proudflax at close quarters.

'Quickstrain will hear ... he's waiting ... it's our last chance.'

'Where is it, where is the bugle?'

'In the furnace.'

Proudflax immediately moved to prevent Bella Crumble from retrieving the bugle. Clutchbolt grappled with him and they both fell to the floor locked together.

'Quick, Crumble, quick.'

'It's not here, I can't find it!'

Clutchbolt had risen on one knee, Proudflax had rolled clear of him.

'Here, here, we have them.' Proudflax shouted to a group of his soldiers, who turned and began to run towards Clutchbolt and Crumble.

'If this is the end, then by the Gods we won't go easy. A pox on Tancredi, a pox on you Brooderstalt curs. Come on.' Clutchbolt shouted as he gathered himself, determined to shed as much enemy blood as possible before inevitable defeat. Proudflax had also regained his feet but was now looking incredulously past the defiant Clutchbolt at Bella Crumble. Clutchbolt looked back over his shoulder to see what was happening.

'What the ...' Mistress Crumble's chest was expanding. Her shoulders were cast back and she was sucking air into her lungs with a ferocious determination. The strings holding her ill-fitting breastplates began to snap, one by one. Her great bosoms leaped from their encasement and trembled like a pair of volcanoes. The onrushing soldiers skidded to a halt and gazed dumbfounded at the unforgettable spectacle of Crumble's unleashed mammaries. Then she plunged her head into the furnace opening and screamed. No one ever heard such a scream before or since. All fighting ceased in the Dredger Hall, dying men stopped moaning and the gargantuan mechanical monstrosity that had been creaking since it was first built, was silent. Those close to Bella Crumble clamped their hands over their ears. Her scream, which later became famous in the annals of Dredgemarsh, spiralled its way up through the flue of the furnace, gathering and increasing in intensity before exploding into the upper air of the ancient fortress. A raven that had idled the years away on this remote chimney stack, dropped dead with fright when the scream gushed forth, and he fell unnoticed into the decaying rubble of rooftops in that long-forgotten region. The scream unleashed, spread throughout the city, in through doors and windows, crockery cracked and glass shattered, and the scream wound its way around towers and belfries, and onto the small veranda off Quickstrain's laboratory, where he was waiting impatiently for a bugle call.

'That must be it, strangest bugle I've ever heard, but that must be it. Do it now!' he shouted to his companions. Keenslide hauled on a long brass lever, and the grinding of gears engaging with the great anemometer spindle could be felt below their feet in the laboratory machine room. Immediately after this, a dull shuddering sound could be heard as the complex layers of drive shafts and interlocking wheels reached down into the depths of the castle, and opened the sluice gates that would release the water to drive the Dredger.

Before Bella Crumble's famous scream died, the Dredger Hall began to crank into life. Those just recovering from the spectacle of Crumble's bosoms and the head-splitting scream, spun round on hearing the thunderous grinding and screeching of the Dredger engine. It swayed and moaned dreadfully.

'Crumble, you've done it. Now quick, this way, Lowslegg quick.'

'What have I done, Cook Meister?'

'Never mind, just follow me.'

Clutchbolt began to zigzag back across the hall, stopping at each of his own men and shouting instructions into their ears.

'Now pass the word, quickly.' In the mind-numbing clamour, the remainder of Clutchbolt's bloodied crew had managed to move back from their defensive positions without any great response from Pentrojan's soldiers, who were confident at this stage that the day was won. Clutchbolt and his little group began to move cautiously backwards towards the punts, which were now beginning to move. Lieutenant Proudflax and his troop of soldiers, who had increased all the while as more and more of them entered into the hall, now stood in the centre and waited, somewhat amused and curious, for Clutchbolt's next move.

'Lieutenant, quick, they're going to escape in the punts.'

'Hold on, young man, look over there.' Proudflax pointed to where the punts made their exit from the Dredger Hall. When he saw what was being pointed out, the young man laughed and one by one, all of the soldier's began to point and laugh derisively. The cause of their merriment was the observation that as each punt approached the exit, an ingeniously designed cam spun the punt completely upside down and righted it once more just before exiting. This was a special security feature invented by Professor Quickstrain.

'I think they have outsmarted themselves, men. Let's sit back and enjoy the spectacle.'

Clutchbolt was now directing his men into the punts, to the enormous amusement of the Brooderstalt.

'Cook Meister they are not attacking any more. They're just laughing ... Oh no, look, the punts, they're turning upside down.'

'Never mind, Lowslegg. Men! Don't worry; just get into the punts with the X chalked on them. And keep your heads down.' He spoke just loud enough for his own little cluster of fighters to hear. It did not take long until all of the small crew was aboard the punts marked with an X and moving slowly towards the exit. As the first punt containing four of Clutchbolt's men approached the point where all previous punts had turned upside down, Proudflax and his men held their breaths and leaned forward in anticipation. Nothing happened. The punt just disappeared through the exit without capsizing. Then the next and the next passed through without incident.

"Shit, we've been tricked. After them, follow them. Into the punts, quickly, quickly.' Proudflax was screaming orders. His men dashed down and scrambled into the moving chain of punts. Clutchbolt, who was the last to exit the hall, waved cheerfully to Proudflax, ducked his head and vanished.

'Bastard, bastard, we'll get you yet. What are you waiting for? All of you, get down there and ... wait, wait, come back ... idiots ...look, they're turning upside down again. What the ... get those men out of there. Come back ... no ... sound the retreat, someone.' The consternation and panic quickly spread to all the men and they scrambled back to the centre of the hall and waited fearfully for Lieutenant Proudflax to tell them what to do.

Far above their heads in the university laboratory, Keenslide, on instructions from Quickstrain, who was counting out the seconds on a water clock, reversed the brass lever into its initial resting place and within seconds, the Dredger machinery squealed to a halt and an eerie silence filled the Dredger Hall. Proudflax and his soldiers were as startled and alarmed at this sudden quietness as they were with the initial thunderous start-up of the rusting monstrosity. But the cessation of the hellish noise was a relief, and Proudflax began to collect his thoughts and assess the situation in a cool, professional manner, which was his normal disposition. He addressed his disheartened troops.

'They think they are clever, but they have abandoned their own castle. There is nothing but swamp beyond these walls. We have won the day. I will leave enough of you here to deal with them should they attempt to re-enter, though I doubt it, and the rest of you, come with me.'

'Lieutenant, what's that noise?'

'What noise?' The soldiers, who were beginning to relax and chat instantly stopped talking and listened. A deep rumbling, almost a vibration rather than a sound, came from somewhere far below them. They were frightened and began to look nervously from one to the other.

'Blast this stinking cesspit. Come on everyone, let's get out of here quick.' Proudflax led them towards the corridor through which they had entered the Dredger Hall. But the sound and vibrations began to increase in intensity and as it did they began to run until eventually they were dashing in disarray towards the corridor, disregarding Proudflax's shouts for order.

As the first man reached the entrance, a roaring torrent of water, muck, and debris spewed from the entrance and sent him and several others sprawling back across the Dredger Hall floor. The rest ran back immediately to the centre and watched with mounting consternation as the geyser of water increased in intensity and the hall began to flood rapidly.

****

The author of this internal river was Quickstrain. Having shut down the Dredger, he then set up a pre-planned pattern on a bristling array of levers that controlled the flow and concourse of Dredgemarsh's subterranean canals.

'I have never tried this before,' said Quickstrain, 'but if my calculations are right, Pentrojan's army will be swimming in forty feet of water very shortly.'

'But what about Clutchbolt and the others?' Keenslide asked.

Quickstrain tapped the side of his nose, winked and said, 'We'll see, but now let us go up to the Dome parapet. We can see the main gate from there. It should be open and our pennant flying if that old windbag Gastsack has woken up today.'

'Gastsack, does the old bugger know what century we're in? ' said Dipslick.

'Spline the philosopher is with him.'

'Wonderful, he'll talk the gate open.'

'Flingthrift is also helping.'

'Flingthrift?'

'Yes, you know, the treasurer.'

'Oh him, tight bollix. He'll charge the King to come in.'

'They're all we've got, Dipslick, now let's go.'

When they arrived on the parapet they could see that the gate was not yet open, but more alarming still, a very large contingent of Pentrojan's soldiers were gathered in the Four Towers square.

'Damn it, he's only sent half his troops below after Clutchbolt. This looks bad.' The three old men watched with mounting despair as the soldiers moved from the centre of the square and into the line of stables that ran north and east from the Blue Tower.

'They know,' said Quickstrain. 'They are waiting for the King. It's an ambush.'

'We must do something,' said Keenslide.

'What?'

'We can't just stand here. We'll try to get to the main gate.'

'Too late, look.' Quickstrain pointed into the far distance beyond the castle walls. They could just discern a tiny column of horsemen moving at speed across the Vildpline and towards Dredgemarsh.

'It's the King, it must be.'

'We've got to do something, we've still got to try. Come on, hurry.' Keenslide led his three old companions from the parapet.

Dredgemarsh

Chapter 40

When he caught the first glimpse of Dredgemarsh, Cesare was astonished at the ache that suffused his whole body. He gazed at the castle in the far distance and felt the pain of guilt and remorse and with that pain, there was a longing so powerful that he trembled with the intensity of it. Never again will your King desert you, never again, he said to himself and surreptitiously wiped a tear from his eye.

'Sire!' It was Jerome, who had moved quietly to the King's side and spoke softly, 'Do not grieve for what is past. Before the sun sets over Grak's Forest, you will be home. Dredge-marsh will have its King once more.'

Cesare reached out and patted Jerome on the forearm.

'Yes, indeed, my dear friend, you are right. It is time for action, not tears. Tomorrow we will celebrate. Lead on,

Grunkite! Lead on.'

'Yes, yes, Sire.' Grunkite was aglow with happiness. It was clear to all that the old man could hardly believe that he, at this stage of his life, was leading his King and the knights of Anselem into battle. This was the crowning honour for all his years of labour and dedication. He showed not a moment's hesitation or anxiety at the approaching conflict. Sitting proudly in the saddle he spurred his mount into a brisk canter. There was a smile of sheer joy on his face. Like the hawk that was emblazoned on their pennants and sashes, the knights of Anselem swooped down on Dredgemarsh.

They were less than half a league from the castle when they heard Bella Crumble's scream.

'What is it?' Cesare reined his horse to a standstill.

'I don't know, Sire. I've never heard anything like it,' Grunkite shouted over his shoulder as he struggled to haul his cob to a halt. The scream began to fill the whole valley until it seemed that every living creature, on hearing it, had ceased all activity. The knights sat motionless, frozen like chess pieces, listening. Cesare, despite his logical mind, could not dispel the idea that it was the castle itself which was crying out to him.

'Jerome?'

'Sire?'

'What do you think it is?'

'I have not heard its like before, Sire.'

'It sounds almost human.'

'It is coming from the castle.'

'Yes! From the castle. Pray, Jerome, that we are not too late. On, on Grunkite, we must not delay further.' As the eerie wail died away, Grunkite and the knights spurred their mounts forward into a fast canter.

In Dredgemarsh itself there were others, apart from Professor Quickstrain and his comrades, who had heard Bella Crumble's scream. In a small cramped fuel shed, where they were hiding, Colonel Gastsack, with moustache bristling, stood shaking his head in disapproval at Flingthrift.

'But Colonel Gastsack, what else could it be? It must be the signal, it must.' Flingthrift said.

'Damn disgraceful horn blast. Worst I've heard in my whole military career.'

'What does it matter, so long as we know it's the signal?'

'Of course it matters. Every last detail ... stand up straight, soldier ... must be correct.'

'Yes, I know, but ... but ... Spline, please talk to the colonel.'

'The stones have spoken,' Spline said.

'What? What does that mean? Colonel Gastsack! Spline! Listen, please listen; we are supposed to open the gate when we hear the signal. If we don't, then Clutchbolt's plan will not work.'

'Clutchbolt, what does he know about military affairs? Give me a thousand good men and I'll sort the whole thing out.' Gastsack twirled the end of his left moustache.

'We don't have a thousand good men or even indifferent men. General! King Cesare will be arriving shortly. The gate must be open.'

'The King's coming?'

'Yes, yes, don't you remember? The gate must be open for the King. That's the plan, we've gone over it a thousand times.'

'Damn it, soldier, you're wasting our time prattling. To the gate at once, the trumpet has sounded.'

'But you just said ... oh, forget it.'

'Stop talking in the ranks. Company forward.' Gastsack, with shoulders thrown back, marched out of the fuel shed and set out for Grak's Gate.

'Colonel! Come back! You can't just walk out in the open like this. We'll be seen. It's better if we sneak around to the back of the guardhouse.

'Sneak, sneak, you snivelling cur. Gastsacks never sneak. No, by thunder, we'll march and attack the enemy. There's only one way for a soldier, now shape up and move out. You too, Spline.' The colonel unsheathed his sword, held it erect just inches from the tip of his nose and marched forward onto the open square heading for the main gate.

'Spline, do something, he'll get us all killed.'

'The fool is hero.'

'What, what are you talking about? You're worse than him.' Flingthrift pressed his palms to his temples and squeezed his eyes shut as if in pain.

'I'm only a simple bookkeeper; what am I doing with these madmen?' he muttered. At this point, Gastsack was proudly stepping along in the open square, a one-man military parade. Flingthrift began to follow, dodging in and out of doorways on his spidery legs, all the while trying to coax the colonel to come off the centre of the thoroughfare, but the old man would have none of it.

'You stubborn old bastard, they'll see us. What will we do then?' Flingthrift hissed from the cloistered pathway that ran along the stable fronts.

'Of course they'll see us. All part of the plan. These scoundrels will turn tail when faced by real soldiers. Now tighten up, stay close and follow me, lads.' They continued on their way, Gastsack out in the open, Flingthrift slinking along the shaded path in parallel. Spline the philosopher was strolling casually behind Gastsack, apparently engaged in some deep personal reflections.

They were seen, of course. Captain Pentrojan, as he delivered his final instructions to one group of hidden soldiers, was at the same time watching Gastsack's progress. At least five of the stables, below the Blue Tower where Cesare had so recently lain wounded and close to death, were packed with Pentrojan's men.

'No matter what, you wait for my signal. Taste blood with every arrow and bolt, and remember the King is mine. And not a sound until then.' Pentrojan had addressed all his troops from the square just moments before Gastsack came into view. They had quietly slipped into the stable where he, Pentrojan and Tancredi had plotted the ambush, and where unknown to them, Verm had heard every word. Tancredi was there, expectant, excited.

'Quiet.' Pentrojan turned to peek through the stable shutters. Tancredi joined him.

'How many?'

'Just two.'

'They have come to open the gate no doubt, the traitors.'

'Here they are now ... what is that?'

'Gastsack, the old windbag, I don't believe it.'

'And look what's coming behind him.'

'Spline the philosopher?'

'This is quite a castle you have here, Chancellor. Lucky for those crazy old fools that my men at the gate know what to do.'

'Psst, psst.' It was Flingthrift, who was now crouched right outside the shuttered window, only inches from Pentrojan and Tancredi.

'Psst, Gastsack, you deaf old whore monger.'

'What is it, man?' Gastsack stopped for a moment and turned towards Flingthrift. 'Speak up; what are you whispering for?.'

'There, down there, at the gate, four soldiers, they'll slaughter us.'

'Nonsense, man. Pull yourself together.'

'Stop shouting, Gastsack.'

'When I give the order, charge in close formation.'

'Oh bollix.'

'Are we ready, extend arms ... CHAAAAAARGE!!!!!'

'We're finished, it's all over.' Flingthrift sank to his knees and watched Gastsack, who had now broken into a gallop. The old man was surprisingly fast for his age. His buckles, medals, braid and chains were flapping up and down, and creating a heinous racket as he bore down upon the guards at the gate. They, on hearing and subsequently seeing the charging Gastsack, were quite happy and relieved to follow their earlier briefing from Pentrojan, so they threw down their weapons and ran away.

'He's done it. The mad old bugger has done it. Gastsack, you've done it. I don't believe it. Spline! Look, the guards have run away, the cowards, they've run away.' Flingthrift was now racing after Gastsack. When he finally caught up with him, Gastsack was standing proudly by the gate winch.

'You did it, Gastsack.'

'Of course, can't beat the old school. Now open the gate, lad.'

'Yes, sir! Colonel!'

Cesare and his troops were now only half a league from the castle. They had stopped and were looking anxiously towards Grak's Gate.

'Look, look, the gate is opening.' Grunkite was excited.

'Yes, but that is still a Brooderstalt flag over it.'

'What matter, Sire?'

'Patience, Grunkite, we cannot jeopardise these men or our friends inside by too hasty an action. We will wait.'

Inside, Gastsack was still barking out the orders.

'Spline, raise the flag.'

'What flag.'

'The flag, the Dredgemarsh flag.'

'All flags are equal.'

'Shit, he didn't bring the flag.' Flingthrift panted after his efforts on the gate winch.

'I'll have you court-martialled sir. Dereliction of duty, stupidity in the face of the enemy.' Gastsack bellowed at Spline.

'I've got it, I've got It.' shouted Flingthrift, who jumped on Spline and began to haul the philosopher's ankle-length shirt off his back. 'His shirt, it's the right colour ... got the hawk on it as well ... stay quiet, Spline.'

'Well done, lad. You'll be decorated for this, and you, Spline,' the colonel addressed the now naked philosopher, 'you're a disgrace to the army, into the guardhouse immediately and straighten yourself up, man.'

Outside, Grunkite was growing more and more impatient.

'Something has gone wrong, we will have to do ... wait, it's happening.'

Cesare watched Pentrojan's flag being lowered.

'As soon as we see our flag, we go in,' Cesare said. Grunkite, Jerome and the knights made last-minute adjustments and poised themselves for battle. Moments later Spline's shirt was being hoisted over the gate.

'What's that?' Grunkite gave voice to the thought that was in everyone's head.

'It's our colours, that's enough. For Dredgemarsh! For

The Kingdom! Forward!' Cesare lowered the visor on his helmet and led them out at a walk, then a canter, and finally full gallop towards the open castle gate. The only thing that distinguished Cesare was the black ribbon tied around his left arm.

'Listen,' Pentrojan beckoned for complete silence, 'they are coming. Your troubles are over, Chancellor.' Tancredi smiled and rubbed his hands in satisfaction.

It was obvious that the soldiers in all of the other stables had heard the distant thunder of Cesare's knights. A hush settled over them and they waited for the quarry to enter the trap.

'Gastsack, Gastsack, close the gate, it's a trap, close the gate.' The voice was that of Keenslide, who came running along the square where Gastsack had just recently marched. Dipslick and Quickstrain were close on Keenslide's heels and gasping for breath. Neither Gastsack nor Flingthrift could hear the desperate cries of Keenslide.

'You three come with me.' Pentrojan flung the door of the stable open and dashed out. Within seconds, he had grabbed the exhausted surgeon and began to drag him into the stable. Dipslick and Quickstrain were easily overcome and hauled in after Keenslide.

'Well, well, well, what heroes have we got here?' Tancredi sneered at the three bedraggled old men. 'You should not have meddled in this affair, you old fools.'

'Shit bag. Traitor!' Dipslick had just recovered enough breath to hurl the insult.

'Oho, our scribe can talk after all. Gag them all, but let them watch. They might learn something, despite their age. Listen, listen you old fools, can you hear? Your brave stupid King is coming to rescue you.' Pentrojan sneered.

The thunder of Cesare's knights was growing distinctly louder, and old Colonel Gastsack was now standing on the castle wall above the gate waving to the approaching knights.

'It's Gastsack, Sire,' Grunkite shouted, 'the castle is ours. Well done, Gastsack.'

'They're ours,' said Pentrojan when he heard the clatter of the horses' hooves on the cobbles of the Grand Plaza.

'They are in the net.' Fifty crossbows were cocked and ready for the slaughter.

'At last,' said Tancredi, and a tiny tremor of delight ran through his body.

'What's that?' said one of the archers, looking towards the ceiling of the stables, on hearing a dull thud followed by another, and then another and another.

'Forget it. Quiet! Any minute now. Archers! Ready.' Pentrojan had opened the stable door slightly to watch the approaching horsemen. Another thud hit the roof and a roaring sound began to grow in volume above their heads.

'What is it?' A nervous soldier whispered. 'It's surrounding us. Listen, it's coming from the walls now. Look! Look!' They all turned to see a dense black smoke pouring into the stable, through every crack and crevice in the surrounding walls.

'Fire! Fire!' shouted the soldier. Within seconds, the stable was filled with smoke, and the roar of the fire that had enveloped them drowned out their screams of confusion.

Cesare, Grunkite and Jerome stormed through the castle gate and rode into the centre of the square. An amazing spectacle was unfolding before them. Pentrojan and all his archers were tumbling out of the stables. They were blinded by acrid smoke and as a result were crashing and barging into each other, cursing and swearing. Many were on their knees and bent double coughing and gulping for air. Practically all of the stables on the west and south wings of the square were in flames.

'Look! There!' Cesare and his knights had reined in their mounts. He pointed to where a continuous stream of lighted torches was being thrown from the upper window of the Blue Tower overlooking the stables. Every now and then there was a brief cessation in the flow and a head leaned out from the window to check the handiwork, gave a whoop of delight, disappeared once more and the stream of lighted torches recommenced.

'I think it's that maniac of a Candle Lighter Sire,' shouted Grunkite.

'Let us finish his handiwork.' Cesare drew his broadsword and spurred his horse forward, into the smoke and flames. The Brooderstalt soldiers heard the thunder of hooves approaching and turned to face whatever danger approached. A knight in strange armour, with a black ribbon on his raised sword arm, loomed out of the swirling smoke.

'Hold firm.' A Brooderstalt officer screamed. A thick cloud of smoke engulfed the knight momentarily, and then dissipated to reveal, not only the black ribboned knight, but behind him, a solid phalanx of knights in similar armour, and maroon surcoats emblazoned with a golden hawk.

'Hold firm. Hold firm.' The command somehow lacked conviction and, battled hardened as they were, the Brooderstalt arbalesters fired their weapons without waiting for the order and retreated back behind a ragged line of spearmen.

'Cowards!' A Brooderstalt officer struck down one of the retreating arbalesters.

The oncoming knights sliced through the Brooderstalt, whose spears shattered or bounced harmlessly off the heavy poitrels protecting the horses' chests. Pentrojan and Tancredi looked on grimly as their men were hewn down by the strange knights. Along with a few arbalesters, they retreated with their horses in tow into the nearest farrier's yard and watched as the knights turned in tight formation, time and time again, their swords and war hammers soaked in Brooderstalt gore.

'It is over. You will not be King this day, Chancellor,' Pentrojan shouted, 'flee for your life.'

Tancredi and Pentrojan mounted their horses, and moments later they both galloped out of the farrier's yard and turned towards Grak's Gate. They were more than halfway to the gate when they were spotted.

'Tancredi is escaping,' Dipslick emerged from the fray, shouting to anyone who would listen.

'Where, where is he?'

Grunkite came pounding out of the smoke in answer.

'There, there he is, heading for the gate.'

'Grak's guts, the baud's dungworm crawls away.' Grunkite spurred his foaming cob in pursuit but there was little hope of catching the escapees. They had fresh mounts, and his poor animal had just endured the long trek from Anselem and the battle that still raged behind him. The fleeing pair were approaching the gate when old Gastsack ran out to block their escape.

'Out of the way, you old idiot!' shouted Pentrojan, but Gastsack would not give ground and began to flail around with his sword. Pentrojan slowed his mount to a controlled trot, drew his sword and advanced on the old man. Tancredi did likewise and drew up beside Pentrojan. Gastsack began to back away but still blocked their path. They both struck out at the same time. The old warrior sank to his knees, blood bubbling up through his gorget, where Pentrojan's broadsword had pierced the antique chainmail.

'Meddlesome old fool.' Tancredi spat on the inert but still kneeling figure of Gastsack.

'Bastards!' Grunkite groaned, but he was still much to far away to be of concern to the escapees, who were now galloping once more towards the half-open main gate.

'Try me, Tancredi!' a voice rang out, and a mud-spattered Clutchbolt appeared at the entrance of the gate, his war axe raised and ready to strike. He was joined immediately by his band of gallant insurgents who had so recently fought by his side in the heroic battle of the Dredger Hall. They spread out across the entrance, a solid wall of torn and tattered men bristling with spears and swords.

Amongst the ragged group, Bella Crumble, like a muddy Boadicea, heaving breasts barely covered by rough sacking, bellowed out, 'You despicable curs.'

The startled mounts of the would-be escapees reared and bridled away from the muddy creatures that had so suddenly appeared as if from nowhere. Tancredi wheeled his horse around. A mixture of fear and loathing contorted his features when he beheld his hated enemy, Grunkite, pounding towards him on his great cob.

'This way, this way,' Tancredi shouted to Pentrojan, and the pair turned right and spurred their mounts frantically towards the eastern side of the grand plaza.

'The Sky Road, the Sky Road ... they are headed for the postern gate ... cut them off, cut them off.' Clutchbolt was shouting and waving his axe. Grunkite desperately hauled his cob to the right to cut off Tancredi's escape, but the great ponderous animal's forward momentum allowed only a wide swerving change in direction rather than a quick turn. Tancredi and Pentrojan raced past the approaching Grunkite. There was no one to stop them now and as they vanished through the ornate archway that opened onto the Sky Road, Grunkite cried out, 'Villians, damned villains.' He reined in his cob to a slow walk and patted the exhausted animal's neck.

'You did your best, your very best,' he said, looking back ruefully to where the main battle appeared to be reaching its conclusion, and saw an Anselem knight riding rapidly towards him. As the knight drew closer, Grunkite saw the black ribbon on this left arm.

'Sire,' he called out. 'Tancredi ... the Sky road ... he is making for the postern ... couldn't stop him.' After a moment's hesitation Cesare, his visor still down, spurred his mount towards the main gate and shouted over his shoulder, 'You take the Sky road.'

Dredgemarsh

Chapter 41

L ucretia was greatly alarmed by the laboured breathing of her father. 'Brother Eugene,' she called out, 'where are we? My father needs to rest.'

'It's not much further. We will emerge in the Mendicant's chapel next to the postern gate. But we must hurry, this torch will not last if we delay.'

'Keep going, keep going.' Beaufort gasped.

The small party of the monk, Lucretia, her father and Celeste, all wearing monk's habits, shuffled in single file through a corbelled passageway just wide enough for the passage of one man. The insipid light from brother Eugene's torch barely penetrated more than a few feet into the inky blackness ahead of them.

'At last. Hold the torch.' Eugene handed the torch back to Lucretia. 'Higher, hold it higher.' Lucretia raised it above head-height. Then the sound of a bolt, a heavy bolt, being drawn was followed by the grinding of long-unused hinges.

'Stay close.' Eugene turned and took the torch once more. In an instant, he disappeared and the impenetrable blackness enveloped Lucretia, Beaufort and Celeste. Celeste cried out, 'Where are we?'

'Don't panic.' The torch reappeared from the side of the passageway. 'We're almost there. Follow close,' said Eugene.

'Your hand, father.' Lucretia reached behind her and grasped her father's hand. He, in turn, reached back for Celeste's hand. They followed Eugene through the doorway and began to climb a spiral stairs. Just when Beaufort seemed on the point of collapse, Eugene handed the torch once more to Lucretia. Another door was opened. But, this time, the silhouette of Eugene was just discernible against a grey glimmer that framed the doorway through which he passed.

Supported on both sides by Lucretia and Celeste, Arnulf Beaufort staggered into a tiny circular chapel and collapsed into a wooden seat set into an alcove. His face had turned ashen and he struggled to catch his breath. Eugene, stepped back inside the passageway from whence they had come, jammed the almost extinguished torch in a sconce by the doorway and returned to the chapel, closing the door behind him. He looked anxiously at Beaufort.

'You may rest for a short while, but the sooner we can get you all outside the castle walls and hide you, the better.'

'Can we not stay here 'til nightfall?' said Lucretia.

'No. Once they discover you're gone, they will triple the guards on this gate and no one will be allowed in or out, not even monks.'

Light trickled into the chapel through three small lancet

windows set at least ten foot above the floor. One window was opposite the door through which they entered the chapel, the other two windows provided views ninety degrees left and right of this window. Several steps led up to a small stone walkway that ran partially around the inner perimeter of the chapel wall and allowed an observer to look through the narrow openings. Brother Eugene stepped up unto the walkway and peered carefully out of each window in turn.

'Good, good,' he said and turned back to his charges. 'There is only one guard on duty. We should go now.'

'My father is still too weak –'

'No, Lucretia, I'm fine ... there is no time to lose.' Beaufort staggered slightly as he rose to his feet but still brushed aside Lucretia's proffered help. 'Lead on, Brother Eugene.'

It took the monk some time and effort to draw the heavy metal bolt of an almost invisible squat door buried in the thick wall of the chapel. The four emerged onto the cobbled garth of the postern gate.

'Prop your father up, both of you, as if he is seriously ill. Pull your capuchons well forward.' Brother Eugene's tone brooked no argument. Lucretia and Celeste immediately stepped in to support Beaufort. They made their way slowly across the cobbled garth. A lone guard was sprawled on a bench outside a sentry box to the right of the postern gate. The remains of a loaf and an overturned mazer with a small puddle of wine lay at his feet. His head was drooped forward and even though they were twenty yards away from him, they could hear him snore.

'It's closed, the gate is closed, it's closed.' There was raw fear in Celeste's voice.

'Quiet, quiet, our sick brother must be removed from this city at once.' Brother Eugene commanded in an over-loud voice. Immediately the recumbent guard shook himself awake and scrambled to his feet.

'Who goes there?'

'Friend,' Brother Eugene called out, pulling back his capuchon and striding towards the startled guard. Lucretia and Celeste stood transfixed and watched as Brother Eugene engaged the guard in earnest conversation. The look of puzzlement on the guard's face began to change to one of panic and he backed away from Brother Eugene.

'Go, go,' the guard gesticulated towards the closed postern gate. He ran to the gate winch and began to rapidly crank the handle.

'Quickly now,' Eugene said to Celeste and Lucretia and the four entered the dark tunnel in the castle wall and waited for the iron postern to slide open.

'How did you do that?' Celeste whispered to Eugene.

'A hint of plague works miracles,' Eugene chuckled.

As they moved out onto the promenade of the castle they stopped for a moment, but, if they felt a sense of relief, it was quickly banished by the sound of galloping hooves and loud shouting,

'Keep the gate open, imbecile.' The thunder of the hooves magnified to a deafening level as the horses galloped through the tunnel of the postern gate. Two riders burst forth onto the promenade.

'Father!' Lucretia screamed involuntarily when the lead horse barged past within inches of them and Beaufort fell to the ground. She rushed to her father's aid. The capuchon fell back from her head, releasing her shimmering tresses. Both riders slowed their mounts and looked back. The lead rider,

Captain Pentrojan, tugged viciously at the reins of his mount and turned back to where Lucretia was helping Beaufort to his feet.

'I'll not leave totally empty handed.' He leaned down as he rode back past the distracted Lucretia, who was turned away from him, and swept her off her feet with one arm. He threw her across his horse's withers. Beaufort, who was now standing, had seen the approaching rider and, despite his infirmity, threw himself forward and grabbed the horse's reins. The terrified horse began to spin round in circles. Beaufort hung on doggedly.

Pentrojan, who was holding the struggling Lucretia with one arm and the reins with the other, bellowed at Tancredi.

'Cut this leech down, now, now.'

Tancredi hesitated for a moment and seemed torn between flight and helping Pentrojan.

'Curse you Tancredi, get back here if you wish to live another hour,' Pentrojan shouted. Tancredi drew his sword, rode back and as Beaufort swung past him, still gripping the reins of Pentrojan's horse, he delivered a deadly stroke to the back of the old man's neck. Beaufort fell instantly to the ground. After some considerable struggle, Pentrojan managed to calm his mount.

'Now, let us depart this cursed place,' Pentrojan said. Lucretia still lay face downwards across the horse's withers, clamped there by the powerful pressure of Pentrojan's forearm.

The two fugitives moved off the promenade and gingerly made their way down the castle glacis through a small copse that opened unto the great plain of the Vildpline. As they emerged from the copse, a lone knight with a black armband faced them. He held his broadsword casually by his side and spurred his foam-flecked mount towards them. Tancredi tried to veer off to one side, but he was not fast enough, and leaned away from the arc of the knight's sword, while at the same time raising his own sword to deflect the blow. The speed and impact of the strike toppled him from his mount and he crashed to the ground. His horse bolted. Tancredi scrambled to his feet and began to run along the bottom of the glacis towards the eastern boundary of the Vildpline, Meregloom Gorge. The knight glanced briefly at the fleeing Chancellor; then turned and began to advance on Pentrojan. The Brooderlunder grasped Lucretia by the nape of the neck and flung her to the ground. He drew his sword.

'Come, knight, and taste Brooderlund steel.' He spurred his horse forward.

Lucretia had risen to her feet and began to scramble back up the glacis towards the castle promenade, heedless of the clash of arms behind her as the two combatants engaged.

'Father, father,' she cried. When she reached the promenade, Brother Eugene was kneeling in prayer beside her prostrate father. A dark pool of blood surrounded her father's head. The bloody halo was spreading and already was soaking the hems of Eugene's robes. Celeste sat on the ground to one side, her head bowed, shoulders hunched, as if her body was imploding. She stared at the inert body, a look of incomprehension on her face. Lucretia raced to her father's side. She knelt in his blood and lifted his head onto her lap. He looked strangely tranquil.

'Dearest father,' she whispered and tenderly kissed his pale cheek. She raised her lustrous eyes, now brimming with tears, to the sky and cried out, 'Don't leave me, father.' She did not notice the small crowd that was assembling around her. Clutchbolt and his followers had taken their cue from the knight with the black armband and had run as fast as they could back along the promenade of the castle, with the intention of heading off the escapees at the postern gates. Too late, they realised, as they gathered around the bloody tableaux of the distraught Lucretia, Celeste, Eugene and the slain Arnulf Beaufort.

'Where are they, the curs, where are they?' Clutchbolt called out to no one in particular. At that moment, the crowd's attention was diverted to the re-appearance of the knight with the black armband. He was still mounted and driving before him, on foot, a shocked Pentrojan.

'Take him,' the knight called out to Clutchbolt.

'And the other one, the traitor Tancredi. Where is he?' Clutchbolt enquired.

'He is on foot. Heading towards Meregloom.'

At that moment, Grunkite emerged from the portal gate on his great foaming cob.

'Just in time,' Clutchbolt shouted, 'come, Grunkite, we have a snake of a Chancellor to catch.' He pushed the now bedraggled Pentrojan onto his knees.

'Mind this one,' he said to his muddy companions, and ran off towards Meregloom. Grunkite rumbled along behind him on the cob, but not before shouting to the small gathering, 'Watch her, she has questions to answer.' He pointed to Lucretia, who was seated on the ground, nursing her father's head in her lap.

The knight of the black armband had meanwhile dismounted and made his way through the small gathering to where Lucretia sat.

'Are you hurt?' he asked, raising the visor of his helmet. She barely glanced in his direction and then turned her attention back to her dead father.

'Hurt?' she said, 'hurt? No, I am not hurt.' Tears were flooding down her pale cheeks. 'Would that it were me that lay here lifeless. What use is life to me when those I love,' her voice trembled out of control, 'those I love beyond all else are dead. My poor father and ... and ... ' she was whispering now, 'Cesare Greyfell, my only love ... ' She laid her cheek on her father's cold forehead and a low wail of desolation escaped unbidden from her lips. The knight knelt down beside her and removed his helmet and gauntlets.

'It's the King,' someone shouted.

'The King,' another echoed and it appeared that everyone in the small gathering had to repeat the words, as if to convince themselves of the truth before their eyes. Within moments, the only one there who did not realise what was happening was Lucretia. Cesare reached down and gently turned her face so that she was looking directly at him. Slowly, her look of anguish changed to one of total bewilderment. She wiped the tears from her eyes and very hesitantly raised her hand to touch Cesare's cheek.

'Cesare?' It was the faintest of whispers, as if anything louder might dissipate the mirage before her eyes. 'Cesare?' she said again. He stood up and, taking both her hands, raised her to her feet.

'I thought ... they told me ... this is not real.' She looked around at the gathering, as if to confirm that they saw what she saw. She turned back and looked at Cesare again. 'It's really you.'

'Yes: back to claim my kingdom,' Cesare took both her hands in his, 'and my queen.'

Chapter 42

When they came to the edge of the copse through which Tancredi had fled, Grunkite and Clutch-bolt could clearly see where the shoulder-high oat grass of the Vildpline, with its pale violet haze shimmering in the breeze, was trampled down by the panic-stricken fugitive.

'We have him,' Grunkite said, and then shouted out, 'Tancredi! The day of reckoning has come for you.' His voice echoed across the vast expanse of the Vildpline. They stopped and listened and Gruntkite, from the vantage point of the cob's back, scanned the tall grasses where they began to merge with the sedges and bulrushes of Meregloom Gorge.

'Aha, I see where the fox shakes the rushes. You wait here. I will steer the vermin back towards you.'

Grunkite ploughed off in a wide arc to encircle the quarry. Within five minutes, Clutchbolt could just see the upper body of the Marshall above the vegetation moving back towards him, halloing and whooping. Not long after, a wild-eyed Tancredi dashed back out of the swaying oat grass of the Vildpline and ran straight into Clutchbolt's sturdy arms.

When the triumphant pair, with their prisoner, arrived back at the scene of Beaufort's slaying, the last of the gathering were disappearing through the portal gate. They followed them through to the garth of the portal gate and onto the Sky Road, along which the crowd were walking in quiet procession. At their head Cesare Greyfell, armour now discarded, led his mount upon which Lucretia Beaufort sat in a state of utter confusion. Celeste was walking beside her mistress, and at times it was clear that the dazed Lucretia would have fallen to the ground were it not for the strong and vigilant hands of Celeste. Behind them was brother Eugene and six mud-spattered men – Clutchbolt's insurgents - who bore the lifeless corpse of Arnulf Beaufort on their shoulders. Mistress Crumble, Nellie Lowslegg and the rest of Clutchbolt's crew brought up the rear. In their midst, Albrecht Pentrojan, hands bound behind his back, face contorted by the shame of his ignominious re-entry into Dredgemarsh, was pushed and shoved along in the procession. A piece of rope was handed to Clutchbolt. He made a noose at one end, tightened it around Tancredi's neck, and joined the tail end of the cortège with his terrified prisoner stumbling along behind him. A triumphant, but subdued, Grunkite, still mounted on his cob, brought up the rear.

As the sombre procession made its way along Sky Road, the walkers unconsciously took up the rhythm of the great

cob's hooves, that echoed back and forth against the towering walls on each side of them. The noise of battle had
ceased, and the cathedral bells rang out in the far distance. A
strange, muted euphoria was palpable when the cortège finally spilled out onto the Grand Plaza. As the crowd spread
out, they were joined by a group of blood-spattered knights.
They had removed their helmets and sheathed their swords.
Jerome was at their head. He dismounted and knelt before
Cesare. The crowd watched in fascination as Cesare raised
the knight to his feet and embraced him. They talked briefly
and then the knights led the still-dazed Lucretia away with
Celeste by her side, followed by the men bearing the corpse
of Arnulf Beaufort. More people from all quarters began to
join the throng around Cesare Greyfell.

'Oh look, Mistress Crumble, they've caught them both.
Look,' said Nellie Lowsleggg . She was pointing at Grunkite
and Clutchbolt, who had made their way forward with their
two prisoners, Pentrojan and Tancredi. They were talking
earnestly with Cesare.

'Oh, he deserves that. Look how proud he is.' Bella
Crumble clapped her pudgy hands as they watched Cesare
embrace Clutchbolt. When they disengaged, Clutchbolt
turned and pointed into the crowd.

'He's pointing at us, Mistress Crumble.' Nellie Lowslegg
grabbed Bella Crumble's arm. 'They're coming towards us.
What will we do?'

'Oh dear, oh dear, oh dear. The foolish man is bringing
the King this way.' Bella Crumble looked wildly around, 'Just
look at the state of us.' She was desperately trying to manip-
ulate and smooth the two sacks into some semblance of decorum on her great bosom.

'Crumble, I don't think the King is coming to examine

our clothes.' said one of her muddy companions.

'Of course not. Relax, woman, you are a hero,' another said.

'It's all very fine for you, you, you ... man you. I'm a wo-man.'

'You are indeed a woman, and a damn fine woman at that,' a third man chipped in.

'Get over here at once, Nelly Lowslegg. Stand in front of me,' Bella commanded.

'Yes, Mistress Crumble.'

Nellie Lowslegg stood meekly in front of Crumble, but she was sadly inadequate as a screen for the distraught kit-chen matron. It was too late, anyway, because the King was just yards away and striding towards them.

'My good and loyal friends, ladies,' Cesare was extending his hand, 'Mistress Crumble and ... and?'

'Low ... Low ... Lowslegg, sire.'

'Lowslegg, yes of course, Miss Lowslegg, come, let your King embrace you.'

Nelly Lowslegg leapt back in fright into the arms of Mrs. Crumble.

'Oh Mistress Crumble...' and Bella Crumble stood trans-fixed, for once as vulnerable and unsure as the pan-ic-stricken Lowslegg. She opened her mouth but was unable to utter a word.

'Your highness.' Incredibly, it was Leopold Ratchet who had arrived, as if from nowhere. 'These ladies, Sire, feel un-comfortable in their present state of dress, especially in your presence.' Cesare stopped, and after a moment spoke again.

'Of course, forgive me, ladies. And you are ...?'

'Ratchet, Leopold Ratchet, Sire.'

'Thank you, Leopold, you are quite correct. Ladies, gentlemen, we will celebrate another day, in more fitting surroundings where I can thank you properly.' Cesare had his arm around Ratchet's shoulder and Bella Crumble was now staring enraptured at the same Ratchet, her saviour. All the physical dangers she had encountered that day were as nothing compared to the trauma of the last minute, and he had rescued her. At that moment, in Bella Crumble's eyes, Leopold Ratchet towered above all men, including the King himself, who had turned to the assembled crowd.

'This day, my friends, will go down in history. Your names will be forever inscribed in the annals of Dredgemarsh, as will yours,' Cesare spun round to face the bound and dishevelled figures of Tancredi and Pentrojan. 'Take the vipers out of my sight.'

Dredgemarsh

Chapter 43

The joy and triumph of victory was soon replaced by a deep sorrow for those who had died in the battle to regain Dredgemarsh. None felt that sorrow more deeply than Cesare Greyfell. He barely slept in the ensuing days and long restless nights. A great burden of guilt weighted him down when he thought of the sacrifices that his loyal friends and subjects made to win back what, he felt, he had lost by his own carelessness and self-indulgence. How could he have not noticed the insidious manipulations of Tancredi? He tortured himself with every instance he could remember of what, he now realised, were the deceits and lies of the Chancellor. Worst of all, the love and desire he had for Lucretia now seemed tainted by the gnawing guilt that it had blinded him to the subterfuge of Tancredi. Had he been more alert, the uprising would not have taken place, his subjects would not have suffered and Lucretia would not have lost her father. In his anguish, he denied himself the consolation of meeting with her. Even at the quiet burial service of Arnulf Beaufort, Cesare attended only briefly, and confined himself to a respectful but perfunctory few words of condolences with Lucretia.

'He tortures himself with guilt,' Grunkite said to a bewildered Lucretia, when Cesare rushed away the instant the burial service was completed. 'He blames himself for everything, for your father's death, everything.'

'But that is not right, Marshall Grunkite, he is not to blame for any of this. All he did was trust people,' Lucretia said. 'What can we do?' Grunkite placed himself directly in front of Lucretia and took both her hands.

'I am not good at this … this kind of talking … and I know you are grieving for your father. But he is at rest now, and it's up to the likes of me to …'

'Please Marshall, what would you have me do?'

'He loves you, but he can't see past his own guilt. He is caught, caught. I can't put it into words but I know this, even when I and others doubted your loyalty, forgive me …'

'There is nothing to forgive, I would have thought the same. I understand that. But please go on.'

'Even when I, fool that I am, gave him what seemed like clear proof of your … you know. Even then, he could not bring himself to believe you would ever wrong him. Oh yes, he loves you. More than his own life, and now,' Grunkite paused, 'now he needs you. In truth, we all need you.' Grunkite pulled away awkwardly. 'I'll … I'll leave it in your hands,' he said, and left.

On that very day, in the Cathedral of St. Johannus, twelve knights who died in the recent battle were sung to their heavenly reward by their brother knights, now attired in their monk's robes. As the last couplet of De Contemptu Mundi drifted up and away through the clerestory windows, their plain coffins were closed and the knights of Anselem set out with their dead for their monastery at Anselem. A sorrowful Cesare embraced every single knight as they left the Cathedral. Jerome also bid farewell to his brothers. He would remain in Dredgemarsh, and continue in the service of Cesare as chief justice.

Shortly after that, the dead of Dredgemarsh were laid to rest in a special garden beside the Royal Vaults, where Cesare ordered a triumphal arch to be erected in their honour. He then convened a meeting of the Dredgemarsh Council to begin plans for the rejuvenation of the city.

'Sire, you must eat, rest a while.' His squire Jakob pleaded with him before they set out for the council chamber.

'I have rested too long, Jakob. I will eat later.'

'It has been like this for the past three days,' Jakob confided in Grunkite, when he arrived with his master at the council chambers. 'He barely sleeps or eats. Just look at him, Marshall Grunkite, his eyes, his face. He cannot go on like this. We must do something.'

'Wait here,' Grunkite said to Jakob and followed Cesare into the council chamber. It was early and none of the other councillors had arrived. Only the scribes Havelock and Dipslick were there, the former mixing fresh ink and his skinny companion sharpening the nibs on their collection of pens.

'Sire,' Grunkite said, 'I must talk to you.'

'Yes, Marshall,' Cesare looked up from the document which he was busily annotating.

'Forgive me Sire, but, can we postpone this meeting? The

councillors are exhausted. I am exhausted. So much has happened in the last few days. We cannot give of our best.' A flicker of irritation crossed Cesare's face, and it appeared as if he was about to dismiss Grunkite's complaint, but he paused and his look softened as he gazed at Grunkite. He leaned forward in his chair and dropped his head into his open palms with a weary sigh.

'I have driven you and everyone too hard, Grunkite. Forgive me. It's just there is so much left undone ... so much.'

'And it will be done, sire. Have no doubt, it will be done. But we all need clear heads as well as strong hearts. Please, rest yourself Sire. I beg you.' Cesare removed his hands from his face, looked up at Grunkite and nodded his assent.

'Gentlemen, there will be no meeting today,' Grunkite said to Havelock and Dipslick, 'please inform the councillors when they arrive.' Cesare and Grunkite left the chamber.

'Come, Jakob,' Cesare said to his waiting squire. 'Our good marshall has persuaded me to rest.'

'Sire, I would have a word with Squire Jakob. He will follow you instantly,' Grunkite said.

'By all means, Grunkite, you and Jakob can contrive what other restrictions you would impose on your poor King. I'll walk on.'

'Thank you, Sire,' Grunkite said, then lowered his voice, 'make sure he returns to his solar and rests. Keep him there, no matter what. If this,' he tapped the side of his nose, 'is still working, I can, no, I will convince the one person he needs above all others to visit him.'

'Thank you, Marshall, thank you.' Jakob shook the old man's hand and followed his master.

Later that evening, as the light through his solar windows began to fade, Cesare, for the first time in many days, began to relax. He had acquiesced to Jakob's relentless exhortations to eat and now sat before a warm fire, eating the last of a small croustade and drinking a sweet vernage prepared by Jakob. Once he started eating, Cesare was surprised at how hungry he really felt.

The Cathedral bells rang vespers, and Cesare was instantly aroused from the incipient torpor that began to wash over him after the food and wine. He thought immediately of the monks of Anselem and how, at that very moment, they would still be on cold road to their monastery in the mountains. Moments after the bells had ceased, he heard a knocking at the door of his solar. The short respite from the sadness and anxiety that assailed him was over. He jumped to his feet.

'Whoever it is, Jakob, send them away. I cannot meet anyone. Tell them I sleep ... whatever, anything.' Jakob went to the outer door of the vestibule. When Cesare heard Jakob inviting the visitor in, his face flushed with anger. Jakob entered the solar with a smug look on his face. Cesare glared angrily at him.

'Sire, Lady Lucretia Beaufort,' Jakob announced. Cesare felt as if his insides had turned to liquid. He could not speak. When Lucretia appeared in the doorway and looked directly at him, he had the strangest sensation, as if he, Cesare Greyfell, was turning to a vapour and being swallowed into the hidden depths of her eyes. He could hardly breathe as she came to him.

Lucretia took Cesare's hand, and, moving it inside the lapel of her black samite surcoat, pressed it against her breast. He felt the heat of her skin through the delicate silk bliaut and heard her sudden intake of breath. He bent down and kissed her open mouth. She reached both her arms around his neck. Her surcoat slipped from her shoulders. Neither Cesare nor Lucretia heard Jakob saying that he was exhausted and would retire to his own sleeping quarters.

Chapter 44

Demetrius Tancredi cried when Jerome, the chief judge of Dredgemarsh, pronounced the death sentence. The traitor was to be brought immediately to the execution chamber next to the courthouse and beheaded. The sheriff of the court, two household guards and the executioner, along with a court notary escorted Tancredi from the dock. Tancredi, like a cornered wild beast, frantically cast his bloodshot eyes around the court, as if looking for some last chance of escape or redemption. There was none. Leaving through the side door, his legs began to give way and the two guards bore him up. The last sound heard from Demetrius Triculatus Tancredi was an eerie childlike wail as he was carried to his bloody rendezvous with the executioner's axe.

An enraged Albrecht Pentrojan was then brought barefoot and in chains before the court for sentencing. A sergeant of the Dredgemarsh household guard, Anvil Paine, and two of his men escorted the Brooderstalt.

'I demand the respect of this court. I am a Captain in the army of Cawdrult of Brooderlund.'

'You forfeited that respect when you allied yourself with the the traitor Tancredi.' Jerome replied.

'He is your traitor, I am still –'

'Silence.' The court distaff pounded the floor with his mace.

'The remnants of your army has already been sent back to Brooderlund,' Jerome began to speak. 'Your crimes, Captain Pentrojan, warrant immediate execution.' He paused. 'However, we have decided to let you live.' The defiant look on Pentrojan's face and his aggressive posture melted away almost immediately. The judgement confounded him, and it showed in a look of almost childlike relief on his face. His body appeared to fold in on itself, and, in a trembling voice, he said,

'When?'

'Immediately,' said Jerome. 'You will return home, with nothing to report to your King but abject failure. The knowledge that you have been outwitted by a handful of loyal servants of Dredgemarsh is your military legacy, a legacy of hubris and stupidity. Sergeant Paine will escort you from Dredgemarsh. Take him away.'

Without any further exchanges, Anvil Paine and the guards ushered Pentrojan to the exit through which Tancredi had recently passed. All his clothes, apart from breeches and shirt, were removed. A Brooderlund helmet was placed on his head, he was mounted backwards on an ass and led through the streets of Dredgemarsh amidst the heckles and jeering of the citizens who came upon the bizarre scene. Pentrojan hung his head and stared at the ground throughout his ordeal. When Sergeant Paine and his guards escorted the mute Pentrojan through the postern gate, there had gathered behind them a long procession of men, women and children. They gathered around the Captain and his charge when they emerged onto the wide promenade of the castle. Anvil Paine held aloft one hand and a silence settled over the gathering.

'Take him down,' he ordered. The two guards dragged Pentrojan from the ass and stood him before Captain Paine.

'If, after this day is out, we find you on Dredgemarsh land, you will be executed immediately.' Anvil Paine pointed north across the Vildpline to Grak's Forest. 'Go.' The crowd parted just enough for Pentrojan to pass through them. He was slapped, punched, kicked and spat upon. 'The wild boar will get you,' a woman shouted. 'And the Blue Mountain wolves,' another voice responded. 'Die, die, Brooderstalt pig and your rotten king,' an old man said. The smaller children took up the chant 'Brooderstalt pig, Brooderstalt pig, Brooderstalt pig...' Battered and humiliated, Albrecht Pentrojan scampered down the glacis to the Vildpline and vanished from sight into the long grasses of that great plain.

****

Although the citizens of Dredgemarsh went into mourning for the loss of so many friends, fathers, brothers, sisters and wives, there was nevertheless a deep pride underpinning their sorrow. They had endured. Despite everything, they had endured, and that engendered in their hearts a new found love of their country and King. In their eyes, Cesare

Greyfell had been transformed from a mere privileged boy to a king that embodied this new pride and love of their ancient land of Dredgemarsh. And Cesare had indeed changed.

'He's tireless,' Grunkite remarked to his Captain of the household guard and deputy marshall, Severino. It was after one of the many long council meetings, where Cesare had made yet another one of his far-reaching proposals; this time, on the development of the university and the elevation of scientific study within the traditional Trivium and Quadrivium syllabi.

'He has a vision of Dredgemarsh being a great centre of learning, and it will happen, Chancellor. He is utterly determined,' said Severino.

'And he will exhaust us all in the doing of it.' Grunkite laughed. 'But you know,' he continued, 'I think this reborn King, this Cesare Greyfell will be one of the greatest kings in the history of Dredgemarsh. I was close to his father; a great man, a wise man, but this son of his ... he's ... he's a revelation.'

'Yes, indeed, a revelation,' said Severino. 'But now, Chancellor, is it not time to savour one or two of Mistress Crumble's delicious doucets and a tankard of braggot before his highness dreams up some more work for us poor devils?'

'No fear of that,' said Grunkite, and the pair began to walk in the direction of the refectory. 'His majesty will spend the rest of the evening with Lady Lucretia and early tomorrow they will travel to Anselem, where they will be married.'

'Married? Tomorrow?' said Severino.

'Yes, tomorrow. The ceremony will be quiet and small, in deference to her recently deceased father. You know, Severino, she has had the most profound effect on him. I can't wait to see them married.' Grunkite rubbed his hands together. 'Who knows? By the end of next year, we may have a new heir to the throne.' He clapped Severino on the shoulder. 'But come, let's get to those doucets. I think I can smell them already.'

Dredgemarsh

Chapter 45

B ella Crumble pressed her two plump hands to her chest and simpered, 'Mr. Ratchet do we have to?'

'Yes Bella, we do. Pull yourself together. You look perfect. I will be there with you. Come along, Miss Lowslegg, the new Chancellor is waiting.' Leopold Ratchet, the erstwhile second-in-command, apparently destined to forever occupy the role of subordinate and obedient one, was brimming with confidence. No one was more surprised at this incredible transformation than Ratchet himself. From the moment he had dared address the King in defence of Bella Crumble's discomfiture in the royal presence just weeks before, and when he recalled how the King addressed him as Leopold and put his arm around his shoulders, and when he thought about the soldier he had vanquished when he and his companions rescued Quickstrain, then Leopold

Ratchet had a source of inner inspiration and strength that would sustain him for all of his days. In contrast, Bella Crumble had become quieter, more retiring since those tumultuous events. But she was happy. In fact, she had never been happier or more content. What had once been a figment of her imagination was now emerging as a reality.

The transformed Ratchet was not only exercising his authority, as she had always wished he would, but he was also showing distinct signs of affection for her. It seemed that the new Ratchet was transferring his attentions from the tepid Miss Lowslegg to the more amply proportioned Bella Crumble. If truth were known, he could not erase from his mind the magnificent spectacle of Bella Crumble's heroic chest, partially visible under the loosely woven sacking, when she arrived triumphant at the castle gate on the day of their victory, and he yearned for the opportunity of a private viewing.

'At last, at last, the reluctant heroes.' Grunkite raised his goblet.

'Come, come, Mistress Crumble, Miss Lowslegg and Mr Ratchet, you have prepared a wonderful feast. Now I insist that you sit with your friends and eat. Have some wine. I have some very important announcements to make.' Grunkite stood and gestured to where they should sit at the banqueting table. Ratchet gallantly held the chair for Bella Crumble and when she was seated, leaned over her shoulder to enquire if she was comfortable, while at the same time stealing a quick glance down the front of her blouse.

'Thank you, Leopold,' she whispered demurely. Leopold took his seat between her and Miss Lowslegg.

'Hey Ratch, great meal, I see you've brought the tarts.' It was Klip the sharp tongued squire who was sitting opposite and who, though drunk, was still keeping his end of the table in a constant state of hilarity.

'We didn't bake tarts today,' said Miss Lowslegg haughtily.

'Now that she mentions it, they do look a bit stale,' Klip quipped to the old soldier Lek, who was sitting beside him.

'Hold that tongue of yours or I'll cut it off,' Grunkite shouted at Klip in mock anger. He then heaved himself up from the table, goblet of wine in his hand and began to speak.

'Friends, I will not abuse your time with long speeches. We are here today because of your loyalty and courage. It will never be forgotten. We have seen friends and companions die. Their bravery will be remembered for all time. We grieve for them, but we also celebrate them. As most of you know, his majesty and Lady Lucretia Beaufort are in Anselem where they will be married this day, as is the custom, by the abbot Sigismund.

'How wonderful,' said Bella Crumble, looking with doe eyes at Leopold Ratchet .

'A day of wedding celebrations for all citizens of Dredgemash,' Grunkite continued 'will take place after a period of mourning for our new queen's dead father. However, his majesty insisted that we hold this repast today to remember and celebrate the freedom that our brave men and women died for.

We are here also to announce and celebrate the many new appointments made by his majesty. As you may know, his majesty has done me the honour of appointing me Lord Chancellor.'

'To Grunkite!' they all shouted and the new Chancellor blushed scarlet. He gestured for silence.

'Havelock, if you please.' Havelock, who sat close to the

Chancellor, handed over a scroll. Grunkite laid his goblet aside and unfurled the scroll.

'These are his majesty's words.' Grunkite began to read: 'The following appointments are to take place with immediate effect: Our new General of the Dredgemarsh Field Army ... Lazarus Clutchbolt, who will henceforth be titled General Hawksfoot.'

'To Clutchbolt,' they all shouted and Bella Crumble began to well up. The proud Clutchbolt raised his goblet in acknowledgement.

'Our new Cook Meister ... Mr Leopold Ratchet,' intoned Grunkite.

'Hooray, hooray, three cheers for Ratchet .' And Bella Crumble began to cry.

'Our new Assistant Cook Meister ... Bella Crumble.'

'Well done, Bella,' they all shouted.

'You're a scream, Bella,' said Klip, emphasising the word scream, and the whole dining hall burst into laughter.

'Our new Matron of the Kitchens ... Nellie Lowslegg .'

'Hip, hip hooray. Nellie bring us jelly.' Miss Lowslegg quivered with excitement and pleasure.

'Well, Lazarus Clutchbolt,' said Flingthrift the treasurer, who was sitting next to the ex-Cook Meister, 'that's the end of your cooking days.'

'I don't know about that, Treasurer. I think I might still stuff a bird now and then.' He spoke loud enough for Celeste, who was sitting opposite, to hear. She glanced across at Clutchbolt, raised her eyebrows and pursed her lips. The same Celeste, who had up to then looked with disdain on the ex-Cook Meister, had obviously revised her opinion of him in the light of his recent heroics and even more so now, with his exaltation to the rank of general. She, for some reason or other, found the dining room very warm, when no one else did, and had to undo the top button of her blouse to 'cool down'. A short time later, to everyone's puzzlement, she just had to undo several more buttons or 'collapse with the heat'. Perhaps she was over-exerting herself because she frequently found it necessary to delicately ladle tiny portions of the multitude of sauces before them onto her trencher and for some strange reason, the sauces she liked best were all directly in front of Clutchbolt and required the poor girl to bend forward at full stretch in his direct line of sight. Of course, completely unknown to her, the new General Hawksfoot was blatantly taking advantage of the situation. It was hardly her fault that all the nice sauces were so placed, forcing her to lean forward so provocatively and at times it did take quite a little while, making the final selection of sauces, during which extended intervals Clutchbolt stopped eating and stared down the front of Celeste's open blouse.

'I think the new General fancies some melons.' Klip announced in a loud voice as Celeste leaned particularly far forward and Clutchbolt's eyeballs bulged.

'I think he's been offered a couple of helpings,' Lek responded laconically.

'Pay attention, you lot!' Grunkite shouted down at them, trying not to laugh. He cleared his throat and continued in a more serious tone.

'As for the assassin Verm Bludvile and his accomplice Burstboil, his majesty has shown great mercy.'

'No, he deserves hanging,' one of the assembled called out.

'Hanging is too good for the likes of that madman,' another shouted.

345

'I understand your feelings,' said Grunkite, 'but listen to the words of our King, words of wisdom.' Grunkite read from the scroll, 'I, Cesare Greyfell, have given the matter of Verm Bludvile a great deal of thought. Misguided as he may have been, he recognised before anyone that there was something amiss, something poisonous in Dredgemarsh. He blamed me and I am not above blame in my stewardship of Dredgemarsh.'

'No, that's not true,' Bella Crumble said.

'Yes, the King is hardly to blame,' Ratchet added.

'It was Tancredi,' said another. Grunkite held up his hand for silence and continued to read.

'Bludvile knew something was wrong. He set about purging what he saw as the evil in this castle and almost ended my life. But, he recognised his error. He also saved my life and the lives of many of us. He has been the instrument that has renewed and revitalised this kingdom and cleansed it with fire. On balance, he has done more good than harm. I have become a King once more, maybe for the first time, and found not only a kingdom, which was lost to me, but also a beautiful lady who will be Queen of Dredgemarsh. How can I condemn the author of this good fortune? He has delivered himself into our hands for punishment. I decree therefore that Verm Bludvile spend the remainder of his life as Candle lighter in the lower halls of this great castle and the foolish kitchen boy Burstboil is sentenced to assist him for that duration.'

'Bravo, bravo,' said the newly appointed General Hawksfoot rising up and signaling to one of the house guards standing by the half open door of the hall. The guard signaled to someone outside. 'Let us all stand and raise our goblets,' shouted the new General Hawksfoot. A great blast

of trumpets sounded from somewhere out on the battlements and grew in intensity as battle horns and war drums
began to answer them. The whole of Dredgemarsh appeared
to erupt into a stupendous roar of triumph that filled the
skies and the surrounding plains.

'Look, oh look,' a young page, his face bathed in an or-
ange glow. cried out. 'Look.' He was pointing out through
one of the north facing windows of the banqueting hall.
Everyone rose and rushed to see.

Along the northern ramparts, one after another, great
bonfires were exploding into life. The banqueters gazed in
raptures at the scene. They hugged and embraced each other
with tears in their eyes.

'Long live King Cesare!' Hawksfoot had to shout to be
heard above the blaring trumpets and horns and the pounding of drums.

'Long live King Cesare!' They all shouted in unison.

'Long live our Queen Lucretia!' Hawksfoot called out and
they all took up the chant and began to dance around the
banquet hall, transported by the sounds and lights that
reached into the Dredgemarsh night sky in an ecstasy of rejoicing.

****

Perhaps it was fanciful, but Lucretia, just hours after a
simple marriage to Cesare Greyfell, thought she could hear
thunder in the far distance. She was standing by an open oriel that looked down over all of Dredgemarsh from the great
eastern wall of the monastery perched just below the highest
pinnacle of the remote peaks of Anselem mountains.

'Thunder?' she whispered. The question was directed at

Cesare who joined her at the window.

'No, look.' He stood behind her and pointed into the darkness, resting his arm on her shoulder.

'What is it, what should I see.' She reached up her hand and caressed his arm

'A tiny glow. There.'

'Yes, I can just about see.' She leaned into him, turned her head and kissed the soft skin of his inner arm.

'You are not paying attention, my queen.' Cesare moved the dark cascade of her hair aside and touched her neck with his lips.

'Since I am a queen, I don't have to pay attention.' She half turned her upper body and kissed him full on the lips. 'But I will indulge you, my clever lord, and ask you to explain.' She turned back to gaze into the darkness.

'That tiny glow, no bigger than a firefly, is Dredgemarsh.' he encircled her with both arms. She nestled closer into his body.

'A firefly.' she whispered and she felt the rising hardness of him press urgently through their flimsy night attire.

'And that distant thunder is the sound of drums.' Cesare voice was low and hoarse as if he was struggling for breath. He moved his hands slowly upwards and caressed her breasts.

'For us?' She gasped and reached up to press his hands harder against her.

'For us,' he said. Lucretia shuddered as she felt him press even more urgently against her. Slowly she turned in his arms, all the while keeping close bodily contact so that each moment was an intimate and new exploration of every part of their bodies. They kissed open mouthed. Lucretia had the overwhelming sensation that she and Cesare were no longer separate but one single being. He carried her to their bed. It took just moments to discard their clothes. Lucretia lay back, her mind and body suffused with an overwhelming desire that Cesare should enter her in the most intimate act of love.

End of Book 1   The Reluctant King

Book 2, The Lost Prince, will be available
in the fourth quarter 2012

www.dermotmccabe.com

Glossary of Fogotten and Old Words

alaunt:
>hunting dog somewhere between a greyhound and a mastif.

aerquerques:
>a board game similar to checkers

arbelest:
>heavy crossbow requiring a windlass to set and load   it

Ars Amatoria:
>Art of Love by Ovid

barbican:
>a tower situated over a gate for defensive purposes

bardiche:
>long handled war axe

bartizan:
>an overhanging, wall mounted turret on a medieval fortification

belvedere:
>a small pavilion at the top of a building

bladderskate:
>an indiscreet talker

bliaut:
>a medieval dress

braggot:
>a mead made of malt and honey

clotpole:
>wooden head

cresset:
>a metal basket on a long pole which contains pitch   or rope

in resin for light

crustade:

a bowl-like crust containing some filling.

cullion:

a mean, rude person

dortour:

a dormitory

doucette:

a custard tart sweetened with honey and coloured with saffron

falchion:

a one handed, single edged sword

fewterer:

a dog handler and keeper

frummenty:

oatmeal and water boiled to a jelly

garth:

an enclosed quadrangle or yard

gyrfalcon:

the largest of the falcons

glacis:

a bank sloping down from a castle or castle promen   ade.

gorget:

armour to protect the throat

gyre:

a swirling vortex

infirmerer:

a monk who looked after the old and the sick

lymer:

Hunting dog especially bred for tracking, like a bloodhound

mazer:

drinking vessel made of wood or metal

nombles:

portions of venison cut from the deer's inner thigh

orfrois:

embroidery using gold thread

oxter:

armpit

paliasse:

mattress consisting of thin pad stuffed with straw or   sawdust

pannage:

a tax paid for allowing a farmer's pigs feed on nuts in the royal forest

pillaster:

recangular vertical pillar protruding only partially   from a wall

pizzle:

a penis

poitrel:

armour protecting a horse's chest area

polenta:

flour made from maize

posset:

a spiced drink of hot milk curdled with ale or wine

promenade:

a flat area surrounding a castle where people can   walk

samite:

a heavy silk fabric, often with silver thread woven   into it

sconce:

a candle or torch holder attached to a wall

sext:

12 Noon

seax:

a large one-edged knife

sippet:

a thin strip of toasted bread soaked in milk or broth

surcoat:

an outer, sleeveless coat of rich material

swyving:

copulating

tambour:

a frame or hoop used for embroidery

tierce:

9 am

vernage:

a sweet white wine

wastel bread:

white fine bread

ypocras:

a cordial of wine and spice –
often medicinal